The Year the Music Changed

Diane Thomas

The YEAR the MUSIC CHANGED

THE LETTERS OF ACHSA McEACHERN-ISAACS & ELVIS PRESLEY

[signature: Diane Thomas]

A NOVEL

The Toby Press

First Edition, 2005

The Toby Press LLC
POB 8531, New Milford, CT 06776-8531, USA
& POB 2455, London WIA 5WY, England
www.tobypress.com

ISBN 1 59264 122 9 hardcover

A CIP catalogue record for this title is
available from the British Library

Typeset in Garamond by Jerusalem Typesetting

Printed and bound in the United States
by Thomson-Shore Inc., Michigan

To Bill, always

"After 1955, Patti Page would have no more number one records. The same was true for Teresa Brewer and Nat King Cole."

—*Tom Waldman,* We All Want to Change the World: Rock and Politics from Elvis to Eminem

And a woman I used to know
Who loved one man from her youth,
Against the strength of the fates
Fighting in somber pride,
Never spoke of this thing,
But hearing his name by chance,
A light would pass over her face.

—*From "Those Who Love," by Sara Teasdale, as quoted in* Five Women Jawing about Love, *circa 1973, a play by Achsa McEachern-Isaacs*

Introduction

On August 6, 1977, just three weeks after the publication of my biography of Achsa McEachern-Isaacs and two years to the day after the tragic auto accident that took her life, an ordinary-looking package wrapped in brown paper arrived at my office.

I was out of the country, so the parcel sat for three weeks on my desk. On opening it, I discovered a large, battered Hav-A-Tampa cigar box with the words "Grammerar Lessons" gouged into the lid. Two wide rubber bands held it securely closed. Beneath one was tucked a small, cream-colored vellum envelope that contained the following handwritten note:

> Dear Dr. Gelber,
>
> I read in the papers where you wrote a book about Achsa McEachern-Isaacs. She must have meant a great deal to you for you to write about her. She meant a lot to me, too. That is why I want you to have these. I knew her when she was 14 years old. I kept them a long time.
>
> Wishing you all the best.
> Yours truly,
> Elvis Presley

As Mr. Presley's death had dominated the previous week's news, I of course suspected a hoax. Yet the note's wording touched me. I opened the box and found it crammed with literally dozens of letters, all apparently written to Mr. Presley by a young Achsa McEachern more than twenty years before. Creased and dog-eared, they gave off a faint odor of Old Spice, the popular aftershave of my youth.

Unwilling to let excitement get the upper hand, I pocketed several of them, along with Mr. Presley's note, and paid a visit to a handwriting expert across campus. In short order, he declared them all authentic: My cigar box contained pages and pages of revealing documentation, by the subject herself, of what must have been the most formative year of her life. Here was a teenage girl destined to emerge as a lightning rod for New York's alternative theater movement, writing to a young country singer who, arguably, would become America's most recognizable cultural icon—and writing throughout the pivotal year that marked the birth of rock and roll.

It was tempting to re-examine Ms. McEachern-Isaacs' life immediately, in view of this new information. On reflection, however, I determined that before bringing this correspondence to light I would search out Mr. Presley's letters to her, leaving no stone unturned, until I either found them or satisfied myself that they had been destroyed.

Through the ensuing years, that is what I did. I accomplished other projects, of course, including a biography of actor-director Milton Isaacs, whom Achsa McEachern married in 1967. Finally, in January 2004, I received a phone call from their daughter, the singer-songwriter Jesse Isaacs Sanchez. While readying her family's summer home in the Adirondacks for sale, she had found Mr. Presley's letters stashed in an attic suitcase.

The correspondence is, of course, most notable for what it reveals about Ms. McEachern-Isaacs, but it is not without revelations regarding Mr. Presley, as well: The young man of these letters bears no resemblance to the bloated caricature our culture has chosen to enshrine. He is instead a true naif, a country boy as yet unshaped by the wider world. Reading his letters, I had difficulty absorbing the fact that his life has become the subject of so much research that his whereabouts and activities on virtually every day of it are public record—information, incidentally, that assisted in corroborating the letters' authenticity.

Of all the documents, only one emerged as problematic. Written by Mr. Presley, it was destroyed, as described by Achsa McEachern, and then recreated by her from memory. How accurate was her recreation? For that I have no answer—only my sincere belief that, considering her stated familiarity with the original, her extreme attachment to it, and the emotionally charged circumstances surrounding its destruction, she had powerful motivation to reproduce it word for word, and did so.

One hurdle remained before the unlikely friendship between the young Achsa McEachern and Elvis Presley could become public knowledge. Considering the content of several of Achsa McEachern's letters, I felt a moral obligation to lay out the entire correspondence for Ms. Sanchez and allow her the final determination on whether any—or all—of it should be withheld. Her courage in agreeing to its publication *in toto* bespeaks her deep conviction regarding the importance of the material.

The result is this volume. Though slender, it is tendered in the hope that it will represent a significant addition to the extant information on these two too-brief lives.

—Aaron J. Gelber, Ph.D., Department of Theatre Arts,
Westbury College, Westbury, Vermont, May 14, 2004

The Letters

Chapter one

February 2–
March 30, 1955

Dear Mr. Presley:

  I don't know who you are, and I'm not a person who writes fan letters, but I thought I ought to tell you they're playing your record, "That's All Right, Mama," on the wrong radio station. I just heard it, and it really knocked me out. The trouble is, I heard it on a hillbilly station. Nobody listens to hillbilly music, and I don't know why you think you're a hillbilly singer. You're not. You're singing that new music they call "rock and roll." Or "rhythm and blues" if you're a Negro—I can't tell from your voice. I can't tell if you're young or old, either. But I can tell one big thing. I know exactly what you feel with every word. I've never heard anybody sing like that.

  I can pick a hit better than anyone, and "That's All Right" deserves to go all the way to number one on "Your Hit Parade." Unless something changes, however, I seriously doubt it will. I myself only heard it by accident, when I was twisting my radio dial. It reached out from that hillbilly station and grabbed me, and I believe every rock and roll radio show in the country ought to be playing your song.

I thought you would want to know.

Yours truly,

Achsa J. McEachern

* * *

Memphis, Tennessee, Sunday, February 6, 1955

Dear Mr. McEachern,

Thank you very much for your letter. I am real glad you think Thats All Right deserves to be Number One on the Hit Parade show on TV. I do too. You sure know a lot about music. Do you work at a radio station?

You said you cant tell nothing about me from my voice. Here is who I am. I was born in Tupelo Mississippi on January 8, 1935. My mamas name is Gladys. She is the light of my life. My daddys name is Vernon. He is a good man that is had some hard times. My twin brothers name is Jesse Garon. He died getting born.

We moved to Memphis when I was 13. I graduated from Humes High School. It is a white high school. I am 20 years old.

If Thats All Right Mama had not started making me some money I would be a electrician by now. I was going to school for it. I got to say I did not like it much. As for me singing hillbilly I suppose sometimes I do and sometimes I do not. I like all the music there is. Even operas. I dont never try to sing one special kind. Whatever comes out that is what it is.

I really like it how you said all the rock and roll radio shows ought to be playing my record. I will take every one of your words to heart. I hope to hear from you again. If I ever get to Atlanta I sure will look you up.

Yours truly,

Elvis Aron Presley

* * *

Atlanta, Wednesday, February 16, 1955

Dear Mr. Presley,

Never in my life have I been so embarrassed and ashamed! I
have created a horrible misunderstanding. Please believe I never meant
to. I am not a man, and I do not work at a radio station. I am a girl.
I go to Stephen Foster High School. I just turned fourteen.

I should have written you all that in the first place. I have no
excuse, except I guess I don't know how to write a proper fan letter.
I thought it ought to say something useful.

I guess I should not have written you at all. I mean, if I couldn't
do it right. I did try, but writing flirty words to a person I've never
met felt silly. And when I dotted my i's with little hearts and bubbles
like the other girls, it just looked dumb.

Also, there's the matter of my name, a hideous bane that does
not even tell you if I'm male or female. Say it, and you sound like
an Italian woodcutter: "You bring-a the ax-a, I chop-a the wood."
The first Achsa was a princess no one's ever heard of. In Judges 1, a
Bible book nobody reads. I'm named for my great aunt Achsa. She
probably hated it too.

I really can pick hit records, though. I'm not bragging, it's the
absolute truth. I bought "That's All Right" the day I wrote you. When
I told the clerk at the record store that someday you'd have a song on
"Your Hit Parade," he rolled his eyes like I didn't know what I was
talking about. Well, he was sorely mistaken. The very first time I heard
"Rock Around the Clock," I was certain it would climb to Number
One. And that was months before they put it in that Blackboard
Jungle movie. I knew the Moonglows' "Sincerely" would be a big hit,
too—a whole year before the McGuire Sisters recorded it.

I listen to the radio every minute, especially late at night when
Penelope the Dream Weaver comes on. I used to think all disc jockeys
had to be men, but she's wonderful! Her voice makes you think of a
soft, silky Persian cat that lives off cigarettes and coffee, if that makes
sense. She's on WDDO, Daddy-O Radio 1360. They play rhythm and
blues. That's where I heard the Moonglows.

Something else that happens late at night, stations from cities far away drift in and out of my radio like ghosts. I jam my ear against the speaker and turn the dial ever so slowly, listening for them. The tiny orange lights in the vacuum tubes look like a city lit up in the dark. If I've tuned in WLAC in Nashville, I pretend I'm on a bus bound for "Randy's Record Shop in nearby Gallatin, Tennessee." If it's New Orleans, I'm dining and dancing in "the beautiful Blue Room high atop the Roosevelt Hotel." Sometimes on a clear night I can get Chicago. But I never can find New York, no matter how hard I try.

Oh, dear, I've rattled on awfully. Now I'm afraid I owe you a second apology—for boring you. You probably think I'm very silly, as well.

In closing, let me say again how sorry I am I misled you. I wish you the best of everything in life. And may every one of your records climb to Number One on "Your Hit Parade."

Sincerely,

Achsa McEachern

P.S. That is so sad about your brother. I guess it makes you an only child like me. I never thought about it, but twins always have someone to talk to, don't they. I wish I was a twin.

*   *   *

Memphis, Monday February 28, 1955

Dear Achsa,

I would of wrote lots sooner. We been on the road.

You cant be no fourteen! You write like you been to <u>college</u>! You are really something. You know that?

What you said about them radio stations it ~~arent~~ is not silly at all. Lots of times late at night I play like I live in them towns too. Something else I do, I go to Beale Street. Its the colored downtown here in Memphis. Something is always happening there. It dont never shut down. Music slips out the doors and windows of the clubs. I walk down the street and let it find me. It is no Perry Como music neither. It is like nothing you ever heard.

10

Colored church music, it is the same way. Sundays me and some boys sometimes sneak off from First Assembly and go sit in the back at this colored church just to hear them sing. Gospel is my most favorite kind of music. White <u>and</u> colored.

I really like getting your letters. I hope you write me again. I live at 462 Alabama Street, Memphis, Tennessee. You can write me there.

Yours truly,
Elvis

P.S. Thank you for saying that about my brother. Back in Tupelo I used to go sit by his grave near every day. Id talk to him like he had got born alive and him and me was still together. I been gone from there now seven years. I still miss him like it was yesterday.

*   *   *

Atlanta, Thursday, March 10, 1955

Dear Elvis,

Thank you for saying I'm not silly and asking me to write you at your home address. You didn't have to do that if you didn't want to, so I guess you meant it.

I really am just fourteen—but I'll be a senior next year, which accounts for why I sound so old. If you <u>don't</u> sound old when you're three years younger than everyone else in all your classes, they treat you like a kid.

Myself, I think I never was a kid. In grammar school, my teachers kept promoting me up an extra grade every winter until Mama made them stop. She told them I'd never have any friends, but she was wrong. Linda Sheffield and I were best friends five whole years, until her family moved away in December. She got promoted midyear, too, but only once. She's sixteen. She's got a boyfriend now and almost never writes. We used to tell each other everything. With her gone I've got no one to talk to.

I liked your letter a lot, especially the Beale Street part. I can picture the music chasing after you down the sidewalk, like a cartoon fog full of swirls and sparkles. I dearly wish I could hear it. I'd love hearing music that's like nothing I ever heard before.

It's neat, too, about the Negro church. I'm surprised they let you in, considering we don't let them into <u>our</u> churches. They must be very kind people.

I'll tell you something I've never told a living soul. It goes all the way back to when Mama and I used to go to movie matinees, to the first time she let me go by myself to the ladies' restroom. It was upstairs and at first all the quiet made my ears feel stopped up. Then I heard this sound, a rustling or murmuring, like birds settling down for the night. It came from a big, dark archway at the other end of the mezzanine. I was so young I pretended the carpet was a raging river and I used its fat, red roses for stepping stones to cross over.

Inside the archway, a red velvet rope was stretched across a flight of steep, concrete stairs. A gold-framed sign on the rope said, "This balcony is closed," but it didn't sound closed. It sounded full of whispers. I looked around and didn't see anyone, so I crawled under the rope and climbed the stairs. When I got to the top, I could not believe what I saw. It looked like I was standing at the back of this whole other theater. Only, the aisles weren't carpeted, and the chairs weren't upholstered, and all the people in the seats were Negroes. (That's what Mama says instead of "colored people." "<u>Knee</u>-grows." The way they say it in New York.)

Negroes! Up there watching the movie just like the rest of us downstairs! Who were they? How did they get in? I was sure they had to be very special—in all my life I had never seen a Negro in a white movie theater.

I took a step closer, and a girl near my own age turned and saw me. She didn't move or make a sound. Just stared. I wanted to smile at her, but my mouth wouldn't let me. So I stared back until I couldn't bear her large eyes looking at me a second longer. That's when I turned and ran. I didn't stop until I got all the way back to the white people's theater, where I found my seat by the projector light shining on Mama's strawberry blonde hair.

I felt icky inside, like I'd seen something I shouldn't have. That's why I never told. But ever since that day, every time I go to a movie, about half way through my heart starts pounding and I have to excuse myself and climb up to the Negro balcony. When I get there, I stand in the back for a second, almost too scared to breathe. I never know if I'm hoping someone will turn around so I can smile at them or if I'm afraid to death they will. Always, before anything has time to happen, I turn around and run back down. I don't know why I keep going up there. Every time, I'm terrified the balcony will be empty. It's as if my heart won't calm down until I see them there.

Now you know something about me no one else in the whole world knows, not even Linda Sheffield. I hope you don't think I'm weird. Do you believe I'm doing wrong to keep going up there? I worry about that sometimes. I've thought and thought about it and I still don't have an answer.

Sincerely,

Achsa

* * *

Memphis, Sunday, March 27, 1955

Dear Achsa,

I can not believe any girl smart as you is writing me! I almost did not make it out of <u>high school</u>! Guess I should not of told you that, just let you go on thinking I am a brain. A regular Einstein or someone. Ha-ha.

I like it you wrote me about climbing to the colored balcony. I like it too dont nobody but you and me know. I do not think you are weird. You are a very nice girl and you are not doing wrong at all. The Lord says we only do wrong if we have evil in our hearts, and you don't have no evil in your heart climbing to the colored balcony.

I dont have no evil in my heart on Beale Street neither. It is a beautiful place. I even buy my clothes there. At this store where all the colored singers go. They are all sharp dressers. Now I am too. I pull on my black pants with the satin stripe and put on my pink jacket, and I can feel their songs inside me like a thunderstorm. I never before said that. Still it is a true thing.

You told me something about you. Here is something about

me. One day I am going to make enough money to buy my mama and daddy a big house and a Cadillac. Only, that ~~arent~~ is not the half of it. I am going to do something really big. I know it. I can feel it in me like the voice of the Lord. The singing is just a road getting me there.

I think what it is is I am going to be a movie actor. I want that more than anything in this world. I know I will be good at it, same as how I always knowed I could sing.

You ever seen East of Eden? I seen it twelve times. I aim to be just as good a actor as that James Dean. Him and Marlon Brando they are the best. They dont never do no phony stuff. That is going to be me too.

You are such a smart girl maybe you can help me. If you want to that is. I got to learn to talk good. I just lately come to understand how much that means.

What happened is this big deejay put in a word for us with Arthur Godfrey, and last week me and the boys flew all the way to New York City to try out for Arthur Godfreys Talent Scouts on TV. I dont mean to brag or nothing. Its just that is how it come about. We saved all our money for a whole month to get there. I had not never rode in a airplane before. It takes some getting used to.

Turned out we didnt make it onto the show. We didnt even get to meet Mr. Godfrey. Them TV people treated us like dumb hicks that come riding in on a mule wagon. They was all the time snickering about how we talked. Right to our faces too. Did not even turn away to hide it.

Now I may be from Mississippi but I ~~arent~~ am not stupid. I do not want to sound stupid neither. Do not get me wrong. I dont aim to put on airs. It is just I dont want NOTHING not NOTHING AT ALL to hold me back if I can help it!

So I am thinking maybe every time I write you you can write me back and point out something I been saying wrong. Then you can tell me how to say it right.

If you want to that is.

I will be honest I cant pay you nothing for it right now. I am fixing to rent my mama and daddy a house. But I know I can pay later and I will.

 Will you help me? Please? It would truly mean a lot.

 Please write back right away and let me know. I dont want to sound stupid no longer than I have to.

 Yours truly,
  Elvis

P.S. I am six feet tall and got brown hair. Some folks say I look like Tony Curtis sometimes. What do you look like? I bet you are a real pretty girl.

* * *

Atlanta, Wednesday, March 30, 1955

Dear Elvis,

 I will be delighted to help you with your grammar! I feel honored to be asked. Already, you have my deepest admiration for wanting to undertake such a project, which I imagine is not usual among hillbilly singers.

 As for paying me, I couldn't take a dime. Getting regular letters from someone as interesting as yourself will be more than payment enough. I think we should write each other at least once a week, don't you? That way, you will make rapid progress, and thoughts of correct grammar will always stay in the front of your mind.

 Since Linda Sheffield left, I have thought several times about answering one of those pen pal advertisements in the movie magazines. Now I won't need to, I'll have you. There's just one problem. My father is quite strict. If he knew I were exchanging letters with a boy, especially a boy I've never met who has already finished high school, he would almost certainly forbid it and likely punish me into the bargain. Perhaps he would even take away my radio, which I could not bear.

 I thought a lot about this and came up with a simple solution. All you need to do is give yourself a girl's name in the return address

15

on the envelope. "Evelyn," perhaps, or "Eve" might work well, since both start with the same letter as "Elvis." That way, my parents will believe I truly have answered a pen pal advertisement and that that is who you are.

I am positive it will work. My father is not a bad man; he would never open someone else's mail. He is actually extremely God-fearing, maybe because he lost both his parents to the flu epidemic. My great-aunt Achsa, who's a devout Presbyterian, raised him and his sister Dora in a little town in south Georgia so small the only thing you see above the treetops is the water tank.

Daddy works at a book bindery restoring people's worn-out family Bibles. Mama says he likes to think that in some small way it makes him a minister of the gospel. She says he still feels disappointed he never got the call to preach. He went to college to be a surveyor, but he got wounded in the leg during the war and can't climb hills. The Army gave him a Purple Heart. He keeps it in their dresser in a little box.

My mother grew up in a small town, too—in South Carolina—but she taught school for awhile in New York. She almost never talks about it, but when she does her whole face lights up as though she had a lovely time. Someday I'm going to live in New York, too.

Speaking of New York, I've seen <u>On the Waterfront</u> and I completely agree with you about Marlon Brando. He looked as real as someone who might pass you on the street, not actorish at all. You have picked a worthy model to ~~immolate~~ emulate.

Unfortunately, I have not seen <u>East of Eden</u>. Daddy thinks movies are sinful. Anymore, the only way I get to go is to say I have a school assignment at the downtown library—which, as luck would have it, sits across the street from two theaters. So I just take the bus downtown after school or on a Saturday. That's how I saw <u>On the Waterfront</u>, also <u>River of No Return</u>. Both times I went with Linda Sheffield.

I go to the library all the time anyway, mostly to read the magazines. <u>Theatre Arts</u> and <u>The New Yorker</u> are my very favorites. I could read magazines all day, every day, and never once get tired of it. I used to cry because I couldn't learn everything there was to know. I guess I <u>was</u> a bit of a kid way back then, wasn't I?

This has turned into a pretty long letter. I tend to get off the subject quite a lot. It's OK for you to write long letters, too, you know. I won't mind at all. I promise.

As for your grammar lessons, I think it's best if I point out only one mistake each time, so you can really work on it. Here's the first: Never, <u>never</u> say "ain't." Say "am not," "is not," "are not." I haven't seen this word in anything you've written, but I did see "it aren't" crossed out once or twice. If you <u>have</u> been using "ain't" when you speak, you must <u>stop</u> <u>it</u> <u>right</u> <u>now</u>! This is the biggest step you can take toward improving your grammar. It is also the easiest.

That's it, the end of your first lesson. If there's any part I did not explain well, please write your questions in your next letter. I will try my level best to answer them.

In closing, I want to say again how much I admire you for wanting to improve your grammar. Helping you do so may very well be the most exciting undertaking I have ever ~~undertaken~~ been a part of.

I look forward to hearing from you very soon.

    Sincerely,

    Achsa

Chapter two

April 4–7, 1955

Somewhere in ~~Arkansas~~ Mississippi, Monday, April 4, 1955

Dear Teach,

I ain't said "ain't" but 20 times all week, two of them right now, and I put ~~apastrathes~~ apostrophes in both of them. I feel lots smarter already. Even bought me a dictionary. Now I can look up all them big words you use.

I guess you saw how I called myself Evie on the envelope. The way I wrote it, it looks pretty much like Elvis. I even dotted the "i" with one of them little circles you hate. Still I <u>will</u> <u>not</u> buy no writing paper with little ducks or bunnies. Don't get to hoping.

Here's a funny joke. A woman gets on a bus with a grocery sack that's leaking all over the place and sits down next to this prissy man in a suit. He runs his finger across the bottom of the sack, licks the wet off and says, "Pickles?" She says, "No, puppies."

I like a good joke. I always try to tell a few in my show.

Speaking of shows, guess what? Saturday me and the boys was in Shreveport singing on the "Louisiana Hayride" like always. Slim Whitman was singing too, and him and us we tore that place up! They turned away 2,000 people! Maybe some Saturday night you can tune in the Hayride on one of them ghost stations and hear me sing. That is if you are not afraid of a little country music. That's what it is called. Not hillbilly. A smart girl like you will want to use its rightful name.

We're going home Easter. I can't hardly wait. This year is the first time we been on the road like this. I tell you, it is something else. You don't never get no sleep. Sometimes there's a couple hours we can check in at a motor court. Most times we take turns sleeping in the backseat of the car.

There is people around all the time but it still gets lonely. Hearing from you is a real treat. I like it there isn't nobody going to know about my letters. Especially with me looking like a <u>girl</u> on the envelope, ha-ha. I ~~wont~~ won't tell nobody about yours neither. That way it will be our secret. Like we got us a secret life or something.

Being on the road is sort of like a secret life, come to think of it. There don't nothing happen on the road have to do with nothing else back home. What happens with you and me won't have to do with nothing else neither. We can write each other anything we want. Things we might not never tell another living soul. We have both wrote a few of those already, haven't we? I like writing you and getting letters from you very much, Achsa McEachern.

Last time I asked what you look like. You forgot to tell me. Maybe instead you can send me a picture. I would like that even better.

Yours truly,
Elvis

*　　*　　*

Atlanta, Thursday, April 7, 1955

Dear Elvis,

It's great, you getting to go home Easter. I bet you really miss it, being gone so long.

Also, I'm pleased you bought a dictionary. I'll try to come up with lots of big words, so you can put it to good use.

Most of all, I'm really glad we're never going to talk to anyone about what we write each other. With Linda gone, I've got so much stuff saved up I want to tell somebody, that some days I think it's going to burst right out of me and fly around like dandelion fuzz.

Most of it's about Mama and Daddy. Sometimes I think Daddy loves the Lord so much it makes him mean. This afternoon he yelled at Mama for no other reason than that the man across the hall went out and talked to her at the clothes line. When she came in, Daddy grabbed her arm and told her she'd been "carrying on like a brazen hussy."

Mean, spat-out words—I don't know what came over him. My mother is not a bit like that at all. I saw them out there, too, you know, and it wasn't her fault that man talked to her. I'm sure she only listened because she didn't want to be rude. And maybe because he made her laugh. Mama was brought up Methodist and says Methodists by their very nature are much happier than Presbyterians. It's the truth, too. At least as far as I've seen. Offhand, I can't recall my father laughing even once. I wonder sometimes why Mama married him. He's no taller than she is, and looking at him brings to mind one of those long-necked water birds that stand around on one leg all day looking like they know everything on earth and disapprove of all of it.

Maybe the man across the hall wonders, too. He's got a crewcut, and you can tell he thinks he's handsome. Friday, I got home from school, and he was working on his car in front of our apartment building. When I turned in at the walk, he caught my eye and said, "Hon, you got a mama pretty as a movie star." You could smell the whiskey on him. I couldn't think how to answer, so I just smiled and ran inside and shut the door.

The thing is, he may have been drunk, but he sure hit the nail right on the head. Mama is pretty as a movie star, that's the whole trouble. She's got periwinkle blue eyes like an October sky, coppery hair, and a face as perfect as those Breck Shampoo ladies' pictures in the magazines. But she's also got a shy, nervous way about her that makes everybody, even me, want to stay close to her and make sure she's OK. Everywhere she goes, people stare. Even women. And men never let her alone.

When I was young, we had a dentist with an office on the tenth floor of the tallest building in Atlanta. We went to him forever. I used to pretend I was a bird perched on his window ledge, all set to fly away. Anyway, one day three summers ago Mama took me to get my teeth cleaned, and when we got in the elevator to leave it was packed full of men going to lunch. They all moved back to give us room. Except one, who kept shifting his big brown leather briefcase around until he had no place left to stand except smashed up against my mother's back. Every time the elevator stopped to let more people on, we all got jammed in even tighter. The brown-briefcase-man's breathing got all slow and jerky, like nobody's breath I'd ever heard. I remember thinking maybe he had a cold and being scared Mama might catch it. But once the elevator stopped and people started getting off, his breathing turned just fine. Out in the lobby he grinned, tipped his hat to Mama and said, "Have a great day, ma'am."

Mama didn't look at him. She didn't look at anybody, not even me. Just down at the white marble floor tiles. Her face had gone sort of gray, and she kept swallowing over and over like she was going to be sick. I asked what was the matter, and she answered something really strange. She said, "Sometimes I wish to God I didn't look this way," but I don't think she was saying it to me. She sounded like she meant it for nobody but her own self.

We quit riding elevators after that. Mama claimed she'd read that climbing stairs is good for you, but I knew it had to do with the brown-briefcase man. We switched to another dentist, too, in a different building. He's on the first floor.

Not everything that happens to my mother because she's beautiful is bad, though. Last spring a newspaper photographer saw her trying on a hat in Rich's Department Store and snapped her picture. The paper put it in their Sunday Women's Pages. The only bad thing was Daddy said she must be "filled with Godless vanity, wanting all those strangers staring at you." I don't know what got into him. I guess he couldn't figure out she didn't have a thing to do with it.

Daddy stares worse than anyone, if you want my opinion. He's seen her every day for 15 years and he still can't take his eyes off her. All during church he gazes up at her in the choir like he's staring straight at Jesus. She never once looks back, only down at her hymnbook.

One Christmas when I was little, he bought a fancy treetop angel at a jewelry store for no other reason than it looked like her. He came home from work and charged into the kitchen, where Mama was fixing dinner, holding that angel high like a torch in his right hand.

I saw it before she did, and my breath caught in my throat. It looked like a delicate porcelain figurine, only with a cloud of angel hair poking out from little holes in its china skirt and a cylinder underneath so you could put it on a tree. Both its hands showed five perfect fingers, even the knuckles and the tiny, pale pink nails. It had strawberry blonde hair, blue eyes, and high cheekbones—and it really did look like my mother. Not as much as a famous painting I saw once in <u>Life</u> magazine of this red-haired lady rising up out of the ocean in a seashell, but that angel came awfully close.

Daddy held it near her face. "Remind you of anyone you know?" he asked. The start of a nervous smile played around his mouth. Mama leaned away, like the figurine might lunge out and bite her. "We already have a perfectly fine angel," she said gently but firmly. "You should take this one back and get your money back, or we won't have any Christmas."

He didn't. He put it on the tree.

That Christmas, Santa brought my last year's doll a whole wardrobe of beautiful new clothes folded up in a cigar box painted white with purple flowers. After Daddy brought the angel home, Mama must have stayed up sewing every night. She made a tiny sundress from a cotton playsuit I'd outgrown, a travel suit and matching hat out of a pair of long blue velvet evening gloves she had from before she married Daddy, a nightgown from one of Daddy's linen handkerchiefs and a negligee from a silk dresser scarf.

In the very bottom of the box lay an ivory satin wedding dress. For a moment, I thought she'd bought it. Then I recognized the lace. Mama had cut up her last trousseau nightgown, the one she always said was too special to wear. To go with the dress she had stitched a bridal veil out of bandage gauze from the medicine cabinet and she had edged it with seed pearls from my baby bracelet she kept in her jewelry box. Every outfit looked as intricate and perfect as an open rose. I was almost afraid to touch them.

When I glanced up to thank her, she wasn't watching me at all. Her eyes were on my father and filled with the deepest sadness I have ever seen in anyone not crying. Daddy was staring into a silver Christmas ball hanging low on the tree. At first I thought he was gazing at his own face reflected in the ball. Then I realized he was watching hers.

Still, I can't criticize my father too much for looking at Mama all the time. In a way, I stare at her too. For two years I kept a scrapbook about all Grace Kelly's movies because that's who she looks like sometimes in the face. And when I was a little girl the only dolls I ever asked for had my mother's red-blonde hair. I gave them names like Margaret and Melissa, but I might as well have called them all Annette, after Mama, because that's who they really were. I always played the same game with them: that they were Mama before she met and married Daddy—when she was young and living in New York.

So I guess that makes me her biggest fan of all, doesn't it.

I almost forgot. We only had the angel that one year. Mama dropped it New Year's Day when she was packing up the Christmas decorations, and it broke into a million smithereens. Sometimes around my parents I get scared and don't know why.

I'm sorry for going on so. I never meant to say all that. I told you things I never told even Linda Sheffield! I hope you don't mind. It made me calm inside to write them, but I won't do it anymore if you don't want me to.

I owe you a lot for reading this far, so I'll try my best to give you a good grammar lesson.

"Him and us, we tore that place up" is not correct. If you were going strictly by the rules, you would say, "He and we, we tore that place up." However, that sounds really stupid, so it's not a good solution. You might leave the first part out and just say, "We tore that place up." Or you could say, "Between the two of us, we tore that place up." That's probably the best way. Although if you keep on tearing places up, you might not get invited back. (Joke.)

Most people don't realize grammar can be pretty slippery. Lots of times it doesn't give you <u>the</u> <u>one</u> <u>right</u> <u>answer</u>. You have to make a choice. But it's the choosing that makes it interesting and fun. That's how I see it, anyway.

    Sincerely,

        Achsa

Chapter three

April 11–17, 1955

Dear Achsa,

I got to thank you once again for another good ~~grammer~~ grammar lesson. Still I got a ways to go, I think, before it feels like fun.

This letter may not look real great. I'm writing it riding in the back seat of a car. I hope you can read it.

Whatever you want to tell me in your letters it won't get no further. You can rest assured, as they say. Satnin sends me my mail when I'm on the road, but she don't never open none of it. Satnin is Mama. I don't remember how I come to call her that. I been doing it all my life. She is got names like that for me. We got lots of words for lots of things we don't never tell nobody. Now you and me can have made-up words too.

I really mean it you can write me anything. I won't mind it and I'll never tell. You won't mind things I tell you neither. Or tell nobody. Like if I was to say I been scared like you sometimes and don't know why. Or if I say there's times I'm scared like that right now. Or if I say I'm scared everything happening in my life is just a dream I can wake up from and be back driving a truck. You won't never tell.

Or if I was to say I know how it is to not have a friend in this

27

world. Satnin walked me to the high school them first days after we moved to Memphis. She was scared I'd run away and not go in the building. I hated her doing it. Still it hurt my heart to leave her and go through them doors alone.

There's not <u>nothing</u> Satnin wouldn't do for me, even if I don't like her doing it. A mother's love is the greatest earthly love there is. It can save a person's life same as religion.

I reckon a wife's love is some like that too. Maybe your mama's love can save your daddy. That is if he will let it. You say religion makes your daddy mean. I can't think how religion could make anybody mean. Still maybe that is not true for Presbyterians. I done met a few folks that is just plain mean and religion can't do nothing for them. I met some others that want something so bad they do mean things. Or want to hold onto something they got. Maybe your daddy is one of them.

Your mama sure must be one pretty lady. I bet you look just like her.

Write me back real soon and let me know how you are doing.

Yours very truly,
Elvis

P.S. Now that we're writing regular I thought you might want to see what I look like. For all you know maybe I lied saying I looked like Tony Curtis. I might look ugly as a skinned possum. That's what's in the other envelope. A picture. We had them made to sell to folks that come see us play. That's me in the middle. Bill Black on the left plays bass. Scotty Moore plays guitar. We been together since this whole thing started. I signed the picture, "To Achsa, with all my very best wishes always, Elvis." I hope you like it. Maybe someday I'll be so famous you will see my mug all over everywhere and I won't need to send one. But I still would anyway.

Now that you got a picture of me you got to send me one of you. It will sure please me to get it. I'll carry it in my wallet when I'm on the road and show you off to folks all the way from Texas to Tennessee.

P.P.S. Like I said, don't never worry about what you write. Anything at all's OK with me. No joke.

* * *

Stamford, Texas, Friday, April 15, 1955

Dear Achsa,

Did you get my letter I wrote Monday? I put a picture in it. Please let me know.

Also I forgot to ask a question.

You said choosing makes ~~grammer~~ grammar fun. I guess you meant choosing between all the <u>right</u> ways to say something. What I need to know is once a person learns to say things right is it OK for him to sometimes say them wrong on purpose? Or does he have to say a thing the right way every time once he learns how?

The reason I'm asking is I don't want nobody to think I got the swell head. Not my buddies nor my kin. I'm still the same old Elvis I always was. I want them to know that all the time.

This is a very important question to me. I am trusting you to give the answer.

Yours very truly,
Elvis

P.S. Please please send me a picture of you. If you don't have a extra one, maybe you can go to one of them booths that spits out four for a quarter. I can't wait to see your pretty face!!!

* * *

Lydia, Mississippi, Friday, April 15, 1955

Dear Elvis,

I've got a feeling this is going to end up an awfully long letter, so I better do the grammar now. Here's an easy one. Never use "neither" at the end of a sentence. Say "either" instead. "Me either." Not "Me neither."

As for what has taken place since last I wrote you, I really hardly know where to begin. Something terrible has happened. My life's all turned around now. Mama's, too. You say these letters are our secret. I am trusting that you really mean it. If I thought for one minute you didn't, I could no more write what I'm about to tell you than I could flap my arms and fly to the moon.

The whole thing came about because of Daddy. And that man across the hall talking to Mama every time she went out to the clothesline. I could see them from my bedroom window. He'd wander over and stand there with this great, open smile spreading over his face like butter, as if merely laying eyes on my mother was all it took to make him happy. Then he'd pick up her laundry basket and follow after her, holding it so she wouldn't have to bend over to take out clothes or put them in. He never did stand close and always kept the basket between them, like he was trying to tell her, without saying anything, that everything was on the up-and-up and proper. That caused me to think some better of him, although I saw why Daddy got upset. Mama looked different out there with that man. She smiled more, and she laughed.

Yesterday was warm for April. Mama wore her yellow sundress with the pinafore ruffles, the one I call her "happy dress." She had gone to the grocery and went out later than usual to bring in the clothes. I was sitting at the dining table doing my geometry homework when Daddy got home. The instant he came through the door I knew he had seen them. Blood pumped in the blue vein at his temple and his mouth made a thin, tight line. He ran himself a glass of water at the sink, but his hand shook so hard he set it down without taking even one swallow. That's when Mama came in, all flushed from the heat and smiling.

Daddy glanced over at her as she set her laundry basket on the kitchen counter. Then, without raising his voice, he said two words I've only read on bathroom walls: "Fucking whore." That's what he called my mother. Suddenly he wasn't the father I always knew at all.

He took a step toward her. "Damn bitch," he said quietly, "My wife, the Whore of Babylon." He swung his arm in a wide arc, and the back of his hand hit the right side of her face. I can still hear it, a hollow "smack," like when somebody serves a volleyball. The whole rest of my life I will not forget that sound.

For the longest time nobody moved. Finally Mama touched her cheek where he had struck her, and Daddy dropped down on the living room sofa, buried his face in his hands, and sobbed. From where I sat, the two of them looked as large and distant as actors on a drive-in movie screen. Then Mama's hand shot out and grabbed my wrist. "Achsa, get up," she said and pulled me into their bedroom.

She shut the door. "I'm sorry, baby, I'm so sorry," she said, hugging me to her long enough for me to hear three of her heartbeats. I couldn't say anything, just stood there. My mind was an empty box.

Mama started pulling clothes out of her dresser, flinging them onto the bed. Underwear, stockings, a couple of slips, a pair of shorts, a blouse. Then she snatched three housedresses from the closet and a lipstick and a makeup bottle off her dressing table. She was crying and trembling, without making any noise or bothering to wipe the streaked mascara off her face. I thought she'd gone crazy as Daddy, until she pulled a cardboard suitcase off the top shelf of the closet and slammed everything into it. The whole thing didn't take two minutes, almost like she'd planned it out.

Then she ran into my room, grabbed some of my clothes and dropped them in the suitcase. "Get your school books, Achsa. We're going," she said.

I watched myself walk into the dining room—I had got on the same drive-in movie screen with them. Nothing felt real. Daddy sat on the sofa with his head in his hands. He didn't see or hear me, or at least he didn't look up. Mama snapped shut the two brass latches on the suitcase, "click, click," and we were out the door, down the stairs, and in the car before he ran outside to stop us.

We screeched out of the parking lot. Our 1950 Chevy broke the speed limit barreling through town. Mama didn't say a word, but she quit crying. I didn't say anything either, only stuck my hand out the window to feel the air. Every time we hit a pothole her car keys jingled, which for some reason made part of me want to cry. But I also had a mean elf crouched inside me ready to grin and shout. I was alone with my beautiful mother in a car speeding toward the setting sun going who knows where, and I never wanted it to end.

You love your mother an awful lot, so you must know what I mean. How sometimes you want her to yourself so badly, even if it's only for a little while. When Daddy was away fighting the war and I had my mother to myself I was too young to remember much, except how one cold morning I watched the sky turn the same fire color as her hair, and how one hot afternoon she pointed out the shiny red mushrooms fairies leave behind under trees after they dance.

After we turned onto the highway, Mama pulled in at a diner. "I need to make a phone call," she said and left me in the car. I stared straight ahead at a ploughed field that ended in a line of pine trees where the sun was sinking so fast you could see it move. I was pretty sure she was calling Daddy and that we'd turn around and go straight home. She was gone a long time. When she came back she reached through the car window and handed me a hamburger sack and a Coke in a Dixie cup. Her hand shook and she looked like she'd cried more.

"It's got a squirt of lime the way you like it," she said, pressing her palm against my cheek. "You okay, baby?" I nodded. She walked around to her side of the car, jerked open the door, which always sticks, and slid behind the wheel. "We've got a long trip ahead," she said, setting a cardboard cup of hot coffee on the dashboard and opening out its handles. "We're going to visit your Aunt Jane."

Aunt Jane is Mama's middle sister. She and Uncle Henry live in Mississippi, where he owns a hardware store. Mama's oldest sister, Mavis, whom I've never met, works at Macy's in New York.

"How long will we be gone?" I asked. It was the first thing I'd said since we left the apartment, and the words buzzed in my head like a bad telephone connection.

Mama frowned, sipped her coffee. I could see the bruise on her cheekbone, even in the twilight. "Don't ask me any questions right now, honey," she said, "because I sure don't have the answers."

She turned the key in the ignition but the car didn't start, which happens sometimes. "Bastard!" she said. I had never heard her use a word like that, and a tiny thrill ran through me, like I had been trusted with a secret. She turned the key again, harder, and muttered, "All I thought running out of the house was, 'What if the damn car won't crank?'"

The third time, it started fine. "Here, hold this," Mama said, handing me her coffee cup. She groped in her purse on the seat beside her, pulled out an unopened pack of Pall Mall cigarettes, peeled off the cellophane, and punched in the car lighter.

"I've never seen you smoke," I said.

The tip of her cigarette flared against the lighter and its burnt smell filled the car. "I used to, long ago," she answered. "I think it's time I took it up again." She tilted her head and blew out a cloud of blue smoke, before backing the car around and pulling away from the diner. She looked beautiful, and mysterious—like a famous actress I would never under normal circumstances get to meet.

The road unspooled in front of us and it felt exactly like you said, like nothing that would ever happen here had anything to do with things back home. "I want to know everything about you," I heard myself saying. I just blurted it out without thinking.

The air outside rushed past. For a long time it was the only sound in the car. Finally Mama said, very softly, "You want too much, Achsa. You all do." In the rearview mirror her eyes looked wide and frightened, like a little girl's.

When I read how you and Satnin are so close you have your own private language, my heart hurt like somebody punched it with their fist. Mama and I never were that way. Most times, I feel like I've got this huge, gaping hole inside me that can only be filled up with things about my mother that I don't know.

It's not as if she never answers my questions. She always does that. She just never answers quite the way I hope she will. For instance, I know that she and Daddy only knew each other just one week before they got married, and that they spent their honeymoon at Savannah Beach in the dead of winter with no one else around. One time I asked her what that was like. I wanted the whole story, beginning to end: Did their eyes meet across a crowded room like in that song "Some Enchanted Evening"? Did she know she loved him the first time he kissed her? Did he get down on one knee when he proposed?

Did they have a wedding cake with a tiny bride and groom on top? Did they honeymoon in a cottage, or in a motor court? Did he carry her across the threshold, did the bedspread smell of mildew, did she ever—even for a little while—feel sad? I wanted her to tell me all of it, everything. But all she did was sigh and say, "It was so foggy you almost never saw the ocean." Just that, nothing more. Ever.

Mama reached over in the car and took her coffee from me. It was cold. She drank it fast like medicine, tossing the empty cup in the back seat. "I married your father because he was a good man and I knew he would always love me, no matter what," she said, staring straight out at the night. Then all at once she didn't sound like anybody's mother anymore, just tired. "It seemed like a good idea at the time," she said.

She cut on the radio. "The Ballad of Davy Crockett" filled the car, and she started singing in a sweet alto voice, "'Davy, Davy Crockett, king of the wild frontier.' Sing with me, Achsa, honey," she said.

Reluctantly, I joined in. She held her cigarette and steered the car with her left hand, while she beat time on the wheel with the palm of her right. After "Davy Crockett," we sang with the Fontaine Sisters about how hearts of stone will never break. As we headed toward Anniston the station grew stronger. We sang "Let Me Go, Lover," "Rags to Riches," "Dance with Me, Henry," "The Breeze and I," every song that had words. When the Anniston station started to fade we tuned in one from Birmingham. When that one went we picked up Tuscaloosa. We sang with Somethin' Smith and the Redheads, Perry Como, Jo Stafford, Frankie Laine, Theresa Brewer, anyone and everyone who showed up. Around midnight I turned the dial to WLAC in Nashville. Mama didn't know these songs, but she learned the words quickly and always came in on the choruses. We sang with Johnny Ace, Joe Turner, LaVerne Baker—sang and sang to keep from saying everything we might have said. We sang ourselves out of Alabama into Mississippi, through Columbus and all the way to Lydia, where Aunt Jane and Uncle Henry live. The sun was coming up when we pulled into their driveway so hoarse we couldn't speak.

Aunt Jane fed us breakfast and put us to bed. It's afternoon now and we're still here. I guess we're staying, but I don't know for how long. I'll write again the minute I find out.

I am so sorry all this had to happen. Daddy always said it was up to him and me to look after Mama and keep her from all harm. I never thought that harm included him. I don't know how he could have done what he did. Most of the time I hate him for it. I would give anything if I could turn back the clock to when I saw Mama heading for the back door in that yellow sundress. I would snatch that laundry basket from her hands and bring in our clothes myself. I don't think that man across the hall would follow after <u>me</u>.

> Sincerely,
> Achsa

*   *   *

Lydia, Mississippi, Sunday, April 17, 1955

Dear Elvis,

Nobody's said anything, but it's starting to look like we're going to be here awhile. Mama spends a lot of time with Aunt Jane just talking. Or by herself—before lunch I heard her crying in her bedroom; later, I found her sitting in the porch swing, a <u>Good Housekeeping</u> lying unopened in her lap. She scooted over and patted the seat beside her. When I sat down she put her arm around me and we swung back and forth for a long time, never saying a single word. It was nice.

Daddy's called three times. Once, Mama talked to him. Aunt Jane took me into another room so we wouldn't overhear. I suppose she figured overhearing was what I wanted most to do, and she was right. He never asked to speak to me, I guess. I didn't think he would.

That reminds me, it's not a good idea for you to write me here. I'm sharing my 16-year-old cousin Nancy's bedroom, and she's one of those people who just <u>has</u> to find out every little thing everybody in the whole known world is up to. I wouldn't put it past her to steam open someone else's mail. That's why there's no return address on this envelope.

35

I'll write you again the first moment I get any privacy. I'll try to send a grammar lesson, too. Don't worry, Mama and I can't stay here forever. Sooner or later we've got to go back home.

Sincerely,

Achsa

Chapter four

April 20, 1955

Lydia, Mississippi, Wednesday, April 20,
very late—maybe even April 21

Dear Elvis,

I saw you sing tonight!

Truly!! I did!! I went with my cousin Nancy and her boyfriend Ramey Lee to Grenada to hear "that hillbilly singer they're all talking about," and when we got there it was you!!!

I'm out in Aunt Jane's porch swing with a flashlight. It's beautiful. The crickets are deafening and the whole world smells of flowers. Everyone else is asleep, but I can't possibly close my eyes until I write you just how much seeing you meant to me. That is, if I'm able. I have always known a lot of words, but they all seem to have deserted me now, when I need them most. All I can say is from this night I will always think of my life as split into two parts: before I saw you sing, and after.

I guess I better back up some.

I came so close to <u>not</u> going—to <u>not</u> seeing you—it scares me just thinking about it. Nancy and Ramey Lee never in a million years would have asked me, except Aunt Jane insisted. Under normal circumstances I would have said a polite "no." But it was Uncle Henry's poker night, and I figured with both me and Nancy gone, Mama and Aunt Jane could have some time to themselves. Rooming with Nancy is giving me a deep appreciation for that sort of thing. Then, too, I'd been cooped up since we got here and I just plain wanted to get out of the house, away from all the cabbage roses crawling over Aunt Jane's wallpaper. So I said I'd go. And I will <u>forever</u> <u>thank</u> <u>my</u> <u>lucky</u> <u>stars</u> I did!

I have to say the trip over and back was not exactly pleasant. Ramey Lee drives an ancient blue Ford with a back seat that's nothing but springs, so we all squeezed in front with Nancy in the middle. The sun was setting and it was country roads all the way. I rolled down my window so I could smell the honeysuckle, instead of Nancy's Evening in Paris perfume. Ramey Lee gave it to her and she drenches herself with it several times a day. They didn't talk much. Ramey Lee mostly frowned and fumed, I guess because Nancy couldn't stop me from coming. You could practically see steam blasting out of his ears. She stroked the back of his neck and made little cooing sounds to calm him down, but it didn't work too well. He grabbed up a handful of her rose-colored skirt and snarled, "What'd you have to wear that nigger-pink thing for?"

I don't like that word. Mama says nobody uses it but white trash. I sat very still until the air in the car settled down from his hissy fit. Then I told Nancy I thought her skirt looked lovely, especially the color.

Ramey Lee leaned forward so I could see him sneer at me. "You would," he said. Nancy laughed, and I felt stupid clear to my toes. Here I'd gone out on a limb defending her and all she'd done was cackle. She was taking Ramey Lee's side against her very own self.

After that, every time we came to a stop sign Ramey Lee pulled Nancy up against him and they necked until a car drove up and honked. One time he just pulled off the road and started kissing her and sticking his hand down her blouse like I wasn't even there. When she giggled and said, "Just what do you think you're doing, mister?" he told her, "This here road don't got enough stop signs to suit me."

I sat still as lichen on a log. As I saw it, there wasn't a whole lot else I could do. I gave some thought to getting out and taking a walk, but I was scared if I did they'd just drive off and leave me. It was a pretty uncomfortable situation, if you want to know the truth.

Ramey Lee needed to neck so much we got to the American Legion Hut late and had to park in the last space way back past the gravel part of the lot. Nancy said maybe we wouldn't get in and we should go back home, but Ramey Lee grabbed her arm and told her to "quit gimping around, after I done drove you and her all this way."

He sauntered over to the man at the door and came back grinning and holding three tickets. "Man said there's still seats left and Elvis Presley hasn't even come on yet," he said.

"Who?" I was sure my ears had played a trick on me.

Nancy let out a huge sigh. "Elvis Presley, dummy. That's who we came to see." My jaw must have dropped a mile. She told me, "Close your mouth, Ugly, or a bug will fly in." Sometimes she acts just plain mean.

I closed my mouth and tried to make my face a complete blank. Nancy and Ramey Lee are the last people on earth I'd ever want thinking I know anything about you. Except for the unfortunate circumstance that Nancy and I are kin, they're the last people on earth I'd want knowing anything about me at all. We went inside and found seats on some folding chairs at the very back, and I knew right then why people pinch themselves to make sure they're awake. I felt like I had landed in my own dream.

Teenage girls took up at least half the seats, which really surprised me. I don't know a single teenager who likes hillbilly country music, but there they were in droves. They were all still clapping for whoever had just gone off the stage, when the man in the bolo tie came out. I guess you heard what happened after that. He stepped up to the microphone and got as far as, "Ladies and gentlemen, here is a young man who——," when all those girls erupted in one endless, ear-splitting shriek that raised the hairs on the back of my neck straight up. The bolo-tie man gave a shrug and a grin and walked toward the wings, like it was all business as usual—and you ran out on stage. At last I saw the person I have been writing for so long!!

My first thought was, I had no idea you were so <u>handsome</u>!

The spotlight made your dark hair shine and your face glow like you had caught its light inside you. You bowed, straightened, and stood there a moment. Then you shook your legs that funny way and all the girls went wild. Screaming, crying, tearing their hair, I never saw the like of it. I wanted so to hear you, I hated they made all that noise. I couldn't believe they even screamed when you broke your guitar string and it sprang out in a silver spiral.

Before long, everyone was on their feet. Or almost everyone. Nancy was standing with her head flung back, shrieking like the rest of them. But when I glanced at Ramey Lee he was scrunched down in his chair looking mad as a thundercloud.

From then on, I watched only you.

You keep your eyes shut a lot, like you're in your own private world. But you're not, you hear every sound we make. And when you open your eyes, it's as if you look at each and every one of us, one by one. When my turn came, I could have sworn you knew me—that you had searched me out way in the back of the Legion Hut because you knew I was the girl you had been writing to. You stared at me a very long time without smiling, as if you wanted to pour all your music into me. And every sound you ever heard and loved.

As I stared back, a warmth began to spread inside me in slow, shuddering waves. I tried to stop it, clenched my fists so hard my fingernails left bloody quarter-moon prints in my palms, but it only grew stronger. A tear slid down my cheek, then another.

I cannot describe what happened next, except to say I <u>felt</u> so much I became frightened. Years ago, in the same <u>Life</u> magazine where I saw Mama, they had a picture of this Catholic statue where an angel has just pierced a woman's heart with an arrow that is God's pure love. The woman clutches the arrow as she falls, grimacing in mortal pain. The statue was called "The Ecstasy of St. Theresa," and I always wondered why. Why "ecstasy," if something hurt so much?

Now I understood. Tears gushed from my eyes, I screamed; the warmth inside me burst in shimmering stars—and I knew that sometimes pain and beauty are the same.

Then it was gone, every last bit of that strange, sweet agony.

I cried to get it back, but it didn't come. You finished singing, ran off the stage. I wanted only to be left alone, but someone grabbed my arm. Nancy.

"Ramey Lee says we got to go," she said. "He's real mad." He had hold of her other arm and was jerking her toward the exit.

"You dumb cow," he snarled at her, "screaming over that pansy greaseball."

"He is not a pansy greaseball," I told him. "He's going to be a big star."

"How the Sam Hell would you know?" Ramey Lee muttered and shoved us out the door.

Nobody said anything in the car going home. Nancy and Ramey Lee stared straight ahead and didn't neck. Finally, Nancy cut on the radio. I knew by heart the words to all the love songs, but there in the dark it seemed like I was hearing them for the very first time. They filled me completely. I felt what every love song means. During "Unchained Melody," I starved to have someone I loved simply take my hand or touch my arm. "I've Got You under My Skin" made me want my very atoms blending with somebody else's atoms until I no longer knew where I ended and he began. And "Pledging my Love," I felt that one the most of all. It hollowed out a hiding place so deep inside me a white hot fire could burn there always for the one I love, even after I am cold dead in my grave.

In that moment when you looked at me, I learned more than I ever did from all the downtown library's shelves of magazines and books. But I have no idea why this should be so, or what it means. During the brief time we have been writing, you have become my dearest, most cherished friend. But I cannot possibly have fallen in love with you—I've never even <u>met</u> you. Still, something wonderful and important happened to me tonight. If you know what it is, <u>please</u>, <u>please</u> <u>tell</u> <u>me</u>. I feel most unsettled and confused as things now stand.

As for the grammar, I had meant to show you about double negatives, but it is very long and complicated and I do not want to do it here. Mama says we're going home on Monday. I <u>promise</u> I will write you about double negatives the instant we return. Until then I remain,

      Very sincerely yours,

         Achsa

Chapter five

April 26–May 12, 1955

Dear Precious Baby Girl,

I call you that because it is what you are. You are God's own innocent child, sweet and pure as winter snow. And you are growing up into a beautiful woman. That is what happened to you in Grenada. It weren't nothing to be scared about at all.

That letter you wrote means so much to me I carry it in my pocket everywhere I go. I've read it till it is near tore apart. I love it how my singing made you feel so good. Now you know how I feel on stage doing it. It is a beautiful thing. The man that made that St. Theresa statue, he knew. Out there singing I got nothing but God's pure love inside me. So much love it hurts me like a jolt of lightning. Or like my heart is fixing to explode.

Precious girl that is what you felt. All that love running straight from me to you. That you <u>did</u> feel it and that you <u>told</u> me makes you <u>so</u> <u>very</u> <u>dear</u> <u>and</u> <u>special</u> in my eyes. We have an abiding bond between us from now on.

But dearest girl I'd of give <u>anything</u> if you had made yourself known to me after the show! I would of loved <u>so</u> <u>much</u> to see you and be with you, us both still feeling all that love. I would of drove you home in my new Cadillac, the greatest car I've ever owned. You can rest assured I would take precious care of you the whole way. You are a good girl. I never would do nothing to you, not one single thing, to spoil you for when you get married.

Instead you go riding off with that Ramey Lee that don't even like me none!

I got no idea why you done it. Maybe you had it in your head you coming up to me when I'd got done singing was wrong. It is not, not at all!!

Dearest Baby Girl, I am praying to the good Lord every night that we will have another chance to be together. Meanwhile I am <u>still</u> looking for that picture I have <u>begged</u> you for. I <u>do</u> <u>not</u> <u>understand</u> why it does not come. Guess there's more than one thing about you I got no idea about.

Very ~~truly~~ devotedly yours,
Elvis

P.S. Did you get the picture I sent? Please let me know. I reckon you don't have as big a need for it now you have seen the real me. Still I want you to have it.

*   *   *

New Orleans, Louisiana, Sunday, May 1, 1955

Dear Baby Girl,

Did you get home OK from Mississippi? I have not heard from you. I hope nothing went wrong on your trip. I hope I did not say something to make you mad either. I sure did not mean to. Please please write me back real soon and let me know you are all right. And please please <u>please</u> send me your picture!!

Guess what? I am a "Special Added Attraction" on the Hank Snow All-Star Jamboree touring show. They got Faron Young and Mother Maybelle and the Carter Sisters. Country music don't get no better. I am proud to be among them.

"Baby, Let's Play House" and "You're Right, I'm Left, She's

Gone" gets shipped to record stores next week. Too bad I have to still play like I'm a girl or I would send you one. Them new little 45 rpm records don't break even in the mail. They're made out of plastic. Bet you didn't know that.

You can see on the envelope we moved to 2414 Lamar. That's that house I told you I was fixing to rent for my folks. It is the nicest place we ever lived. So pretty it almost don't seem real.

Very truly yours,
Elvis

* * *

Atlanta, Georgia, Monday, May 2, 1955

Dear Elvis Presley,

I will keep your beautiful letter always. I have read it over many times—and every time it breaks my heart.

When I first wrote you, I had no intention to deceive you. The instant I realized you thought I was a man and worked at a radio station, I set you straight immediately. I have, however, let you hold on to another mistaken assumption. Now I fear it is my duty to set that one straight as well.

I do not look anything like my mother. I am small and thin, my hair and eyes are a dull brown, ordinary.

But that isn't all. Were I simply a plain, colorless girl, I could strive to overcome it, maybe cultivate a strong spirit, like Jane Eyre—which I have sometimes tried to do. But there exists another hurdle I do not know how to climb.

I was born with a hare lip. A doctor fixed it when I was too young to remember, and I talk fine, although I couldn't say proper "S's" and "T's" until I was nearly ten. The problem is, the operation left my upper lip thick and lopsided, a crooked, upside down "V" with a white scar leading to it from my left nostril. The kids in grammar school—the not-nice ones—used to call me "Nigger Lip" on the playground. They still do, in a way. Only now they call me "Nig," like it's some sort of nickname. I guess in a way it is.

That's why I never sent a picture. Or thanked you for yours. I figured if I ignored any mention of pictures maybe you'd forget, and just this once the way I look wouldn't matter. It was wrong, and I have no excuse. Except every time one of your letters came, for a little while I knew how being pretty felt. Like living on a perfect island, where the warm sun shines and flowers bloom every day.

I guess Mama's life was always like that. It must be hard on her having an ugly daughter. The way I look—and that I'm smart—makes me what the kids at Foster call a gimp. In the dictionary "gimp" means "cripple." At Foster it means "outcast." You're a gimp from your first day. About the only way anyone ever gets out of it is sometimes if they transfer to a different school they won't be one anymore. That happened to Linda Sheffield when she moved to Florida, but it won't happen to me.

Your new house sounds wonderful. So does your nice new car. I hope it has a comfortable back seat for you and the boys to take turns sleeping on.

I don't imagine you will write me anymore so I don't guess it matters, but we are moving, too. Starting this Friday, May 6, my new address is 1807 Camptown Circle, Atlanta, Georgia. Unfortunately, I'll still go to Foster High.

If I never hear from you again, I will truly understand. And I will always remember you fondly. I mean both those things with all my heart.

Most sincerely,
Achsa

*   *   *

1807 Camptown Circle, Atlanta, Georgia, Friday, May 6, 1955

Dear Elvis Presley,

After I mailed my last letter, I remembered that I promised to tell you about double negatives. As a person of my word, I must keep that promise. So please do not think me forward for sending one last letter. I do not expect you to reply.

A double negative occurs when a person wants to say a really definite "no," so he says it two different ways. But what really happens is, the two "no" words cancel each other out and end up meaning "yes." Double negatives do not all look alike, so they are hard to spot. Usually, though, a sentence with a double negative will have two words that start with "N." "Not nothing" (which really means "something"). "Not never" ("sometimes"). "Not nowhere" ("somewhere").

You often write double negatives in your letters, so there's a good chance you also use them when you speak. Getting rid of them will help you tremendously on your road toward better speech.

I just wanted to make sure you knew. I mean, since I promised.

I really like our new home here at 1807 Camptown Circle in Atlanta. I have never lived in a real house before. Only apartments, like the one we rented on South Highland.

Yours truly,
Achsa McEachern

*   *   *

1807 Camptown Circle, Atlanta, Georgia, Tuesday, May 10, 1955

Dear Elvis Presley,

Forgive me for pestering you with yet another letter, but sometime back you asked me an important question which I neglected to answer. You wanted to know if, once you learned the correct way of speaking, you always had to speak that way. The answer is no, you can speak any way you want at any time.

I think I did not answer you earlier because I could not imagine how proper speech can come between you and the people who care about you. They should admire you for your initiative and emulate it. I'm sure they will—I can't imagine why they would do otherwise.

I hope this answers your question. I apologize for the delay and any inconvenience it may have caused you.

Sincerely,
Achsa McEachern

*   *   *

1807 Camptown Circle, Atlanta, Georgia, Thursday, May 12, 1955

Dear Mr. Presley,

In my explanation of double negatives two letters ago, I forgot to mention that the word "don't" often appears in such sentences. ("He <u>don't</u> never do right.")

Recognizing and eliminating double negatives can be complicated at first. If you ever have any questions at all regarding them, please do not hesitate to write them to me here at 1807 Camptown Circle, Atlanta, and I will answer immediately.

In closing, I want to wish you the best of luck throughout your life and your career.

Yours very truly,
Achsa McEachern

Chapter six

May 16–20, 1955

Dear Achsa,

I don't have <u>no</u> questions about double negatives. But I do have <u>a</u> <u>question</u>. Can I still call you Baby Girl?

Cause you still are, you know.

I got to admit I done some thinking after your last letter. What it come down to is you're the same sweet person I been writing all along and you look just the same to me as always. Which is still a big question mark since you never sent me ~~no~~ a picture.

So it don't make any difference what you look like. I don't think ~~no different~~ any different about you ~~then~~ than I ever did. Those kids calling you a ugly name, it don't mean you <u>are</u> ugly. And you must not ever let it make you <u>feel</u> ugly in your heart. I expect it's just they don't like it you are smarter than them.

I will tell you something. The woods is full of pretty girls. I don't need another one. I done had me enough of pretty girls to last a lifetime.

The day after your letter come I did a show in this huge new baseball park in Jacksonville. After I got done I walked off the stage

49

and came back on a bunch of times and them girls was all still clapping and screaming. So just kidding around I said, "Girls, I'll see y'all all backstage."

Baby Girl, you won't believe what happened. They <u>came</u>!!

Ever blessed one of them! They was chasing after me, grabbing onto my clothes, even yanking out my hair. I pulled my jacket off and threw it at them, thinking to slow them down. Well, they ripped that jacket clean to pieces and just kept on coming! You ought to see some of them girls' <u>fingernails</u>! They tore the shirt right off me. Then they started going for my <u>pants</u>!! That's when I ran in a bathroom, shut the door, and climbed up on a shower stall. All they did was to come in through the window.

I hadn't never been so scared! They was just girls. They didn't mean me no harm. But they was <u>hundreds</u> of them! All them pretty-girl hands reaching up and pulling on me. One girl even yanked off both my boots!

The cops took a couple years showing up. Finally, they got there and chased them girls out and I climbed down off the shower. Even then my heart was hammering.

That night I called Satnin, like I always do. First thing she said was, "Baby, what's the matter?" like she could hear my jackrabbit heart clear through the phone. I told her some girls chased me and I had to hide in a bathroom. I laughed about it, got her to laughing too. I can't ~~never~~ ever tell her how it really was. She worries about me the live-long day. She don't ever stop.

That night I couldn't hardly sleep at all. Just lay awake wondering, what if them girls had got all my clothes tore off and there weren't nothing left to tear apart but <u>me</u>?

Yeah, I got me more pretty girls than I can handle, that's the almighty truth. And all I want is my sweet Baby Girl Achsa sending me letters and teaching me to talk right. Reading what you got to say, writing you back, it brings me peace. Many is the time I found me a hidey-hole in some high school gym or Legion Hall, sat down right there and wrote you. It keeps me from getting scared before a show.

So you write me all about your new house and what you're going to do this summer. You hear? I will write you back. I promise.

You will always be a pretty girl to me.
        Yours very truly,
            Elvis

P.S. We got two shows in Meridian. After that I'll be in Texas a whole week. If you are ever any place we are playing, you better come backstage so I can meet you. If I ever hear you didn't, I <u>really</u> <u>will</u> never write to you again. <u>That</u> is a promise, too.

P.P.S. I got to thank you for answering my question. It is a great comfort to know I do not have to speak right all the time. It is also a comfort learning how to speak right when I want to.

*   *   *

Atlanta, Friday, May 20, 1955, very late at night

Dear Elvis,
        If you had been in Atlanta this afternoon you might have seen me looping and soaring high over the rooftops of Dreamer Hills. Which is another way to say I got your letter!!!
        I dared not open it till my parents went to sleep. So I stashed it temporarily with the others in a box way in the back of my closet and tried my absolute best to contain myself. But I didn't do a very good job. I ate so little dinner Mama thought I'd caught a virus. Later I tried to study, but the whole War of the Roses simply blurred right through my brain. When my parents finally went to sleep and I was about to open your envelope at last, suddenly I feared you might only be writing to say you were never going to write me anymore. But you weren't, you WEREN'T!!!
        So now I am once more holed up in my room answering another of your wonderful letters, flashlight balanced on the bed, Penelope turned low on the radio. All is right again in my world.
        In the past couple of days I've heard "Baby, Let's Play House" twice—and it's <u>super</u>!!! I love all the "b-b-b-baby" stuff at the beginning. And I bet you wrote that part about the pink Cadillac. It sounds just like you.

51

Oh, but I can't believe those girls in Jacksonville! Didn't they know they could have hurt you really badly?!! No wonder you were terrified! And I don't blame your mother one bit for worrying. I hope that kind of thing never happens again! I bet you do, too!

You asked about our house. I guess I'm like you. I love it so much I can't believe it's real. What's really strange is I care about it just like it's a flesh-and-blood person, some long-lost relative shown up at last to circle us with loving arms.

Daddy bought it while we were in Mississippi as a surprise for Mama. He always said he'd never buy a house, even though she wanted one. Can you imagine how sorry he must have felt for what he did to her? The very day we got home, he herded us into the car after dinner, said he was going to treat us to milkshakes at the Tastee-Freeze. But before we got there, he turned down this winding street of little white houses, identical except for different-colored shutters. Two windows in front, a door in the middle, a tiny front stoop—they looked like faces smiling.

He pulled in the driveway of a red-shuttered house, climbed out of the car and opened both our doors. "Come on, I want to show you something," he said.

We followed him single file up the walk. Daddy opened the front door and motioned us inside. I'd never been in a brand new house no one had ever lived in. The cream-colored walls didn't have a single smudge, and the floors still smelled like oak-tree lumber. I tiptoed across the living room holding my breath.

Mama's eyes burrowed into all the corners. "Warren, what have you done? Did you rent this house?" she said.

Right then Daddy did something I never thought I'd see. He stepped back, looked at her, and his face cracked open in a big, broad, ear-to-ear grin. "I bought it," he told her. "I bought it for us."

Mama clenched her hands into fists by her sides and slowly backed away from him toward the center of the living room, sort of like she did when he brought home the Christmas angel. A lot of things happened on her face in a very short time. Her eyes opened wide and panicky and turned moist like she was going to cry. The corners of her mouth twitched. Then she let out a sound somewhere between a snort, a sigh and a sob, opened her hands and turned her palms toward Daddy, like a captured soldier in a war movie who doesn't have any weapons. "OK, Warren," she said, "OK." She raised her chin and gave a little smile.

"OK," Daddy answered. Most of his grin had faded, but he still had a bit of it left.

So now we've got our very own house, nicer than any place we've ever lived. The day we moved in, before the van came with our furniture, Daddy stood where Mama had, in the middle of the empty living room, stretched out his arms, and turned all the way around. Then he walked over and hit one of the walls so hard it shook. "If we want," he said, "we can knock this wall down. It's <u>our</u> wall, nobody cares. That's what it means to own your own home." For the second time in a single week, I saw my father happy.

I guess Mama's happy, too. Daddy keeps following her around the house, but when she turns and catches him at it she smiles. She went downtown yesterday and bought all new bedspreads and curtains. Mine are white with ruffles, and my room looks really good.

The very best thing about my room, though, is the magnolia tree outside my window and the mockingbird that sings there late at night. His song echoes in the stillness, making the dark world seem very vast. I leave the window open so he'll wake me, and my room smells of magnolia blossoms. He's out there singing now. I have never heard a nightingale, but I am sure it could not sound more beautiful. Someday I'll write a poem about him.

Did I ever tell you I'm going to be a poet? I'm going to write plays, too—some plays are nothing but long poems with people in them. If I were pretty like Mama, I might take up acting on the New York stage. Theatre people lead such fascinating lives. I read about them all the time in <u>Theatre</u> <u>Arts</u>. There's a poem that goes, "My candle burns at both ends, it will not last the night. But ah, my foes and oh, my friends, it gives a lovely light." That is how I want to be, a bright, burning flame that shines for everyone around me.

I've got it all planned out. I'm going to live in Greenwich Village. That's the coolest part of New York. Everyone there is either an actor, an artist or a poet! And renting an apartment costs practically nothing if you don't mind climbing lots of stairs and living without hot water. Which I wouldn't mind at all; in fact, it sounds wonderfully Bohemian. I shall live there all my days and never marry. My life will belong only to my art. I read someone saying that recently. It gave me goosebumps.

Of course, it would be lovely to someday have a fire in my soul for someone, like in "Pledging My Love," and him have a fire in his soul for me, too. But I don't think that will happen. It won't matter, though. I'll have so many friends we'll see to it no one is ever left alone on holidays. And when any of us has a birthday, we'll throw a party so big there'll be people there nobody knows.

So you see, you have absolutely no cause to feel sorry for <u>me</u>. I can plan my life any way I choose. The only thing a pretty girl can plan for is to marry well as soon as she gets out of college. If not before.

Speaking of college, my English teacher told me yesterday she's sure I can get a scholarship to any place I want! A scholarship means you go for free. Sometimes they even give you spending money! That means I can go to college in <u>New</u> <u>York</u>!! Then when I graduate, I'll earn my living writing poems for magazines like <u>The Ladies Home Journal</u> and <u>The Saturday Evening Post</u>—and in my spare time I shall write a play. On weekends I'll sit by the fountain in Washington Square Park and compose poems for people right there on the spot and charge them money like those artists who cut silhouettes. I'll burn candles in wine bottles to save electricity, and buy day-old bread so I'll have money left for books and theatre tickets. Mine will truly be a lovely life. People don't call you "Nigger Lip" in Greenwich Village. Or anyway, I can't imagine it.

That's what I think about late at night when the mockingbird sings. My plans. And then I fall asleep and dream about them.

Here's the grammar lesson for today. It's easy. Use "an" instead of "a" before words that start with a vowel. Vowels are a, e, i, o, and u. So it's "an ugly name," not "a ugly name." I think the only reason we're supposed to do this is it makes the vowel words easier to say.

One other thing: You asked if you can still call me Baby Girl, and I don't think so. "Baby Girl" is a pretty-girl name. You called me that when you thought I was pretty, and it doesn't feel right anymore. Actually, it didn't feel right in the first place, if you want to know the truth. It made me think how small I am, and young. So I'd like it if you just went back to Achsa, if it's all the same to you.

In closing, I want to say again how glad I am you are still writing me. I would feel awfully lonely if you stopped.

Most sincerely,
Achsa

Chapter seven

May 26–June 4, 1955

Meridian, Miss., Thursday, May 26, 1955

Dear Baby Girl,

How did you know that about the pink Cadillac? You really are the coolest girl I ~~ever~~ never met!

I just got done riding in my first parade. Sat on the hood of a huge convertible and waved at folks. Nobody paid me any mind. I felt like the Indian on a Pontiac. Had a big time anyway.

I really got a kick out of your letter. Anybody ever tell you you think too much? You done planned everything out, all right. Only, you done planned all the wrong things. For one thing, why don't you think you can be an actress? There is actresses ugly as homemade sin. Not to say you're ugly or anything. It's just, you don't have to be ~~no~~ a beauty queen. And another thing, you're just cheating some poor guy out of marrying you by saying you don't want to when you do. For a smart girl sometimes you don't make good sense.

Here's how I see it. You, me, everybody, we each got us a voice inside our heads. Whatever your voice says you want to be, that's what you got to plan for. You got to listen to that voice and trust it. It is the good Lord talking.

Got to be, else how would I know I was going to be a singer? There weren't ~~nobody~~ anybody but one of my uncles sang and played guitar. So how come back far as I remember did I have music in me? Where else did it come from but the Lord?

Here is how the Lord works. The year I turned eleven I wanted this blue bike from the hardware store for my birthday, only Satnin wouldn't let me have it. She was scared I'd ride it in the street and get hit by a car. That was the Lord working through Satnin. What they bought me instead was a guitar.

After high school, the Lord saved me from being an electrician all my days. He put it in my head to go to Sun Studios and make a record. Anybody that's got the three dollars and ninety-eight cents to pay for it can make a record there. You don't have to be ~~nobody~~ somebody special. By then I was really in the Lord's hands. I met Mr. Sam Phillips and them and my life just took its course.

But like I told you, all this time the Lord's been saying he means me to do more. One time back in high school I dyed my hair black and got a cold wave to see if I could look like Tony Curtis. That had to be the Lord talking. I was not ~~no~~ any kind of handsome brute back then. Kids called me "Squirrel," meaning some ratty, twitchy animal just jumped out of a tree and acting weird. Well, I didn't listen to them. I listened to the Lord. When I got the cold wave curlers out of my hair I <u>did</u> look like Tony Curtis. That's when I knew the Lord meant me to be an actor and I better start getting ready.

He put it in my head to wear dress pants to school so I'd feel special. He told me, "Go to the picture show. Watch Marlon Brando and James Dean, how they walk, how they talk. Then you go walk and talk just like them. And don't you never ever smile. The girls don't go for some man grinning like a silly fool."

The good Lord told me all those things and He is still talking to me. He is saying I am almost there and getting closer every day. The Lord talks to you, too, Baby Girl. All the time. All you got to do is listen. And do what He says.

The Lord brought you into <u>my</u> life so I could learn ~~grammer~~ grammar and the folks in Hollywood won't treat me like them New York folks at "Arthur Godfrey's Talent Scouts." He brought me into

<u>your</u> life so I could tell you what I just done told you. And what I am fixing to tell you now.

Here it is. You got to quit letting other folks make you feel ugly. From right this minute on, you got to forget all about how other folks think you look. How they think you look don't matter. It don't matter ~~none~~ any at all. I promise. Only thing that matters is how <u>you</u> think you look.

So listen now. You go get you one of them blouses girls pull down off their shoulders. Get you a red skirt with bright, pretty flowers, and one of them wide stretchy belts. Then you put on all them clothes the same way I put on the clothes I buy on Beale Street. Pull that blouse off your shoulders far as it'll go, hook that belt tight as you can and still keep breathing. Feel all the beauty of them clothes come into you. Then go outside and hold your head up high like they just crowned you Miss America. And anybody calls you "Nigger Lip," you look on him with pity. Lots of black people I have seen, they got strong, beautiful faces. That person calling you that ugly name, he ~~don't know shi~~ has made a bad mistake.

You do all them things and folks will say, "There goes a pretty girl." I guarantee it. Know why? Cause that's what you're <u>telling</u> them. The way you walk, the clothes you got on, they're saying you <u>know</u> you're a pretty girl. It is a true thing that folks <u>believe</u> what you tell them. I am the living proof.

I mean it, Baby Girl. You do like I said, things will start to change. And always, always listen to the Lord. His Way is one big mystery so complicated it's not meant for us to understand. Still I know this much. He brought you and me together for a reason, and He tells us what we need to know.

Very sincerely,

Elvis

P.S. Me not calling you Baby Girl because you think it is a pretty-girl name is foolishness. You ought to be called a pretty-girl name all the time. Whoever stuck you with a name like Achsa somebody ought to horsewhip them. They should have ~~give~~ gave you a pretty-girl name like Cynthia or Lisa. Achsa is an old-maid-schoolteacher name.

If you don't like Baby Girl I won't call you that again. Still I am not now or ever anymore having any part of calling you Achsa and that's that.

No matter what I call you, you will always be Baby Girl in my mind. How about if I just call you B?

* * *

Atlanta, Monday, June 4, 1955, late at night again

Dear Elvis,

I truly appreciate your generous advice. As you once wrote me, I will take all your words to heart. And I promise I will truly follow them in spirit, but right now that's about all I can muster.

To begin with, I'm afraid I would look the height of silliness decking myself out like the Queen of Sheba and sashaying around. Also, Daddy thinks red is the Devil's color, so Mama and I don't own a single red thing. Without the red skirt I guess there's not much point in the rest of it. I'm pretty skinny, anyway.

As for my name, I daresay I like it even less than you, and you can call me "B" if you want. It beats "Baby Girl," anyway. While we're on the subject, "Elvis" isn't such great shakes in the name department either, if you want my opinion. So if I have to be "B," maybe you should be "E." I will most likely continue to sign myself "Achsa." In spite of all its drawbacks, it _is_ my name and while I've not grown fond of it, I have grown used to it.

So much for all the things I can't—or won't—do. There is one thing I can: Stop sitting with my hand over my mouth at school. I do it all the time. I prop my elbow on my desk and my chin in my hand and rub my fingertips back and forth over the scar on my upper lip. I've done it ever since kindergarten. It makes a cozy place to hide, like a tree's leafy branches. Taking my hand away feels like climbing down from the tree onto flat, open ground where anything can happen. But I _will_ do it. I've already started. A little bit more every day. I guess that's following the spirit of your advice. I hope so, anyway.

That's surely enough about all that. Now I think I've earned a question: Do you really believe God _talks_ to you? Does He say things you can actually <u>hear</u>? I don't think even Daddy, as religious as he is, believes that. I don't consider myself a heathen, but I've always thought of the voice in my head as just me, my own thoughts—and of God as "up there" somewhere, sitting on a golden throne waiting for <u>us</u> to talk to <u>Him</u>, that that's what praying's for.

And I've got to say my whole family does plenty of that. Whether we want to or not.

I've never told <u>anybody</u> what I'm about to tell you now. It's worse, even, than climbing to the Negro balcony. It's so embarrassing I never even once let Linda Sheffield spend the night, because I was afraid she'd blab it all over school. But I know you won't tell, so here goes: The last thing my family does before we go to sleep at night, every night, Daddy makes us all sit on my parents' bed and have what he calls "evening prayers."

I'm sure nobody does it but us, not even the preacher's family. But we've done it as long as I remember, I guess ever since Daddy got back from the war. Back then I'd lie with my head in Mama's lap and my eyes closed, feeling the daisies on her chenille bathrobe press into my cheek, breathing her Ponds-cold-cream smell and listening to Daddy's nasal voice drone Bible words.

Except that I've grown up and lie propped on an elbow, nothing's changed. Like tonight. Daddy read the part from the book of Daniel where King Nebuchadnezzar casts Shadrack, Meshak, and Abednigo into the fiery furnace. He always reads the Bible Genesis-to-Revelation and then immediately starts over. I bet we've heard it a million times. Well, six or seven anyway. After Daddy's through, Mama reads the day-page from this monthly magazine for Presbyterians. Tonight it talked about overcoming obstacles.

I'd die if anybody peeked in a window and saw us: Daddy's scrawny chicken legs poking out from his wrinkled boxer shorts, Mama's housecoat faded and her freckles showing, my pincurls unspiraling and hair sticking up all over my head. It's really strange and creepy, us there like that, but for the life of me I can't figure out why. Maybe it's that that's what we're really like, me and my family. Maybe that's when we're the most like who we are.

I'm not sure what I mean, and maybe I'm not saying it right.

The thing I can't understand is, I <u>hate</u> evening prayers, the whole idea of them embarrasses me to tears. And yet it's then I feel the most like we're a family. I watch us in my mind's eye, the three of us there on my parents' bed, as if I'm hovering near the ceiling. We look small and fragile from that height, my parents most of all.

Tonight, when Mama finished reading about overcoming obstacles, we all knelt on the floor with our elbows on the bed, like always, and we prayed. Mama puts a pillow under her knees and never stays down more than a few minutes, but Daddy stays down sometimes half an hour, his bony kneecaps pressed into the hard floorboards and his war-wound leg quivering like a horse's flank. I can't imagine what he prays for all that time. I used to think he went to sleep, but if he did that he'd fall over.

Myself, I'm always finished in two minutes flat, but I can't just get up or Daddy lectures me for neglecting my immortal soul. Once or twice, just to be mean, I tried staying down as long as he did, but I couldn't do it. Usually I wait for Mama to get up, which is what I did tonight. While I was waiting, I opened my eyes just a sliver and peered out the window on the other side of the bed. You can see the lights from all the houses, way down into the valley part of Dreamer Hills. It made me feel like the shepherd on the hillside in those "O Little Town of Bethlehem" Christmas cards, and I got to wondering if maybe every family out there has something that's like evening prayers only different, something that shows them who they are and that they never talk about—and if that's the thing that makes them a family and makes them keep on being one.

It's like there's this net of tiny lights spread out across the valley. Each light is a family, and each family has got its own secrets and stuff, but they are all woven together in the darkness. When I think things like that I always want to cry, but in a good way. I guess if God's ever going to talk to me, that's when.

Before long, though, my knees started hurting, and when Mama finished praying I rejoiced. Once evening prayers are done, I'm free. I can go in my room, close the door, and listen to Daddy-O Radio.

I don't know how much I've told you about wDDO. They play

gospel music until 5 P.M. Then Johnny Wooten comes on. He's the white man who owns the station, but he plays rhythm and blues just like Avenue Al. That's Mr. Al Willis, a Negro who owns the pawn shop across from the station. He's on right after Jonny Wooten and right before Penelope. He always shows up a few minutes early and kids around with Mr. Wooten on the air. Last night he suggested Mr. Wooten "might want to come on down to Avenue Al's Loans and liberate some money from that gold pocket watch you're always flashing, so you can pay down your possum-choking poker debt." Mr. Wooten chuckled and said he's still on the lookout for the "low-life third party" who marks Avenue Al's cards.

If right then you happened onto WDDO by accident—like I did that ~~hillbilly~~ country station where I heard "That's All Right"—you'd probably think they were both Negroes. Or white, it wouldn't matter. What <u>does</u> matter is they're much, much funnier than Jack Benny and Rochester! It's a pity 99.99999 percent of white people in Atlanta don't have the vaguest notion they exist.

I'm sure most of the white people who do listen are teenagers. At Foster it's pretty much only the hoods—and their girlfriends, of course. I myself found out about WDDO last year from Hank Lawson, this hood who goes to my church when his parents make him. I heard him talking about it with Betty Jean Puckett, who's sort of hoody, too, and dates Hank's best friend.

Betty Jean does a terrific Penelope imitation. She says you can tell from her voice she's white. She used to say Penelope was Mrs. Johnny Wooten, but last week after Sunday school she told me Hank has it on good authority that she is really Mr. Wooten's <u>mistress</u>, that he keeps her in a penthouse on top of the Darlington apartment building and buys her everything under the sun she wants.

Betty Jean is, hands down, the coolest girl I've ever known. She's a year and a half older than me, and she's the only girl I ever saw who can talk jive and not sound ridiculous. She rolls her eyes, says, "Dig it, man," and all the boys just grin like silly idiots. At church we're practically buddies—I'm the only girl anywhere near her age, except for poor Marlene Sprague, who is mentally slow. But even though Betty Jean buddies up to me at church, I don't dare speak to her at school. Since I'm a gimp and she's not, it's up to her to speak to me. If she ever wants to, that is. We had English together all last spring and she never so much as tossed me a mumbling word.

When I said to her at church that maybe Hank made it up about Penelope, she just rolled her eyes. "How <u>else</u> could a <u>woman</u> ever have her own radio show, even on a colored station?" she said. Since I'd never heard of any other lady disc jockeys, I had to admit she had a point.

And whether or not the rumor is true about Penelope and Mr. Wooten, I can see why people might believe it. Penelope talks with her mouth right up against the microphone, so close you can hear her breathe—which is absolutely not creepy at all. She'll say stuff like, "Baby, you <u>know</u> your girl Penelope loves you the <u>most</u>. So don't you go running off now, you just stay right here and listen. Curl up in that big old easy chair, maybe sip a little of that King Cotton peach wine we been talking about, and suck on one of those delicious ribs you got left from Benton Brothers Barbecue—I <u>know</u> you been there, baby. Because right now we got Mr. Al Hibbler coming up to sing his ooh sooo beautiful 'Unchained Melody.' So <u>stay</u> with me, baby, because your girl Penelope is sending <u>this</u> one out e<u>special</u>ly for <u>you</u>."

All the hoods at Foster are crazy in love with her. They're always talking about her—any time they're not jiving around like Avenue Al. Last Sunday, I overheard Betty Jean ask Hank why he kept yawning all through service. He grinned and said, "Man, that Penelope, she keeps me <u>up</u> <u>all</u> <u>night</u>!" Betty Jean giggled, punched him in the arm, and called him a bad boy like he had said something nasty. Which I guess he did, but I don't know what it was.

There's only one bone I've got to pick with Penelope. She never plays your records. I know wddo is a mostly Negro station, but I think she ought to anyway. They'd fit right in. I called a couple of times to ask her to, but she never answered the phone.

I guess I better quit writing this letter now and go to sleep. It's so late the mockingbird's outside. He's singing his heart out. Just like you.

Very sincerely,
Achsa

P.S. School gets out Friday. Can you believe when I come back in September I'll be a <u>senior</u>?!! I'm working this summer at a swimming pool, checking kids in and out. I tried really hard to get a job selling records at Junior's, but they didn't need anyone.

P.P.S. I almost forgot the grammar. Don't ever say "knowed." There's no such word. Say "knew" instead. "He <u>knew</u> all the answers on the test."

Chapter eight

June 7–July 4, 1955

Tuesday, June 7, 1955, somewhere over Texas

Dear Achsa,

I'm afraid it isn't in me to call you "B" right now, or even "Baby Girl." Something bad is happened. My car burnt up! My pink Cadillac! And I like to burnt up with it! It's all I can think about. It's got me so scared I can't sleep.

I need you to be the grownup person for a little while instead of me. You got to help me figure what it means and what to do.

It happened real late Sunday. We'd just got done with a show in Arkansas and I was on my way to Texas. We was playing there the next day. All of a sudden my radio give out, just went dead as a rock. Everything got real quiet. All I could hear was the car speeding along on the road. Then a few miles outside Fulton, where my Daddy's from, there started up a wailing. That's all I know to call it. Sounded like some haint chasing after my left rear wheel.

I speeded up, and the haint commenced to dragging on the wheel like it was trying to stop me. It got to pulling so hard I near about couldn't steer. Then I smelled something burning, like the haint come carrying part of Hades in a croaker sack.

Sweat was pouring off me, and I got to feeling like the car was

heating up. I gripped the steering wheel and started praying, "Lord, please let me make it into Fulton. Lord, please get me to where there's lights and people and a filling station."

To make a long story short I didn't make it. It got to where I couldn't drive no more, so I pulled over. It's a ~~damn~~ real good thing, too. I got out to have a look, and fire was licking at the left rear tire and all around the gas tank.

I ran up a bank alongside the road and sat there staring at the flames spreading out underneath my car, praying they'd stop. They didn't. There come a big "Whooosh!" and fire went boiling everywhere. It rolled in the windows and started burning up the seats. I could feel it heating up my face even from that far away. Then the horn blew one long blast and give out like a dying heifer. It was like that car had been alive.

I hadn't never felt so helpless in my life. I didn't have no water. I couldn't do nothing to put out the fire. All I could do was sit and watch it burn. It like to killed me. When that horn give out, my heart just broke. I started crying like a baby.

Sitting up there on that hill watching my car burn up, it felt like living out my worst nightmare, like it was my whole life going up in flames. It was like the Lord was saying, "Elvis, I done give you everything, and I can take it all away. I can take it in the blink of an eye, same as I just took your car. Cause I done give you this great and wondrous gift, and all you done with it is <u>sin</u>."

It's true. I have. I do. I sin all the time anymore.

Used to be, I could tell Satnin everything I done. My girlfriend, too. Did I ever tell you I had a girlfriend? She's a good girl. She's 16. Except for a few times we was broke up, we been going steady two years now. She stays over a lot with Satnin and Daddy. I call there every night and talk to all of them, tell them what all is going on. "I sung in the same show as Hank Snow." "Mother Maybelle Carter talked to me backstage." Used to be, that was everything. Now seems like every time I dial the phone there's more and more I can't say.

It's been that way ever since we started going on the road. It's real different out here. I'm different, too. I call home and need to check a mirror to make sure it's the real me talking and not some cat the road made up. There is all temptations out here. It's easy to give in. I keep telling myself I got to stop it, but I can't. I'm all the time asking the Lord for help and He don't never give me none. Not none at all.

Unless that's why He burnt up my car. Unless that's Him saying, "Elvis, you keep doing what you're doing and I will take away the most precious thing you ever love."

My girlfriend is a gospel music fan. She would like nothing better than me singing gospel all the time. I used to want that too. More than anything I used to want to be exactly like Jake Hess in the Statesmen Quartet. In Memphis I used to go to all the all-night sings and sit there to the small hours feeling the love of Jesus flood into my heart.

Satnin and my girlfriend they want me to be that way still. They want me to settle down, stay home, buy a furniture store or something. Only, my life is not turning out in that direction. Not at all.

And it's all happening so <u>fast</u>. It's like last time I went to sleep I had a job driving a truck and was all set to be an electrician. Then I woke up and I was singing rock and roll and had women tearing off my clothes and near as many fans as Hank Snow. I'm scared to death to go to sleep again. I got no idea <u>where</u> I'll wake up this time.

The voice inside my head keeps saying, "Elvis, you got to ride this horse as far as it'll carry you." Till two nights ago I thought it was the Lord's voice. Now I got to say I don't know who it is. Sometimes I think it's me. Sometimes I think it's the Devil. Mostly, I don't know. I don't know anything no any more.

Except I'm hurting people, I know that. Like my girlfriend. She wants to get married but I can't do it. Not now, it's not fair. Not fair to <u>her</u>. Them things that happen on the road, they don't mean nothing. Still they happen. And I don't never get home no more. When I do it's not any way the same.

I'm hurting Satnin even worse. She misses me and she is scared for me all day and night. She even worries when she sleeps. Sunday night I called about the car and Daddy said she had earlier sat up wild-eyed out of a sound sleep. She ~~knowed~~ knew something horrible had happened to me. She was already near coming apart before I even dialed the phone. Still she don't never get angry. She just gets sadder and scareder every day. All on account of me, who loves her more than my own life itself.

I love her so much it's hard to talk about. There's times I been away a week or two and then I see her, and I just sit real still and study on her, one little piece at a time. I look at all the small hairs in her eyebrows, the way the skin creases in her neck. I look at how she's got a vein going down beside her little finger on her right hand, and I think how much I love that tiny vein and all her heart's blood running through it.

I'm so scared something bad will happen to her on account of me. It's real bad her worrying like she does. The doctor says she is not a well woman. All in the world I ever want to do is take care of her. Give her a good life and make her happy. And all I'm really doing is causing her grief and pain every time I draw breath.

Right now I'm on a airplane so I can get someplace in time to do a show. She's sitting home worrying about that. My girlfriend's sitting with her. It's like there's two ways I can go. I can quit making all my fans happy. Or I can quit hurting everyone I love. I got to choose.

My grammer is all ~~shot to shi shot to hell~~ shot right now, I know it. I'll do better next time.

Yours,
        Elvis

*   *   *

Atlanta, Sunday, June 12, 1955

Dear Elvis,

You never wrote me you had a girlfriend.

The two of you have been going together a long time. You must love her an awful lot.

Except, I always thought people who really loved people were

70

true to them. I always thought if you really loved someone, you wouldn't <u>want</u> to love anybody else. Not even for an hour, much less a whole evening. I thought that's what having a fire in your soul for someone <u>meant</u>.

I don't imagine anyone will fall in love with me. But if someone ever <u>does</u>, and if he is a nice person, I'd like to be able to love him back. So I am <u>glad</u> you told me you have a girlfriend! And I am <u>glad</u> you told me you date other girls when you are on the road! Because now I will <u>never</u> develop a fire in my soul for <u>you</u> that will burn there throughout all Eternity and keep me from loving anybody else.

I am very sorry about your car. If it gives you any comfort, it will always live on as the pink Cadillac in your song. It was a terrible thing to happen, there is no denying it, but you have got to quit worrying so much. Did it ever occur to you, you might be listening out for the Lord a little too hard? You said yourself His way is not meant for us to understand. Maybe He didn't burn up your car at all. Maybe it was just some mechanical thing that had nothing whatsoever to do with God. Burning up a car that meant so much to you sounds like an awfully mean thing for Him to do. And I'm still not convinced the voices in our heads are anything more than us talking to ourselves, anyway.

As for what you should do about Satnin and your girlfriend and staying on the road and everything, you're the only person who can decide that. All I know is, Mama always says when you've got to make a choice, first look for a way to have your cake and eat it too. For instance, what if you only travel half as much and stay true to your girlfriend when you are away but keep on singing the same kind of music you're singing now? Won't that please everybody at least some?

If Mama can't have her cake and has to decide, she draws a line straight down the middle of a piece of paper. On the left side she writes all the good things about one choice and on the right side she writes all the good things about the other. Then she picks the choice that has the longest list. She even did that in Mississippi when she decided to come home.

I hope this helps.

I think about you all the time. I'm sure I think about you way too much, considering. Maybe I shouldn't write to you so often. Maybe I shouldn't write to you at all. If I were your girlfriend, I wouldn't want you writing letters all the time to some other girl. And I wouldn't think much of that other girl for writing you back, if she knew you were pledged to someone else.

Yours truly,

Achsa

P.S. Here's the grammar. Don't say things like "he done gone" or "they done finished." Instead say "he has already gone" and "they have already finished." Use "done" only for sentences like "The cake is done" or "Have you done your homework?" And don't say "come" when you're talking about something that's already happened. It's "the haint <u>came</u> carrying part of Hades," and "There <u>came</u> a big "whoosh."

*   *   *

Altus, Oklahoma, Friday, June 24, 1955, real late at night

Dearest B,

Your letter finally caught up with me three days ago. This is the first chance I got to write.

I like it you think about me like you do. It's not ~~no~~ anything to quit writing over. I think about you a lot too. I'm all the time thinking, "I got to tell sweet Baby Girl about this," or "I reckon Baby Girl will have something to say about that." I still call you Baby Girl in my heart, you know. No matter what I got to call you in my letters.

Me having a girlfriend is no reason to quit writing ~~neither~~ either. Me writing you don't have anything to do with me and her.

So don't ~~never~~ ever quit thinking about me. Don't ever quit writing me either. ~~I need you~~ I mean, I still don't talk real good. There's times I don't know what I'd do without you.

Like right after I got your last letter. I spent three whole days doing what your mama said. She's a smart lady, it really took some thinking. First I tried real hard to have my cake and eat it, and there was not ~~no~~ any way to work that out. To keep on singing the kind of music I been singing, I got to go <u>where</u> my manager tells me <u>when</u> he tells me. In other words I got to keep on the road.

Still I got to confess, the real reason I can't have it both ways is cause I don't want to. I can't do <u>anything</u> half way. That's just the way I am. If I keep singing country music, or rockabilly or whatever thing they're calling it these days, I got to think about that kind of music all the time. I got to go places where people listen to it. I got to sing it every chance I get. If I sing gospel I got to do it the same. That means I got to choose.

Well, I did. This tour I'm on ends July 4th. They give me two weeks to rest up at home. Then I go out again. Only, this time and forever after I am going as a gospel singer. That is the choice I made.

When I start singing gospel I won't need to be away from home so much. My girlfriend and I can get married. Satnin can start smiling again and live a long, happy life. I wrote all that on the left side of the paper. On the right side all I had was "I can make my fans happy and maybe be a movie star." It was no contest. Satnin means more to me than anything else here on earth.

I haven't told nobody yet. I'll tell them soon enough. Just making up my mind like that brought me an abiding peace deep in my soul. I slept last night like a newborn child. You been a great help to me, Baby Girl. I really got to thank you. I wish you had a birthday coming up, I'd buy you a great big present. You are a very sweet girl. Do not ever quit writing me.

I mean it,
Elvis

P.S. How do you like your summer job?

P.P.S. Here is something I been meaning for a good long while to say. I don't talk jive around girls, just guys. And I don't know why you think this Betty Jean is so cool. It don't sound right some girl saying, "Dig it, man, he's a real gone cat." She might just as well be shooting dice out on a street corner. I hope you ~~don't~~ never do it. Talk jive, I mean. I like you just the way you are.

* * *

De Leon, Texas, Monday afternoon, July 4, 1955

Dearest B,

How are you doing? I have not got a letter from you in several days. Still I am writing you anyway.

Guess who has just been voted Number One Up-and-Coming Country Singer in the whole U.S. of A.? It don't matter you don't listen to country stations. It is someone you know very well.

Give up?

It's Yours Truly! Me!!!!

Every year the DJs all vote and they run it in <u>Cashbox</u> magazine. Can you believe it? They voted <u>me</u> the Number One Up-and-Coming Country Singer in the <u>whole</u> <u>country</u>!

I still hadn't told nobody yet about the gospel singing. But that is not for long!! I am writing you from a Fourth of July picnic this gospel music promoter puts on every year. It's so big they got the Statesmen and the Blackwoods both. I'm sitting in the Blackwoods bus right now. There's windows open and I can hear them singing not 50 feet away. All kinds of folks is sitting out there on the grass with the sun beating down on them. Mamas and daddys, grandmas and grandpas, big kids and little kids. All drinking sweet tea and eating fried chicken and potato salad and watermelon. The least ones got that watermelon juice dripping off their chins. I look out at them and I love them all so much my heart is near to bursting. Big and little, young and old, I love them every one.

At first I thought me winning Number One Up-and-Coming Country Singer was the Devil tempting me. Then right this minute sitting here and writing you it came to me. It is God's blessing. It is His way of showing me He is sorry He burnt up my car. So I say right now, "Get back, Satan. This very day I will lay my prize upon the altar of the Lord."

I got to wind this letter up. The Blackwoods are singing their last song. Soon I will run out on that stage, and from that very moment on all I am ever going to sing is gospel music!

I mean it. I count it the greatest honor of my life to sing in the same show as the Statesmen and the Blackwoods both. I can't think of ~~no~~ any better place to start.

I am going to hand my talent over to Jesus Christ, our Risen Lord! Right here today in front of all these people! Baby Girl, I'm so excited I can't hardly wait!!

Yours in Eternal Joy,
Elvis

* * *

Atlanta, Monday night, July 4, 1955

Dear Elvis,

Once again, thank you for your advice, but I shall talk jive if I wish. I don't see why my being a girl should make one whit of difference.

I am pleased for you that you have come to a decision about your life and found peace. I must say, though, that your choice surprises me. It will be a big change, I suppose, being a gospel singer. But I am sure you will be good at it. I wish you much success.

Also, I hope you and your girlfriend have a happy life. This is my last letter. I do not feel right writing to a boy who is engaged. I am sure you will understand.

You asked about my job at the swimming pool. It's OK, I guess. I work in the mornings and it's mostly little kids. I give each kid a locker key, which is on a thick elastic cord, but they are always losing them because they put them on their toes or in their swim trunks pocket instead of wearing them around their ankles like I tell them to. Every night a lifeguard dives in and brings up a fistful of locker keys from the bottom of the pool.

I am too sad to write any more. I will miss you so very much.

Sincerely,
Achsa

Chapter nine

July 7–12, 1955

Dearest B,

You really meant it about not writing me, didn't you.

Well, you don't need to worry ~~none~~. You can write me all you want. Me being a gospel singer didn't work out, and I reckon my girlfriend and me are breaking up for good pretty soon. It's a sad time all around.

I don't know what happened with the gospel singing. They called my name and I ran out and people screamed and clapped like always. The Lord's own hot sun was shining in my face, brighter than any manmade spotlight. It was all I could see. Nothing but light, everywhere I looked. I shut my eyes, stood real still, and the most glorious feeling came into me. Like I was standing on top of a high mountain with all God's music pouring out of my mouth. I couldn't hear nothing else no more. Just a sound in my head like a running stream or the wind in the pine trees, and my own voice singing in the center of that light.

I stood there with my eyes closed and sung song after song. All my gospel favorites I hold in my heart, and each one the best I ever sung it. I thought of them like presents wrapped in silver paper, tied with golden ribbons. I wished I could ~~have~~ give one to every man, woman and child sitting out there on the grass, just for being with me at such a beautiful time. I sung all my songs. Then I bowed my head, said "Thank you very much," and walked off. Right then I felt the best I ever felt my entire life. I knew in the marrow of my bones I was traveling the right path.

All I wanted was to go off by myself and thank the gracious Lord for bringing me to this place in my life. It was not to be. Already folks was running up to me. This friend from Memphis clapped me on the shoulder and said, "Man, I sure am sorry. I'm just real sorry." Other folks was coming too, patting me on the back and shaking their heads like somebody died.

I said, "What is it? What's the matter?" I was scared there had been something bad happened to Satnin.

Then this one man, he might of been with the show, I don't know, he come up and said real gentle-like, "Son, what come over you out there? Didn't you hear all them people calling out to you?"

I said, "No, sir. I didn't hear nothing at all."

He said, "They was calling out the names of all your records that they come to hear, and you didn't do a one of them."

Then some other man I'd never seen stepped up and said, "Them folks weren't sitting out there in the gnats and the flies just to see Elvis Presley stand still as a post and sing Jesus at them. You got a responsibility, boy. By not giving people what they want you're going back on it."

The way them men sounded made me feel about three inches tall. Here I'd gone and done this thing I meant for a gift to all the people there that day, and turned out nobody wanted it. I like to cried.

I had to get away. I said, "Please excuse me" and went over to this group of girls standing a little ways apart and looking at me. There weren't real many, not like usual. They was all real quiet. Mostly they had stuff for me to sign, and I signed it.

This one girl, she was the last one. Kind of heavy and wearing glasses and she had her right leg in a brace like she'd had polio or something. She handed me a record. It was "Baby, Let's Play House." I smiled at her and signed it and gave it back without saying ~~nothing~~ anything. I didn't feel real much like talking.

She looked down at where I wrote my name and then looked up at me. "My mamma and daddy drove me 50 miles to hear you sing that song, and then you didn't," she said. Her eyes were filling up with tears.

Right then I didn't care what I'd told the Lord. I said, "I'll sing it next time, I promise you."

She said, "But I won't be there to hear it." She looked me square in the face with this tear hanging on her lower eyelashes just waiting to fall.

Man, it really got to me. That and her leg brace, how the sun kept bouncing off it like in some movie. I reached in my pocket and pulled out a ten-dollar bill. Then I took her hand and closed her fingers over the money. I told her, "Look, I'm singing this afternoon in Stephensville. It's not but a little ways away. This will cover all y'all's tickets and everything." I asked her, "What's your name?"

She said, "Susan Williams."

I said, "Susan, when I get on that stage in Stephensville I'm going to sing that song for you."

I did, too. I hope she got there to hear it. I didn't see her again.

I reckon them men that talked to me was right. I been selfish. Just singing what I wanted and not thinking about nobody else. I been acting like I was hot ~~shi~~ stuff on a stick, like I found me a job where I don't have no boss. Turns out them folks that come see the shows, they been my bosses all along. I just didn't know it. They quit coming, and I'm out of a job sure as shooting. They're good folks. I don't never want to let them down. And that's what I done to them that day.

I got to thinking like that in the car and got so ashamed I wished I could crawl off and hide. After I sang in Stephensville I had to sing someplace else that night. I did both shows same as I always do, shaking my legs and everything. I tried my best to put my whole heart in it. Nobody said nothing else about the gospel singing. I reckon maybe they forgot about it. I won't never forget. It hurt to think my whole life might have been that beautiful, only I come to it too late.

I got home pretty sad. Near about all I did the next two days was sleep. Then I woke up and I wasn't sad ~~no~~ any more. I went in the bathroom to shave and looked at my face in the mirror. I said, "Elvis, you aren't ever going to be a gospel singer. You best put that behind you this day. The Lord has blessed you with a talent that pleases folks and lets you make a good living. You got a <u>duty</u> to keep on doing it."

And it's true. The way I see it, Satnin brought me into this world. Her and Daddy took care of me from when I was a tiny, helpless baby. Now it's my turn to take care of them. If it means I got to be gone from home, then that's what I got to do. Even if it takes Satnin some getting used to. She knows I love her more than anything. She'll come to see it's for her own good in the end. There's not no other way to look at it.

I finished shaving, brushed my teeth and ate some breakfast. Then I went out and bought me a car.

And Baby Girl, I got to say it is the <u>gonest</u> car I ever had! A 1955 Caddy, my first brand new car! It's off getting painted now, getting a pink body and a black top and my name written on the side. When I go cruising down the street <u>everybody</u> will know who I am.

And if I get to Atlanta in it I'll take you for a real long ride.

You write me real soon. You hear?

Yours very truly,
　　Elvis

*　*　*

Memphis, Saturday, July 9, 1955

Dear B,

I got a few minutes, so I figure to spend it writing you another letter.

80

Except for a night here and there, I been gone from Memphis almost since we started writing back in February. It's good being home. Only, everything's different. I'm not this kid hanging around anymore. Everybody's glad to see me, even folks I never met. They honk their horns and wave at me on the street. The paper had my picture in it and there's three country song magazines got stories on me. That's how all them folks come to know me, I guess.

Yesterday I was in the drugstore drinking a malted at the counter. This lady sitting at a table with her little girl smiled at me and said, "You're Elvis Presley, aren't you."

I told her, "Yes, ma'am, I am."

Then she said, "I thought so. I got to run call Bea and Dot and tell them I saw Elvis Presley in the drugstore drinking a chocolate malt."

She didn't say anything else, just put money on the table and got up with her little girl to leave. They got about ten feet and she turned around and said, "'Bye" and bolted out the door. She had rather call her friends and tell them how she saw me than talk to me sitting right there in front of her. People sure are getting strange.

This week's the first chance I've had to spend time with my girlfriend since I took her to her junior prom. Last night I took her with me to this club to see some boys I know. I don't ~~neither~~ drink or smoke, except I might sometimes chew on a cigar without lighting it. They was all smoking and they'd had a drink or two. I could tell she didn't want to be there. She sat the whole time with that same scared, worried look Satnin gets. I haven't broke up with her yet, and I know I got to. My whole life is different now. It's no fit life for her.

So you can write me any time you want, like always. I'm not going to be ~~no~~ a gospel singer. And I'm not getting married any time soon. I plan to work real hard on my grammar. I look forward to hearing from you.

Yours very truly,
Elvis

P.S. While I'm thinking about it, it's OK with me for you to talk jive all you want. Only, I hope you don't do it around me. That's the last

I got to say about that. I think we've wrote back and forth about it long enough.

*   *   *

Memphis, Monday, July 11, 1955

Dearest B,

It's real late but I'm too keyed up to sleep. Me and the boys cut three songs with Mr. Phillips today. The last one was about this cat traveling night and day and running all the way to see some girl he'd been writing. I thought about you the whole time I was singing it.
Yours truly,
Elvis

*   *   *

Atlanta, Tuesday, July 12, 1955

Dearest E,

How wonderful to get two letters from you in one day! They came yesterday, and I literally <u>ran</u> to Greene's drugstore to buy those country song magazines. They only had the one that called you a "Folk Music Fireball." It thrilled my heart to see it.

How fast and exciting your life must be now. Sometimes I sit still and try to imagine it, but it all just whirls around me.

Right now, I am sitting in the very back of our yard, leaning against a giant water oak in the dappled sunshine. Its broad trunk hides me from the house, and two of its huge roots make a lovely and comfortable armchair, a throne fit for a woodland princess. I bought a new ballpoint pen at Greene's to write you. My hand feels good holding it. My knees feel good with my writing tablet propped against them, and my eyes feel good watching my hand write "Dearest E" once again.

I must remember that this time my letter goes out to "<u>the Number One Up-and-Coming Country Singer</u>" in <u>the whole United States</u>! What an honor!!! Yet I must say it does not surprise me in the least. Remember how I told the clerk in the record store you'd have a number one hit and he just rolled his eyes like I was stupid? Well, so much for him.

I'm sorry the gospel singing didn't work out, especially since you wanted it to.

No, that's not true. Nobody sings the songs you sing the way you sing them, and I hoped you wouldn't ever stop. I owe a huge debt of gratitude to that Susan girl at the picnic.

The irony is, if you <u>had</u> become a gospel singer, in a way it would have been my fault. For giving you bad advice. Mama was wrong, picking the longest list doesn't always work. I know now that sometimes one reason for doing something can outweigh ten, or even a thousand, reasons for doing something else. I'm afraid she's finding that out, too—but I don't want to think about it now.

Here's the grammar. This is sort of like double negatives because you have to look for it. Always make sure your subject and your verb agree in a sentence. In other words, don't say "they is" or "they was," because "they" is plural and "is" and "was" are singular. Say instead, "they are" and "they were" because "were" is a plural verb. Don't say "he don't" for the same reason. Say "he doesn't" and "they don't." And still watch out for double negatives. Now and then you let one slip by.

It feels so good writing you once again, I could go on forever and end up with a letter that stretches all the way from here to the moon, but I'm being called to dinner. Right now I'd much rather write to you than eat, but I don't think I could explain it very well.

Sincerely,
Achsa

P.S. We learned "irony" in junior English. It's when something turns out the opposite of what you want or think it ought to be, which you may already know since you had junior English, too.

Chapter ten

July 19–24, 1955

Atlanta, Tuesday, July 19, 1955

Dear E,

Guess what!! Mama and I just saw <u>East of Eden</u>. I <u>finally</u> got a look at <u>James Dean</u>!!!! He was fantastic!! At least as real as Marlon Brando!

Until today I never thought movie acting was anywhere near as serious a profession as acting on the New York stage. Well, I was wrong. I see why you want so much to do it. And I bet once you get started you'll be every bit as good as James Dean. Maybe even better, although right now that's pretty hard to imagine.

Mama made me promise not to tell Daddy about the movie. She said maybe sometime we can see another one.

Got to go. Dinnertime again. I'll write a longer letter later (so many L's!). This was just to let you know about the movie.

Sincerely,

Achsa

P.S. I can't wait to hear your new songs. Especially the one that made you think of me! Please let me know immediately when I should start listening for them on the radio and pestering the folks at Junior's.

P.P.S. A very short grammar lesson: It's not "cause." It's "<u>because</u>."

*   *   *

Memphis, Tuesday, July 19, 1955

Dearest B,

Sometimes I think you know me even better than I know myself. You know how you said you feel my life whirling around you? Well you're right, it whirls around me too. You said what I was thinking before my mind could put it into words. That means a lot to me.

Tomorrow my little time at home is done and everything starts up again. Only, these days there's more to it. Like them men said at the gospel picnic, it's not just me going out on stage and singing what I want to anymore. Everything I do has bearing on the folks around me. On my manager and the boys that back me up, on Mr. Phillips at Sun Records, and on Satnin and Daddy.

And now there's something I want so bad I don't dare tell ~~nobody~~ anybody else but you I want it.

There's this man. He's a honorary Colonel in the state of Louisiana. That's what people call him. Not <u>the</u> Colonel, just Colonel. He manages Hank Snow, who is <u>the</u> <u>number</u> <u>one</u> country singer in the world. It was Colonel got me on Hank Snow's Jamboree Attractions tours, and Colonel was in Tampa when them girls tore off my clothes. Ever since then he's been calling, showing up, talking to folks about me.

Now he's saying he can get me a big record contract. He knows all the top brass at RCA Victor, and he says I ought to be making records for someplace like that. I want to, too. I want to so bad my heart starts jumping every time the phone rings ~~cause~~ because it might be Colonel calling. It's like he's some girl I'm dying to go out with. Colonel even knows people in <u>Hollywood</u>! He says soon as I have a real hit record he can get me in the <u>movies</u>!!!!

86

Seems like everything I ever wanted, Colonel can get it for me. Colonel can make my every dream come true.

But like I said, it's not just me doing how I want to anymore. There's all these people talking behind my back about what's going on. They're scared how it's going to bear on them. It's got to where every time I walk in a room things get real quiet. People smile and say, "Hey, Elvis, how you doing, man? Life treating you fine?"

I want to say back, "What was y'all talking about? Was y'all talking about me?" But I just smile and answer, "I'm cool, man. Yeah, I'm cool."

Because I don't want to hurt nobody. I don't ever want ~~nobody~~ anybody saying, "You know Elvis Presley? Well, he hurt a lot of people on his way up." What that means is, if Colonel gets me a big record contract I want my same manager to keep on managing me. And I want Mr. Phillips to get a real good price for the contract him and me got going now. I want him to get the best price in the world. If it wasn't for Mr. Phillips I never would have got to where I am today.

I told all this to Colonel, and he give his promise that's how it's going to be. He wants to get with me and my folks the first of August, and we'll sign papers letting him go after the record contract. Trouble is, I can't sign nothing on the dotted line till I'm 21 without Satnin and Daddy signing too, and I'm not sure they will. They both like the man that's been managing me all along. They're scared this'll change things.

I told Colonel, and he says they'll come around. When it gets down to it, I think they will, too. Colonel's like you. Someone the Lord put in my life to serve a special purpose. It'll all work out. You wait and see.

So that's what's going on with me. Business. And business flat gives me the heebie-jeebies every time. That's how come I trust in other folks to do it for me.

Now it's your turn. Write me how you are and what's been going on with you.

Yours very truly,
Elvis

P.S. Yesterday at last I got to spend some time on Beale Street. Wished I could take you with me. You'd like it. Them cats don't treat me ~~no~~ any different than they ever did. We had a real cool time.

*   *   *

Atlanta, Saturday, July 23, 1955

Dearest E,

Got your nice, long letter today. So much great news!! And so exciting about that colonel!!! I bet he's delighted you've set your sights on being a <u>serious</u> <u>actor</u> like James Dean. I bet he's got you picked to be a <u>star</u>!

I'm sitting in my "armchair" at the base of the water oak. We've had a lot of rain lately, but today the sun's shining and I've come out here to let it cheer me.

You asked how I am, and "troubled" is the best answer I can come up with. I guess I've been that way for some time. I didn't say anything, because I didn't really want to think about it. You know what you said about things going on behind your back? Something like that is going on in my life, too. I guess I feel like you did when your Cadillac caught fire—I need someone to help me sort things out.

Here's my biggest question: If someone imagines things about another person but there's never ever any proof, does that always mean those things aren't true? Or could someone's imagining them mean they <u>are</u> true, that they're in the very air around that other person and in that other person's mind?

I guess what I'm trying to say is, I keep feeling something strange is happening, but I don't know what or why—only that it has to do with Mama.

It's been going on ever since we moved. Maybe even since Mama and I ran away to Mississippi. It's like our house is haunted, like there's something here that's very real, as real as another person, only Mama's the only one who ever sees it. I've tried telling myself it's just all the rooms are in different places now, not like in the apartment, and so we see each other different ways. But I know deep

88

down what's happening doesn't have a thing to do with the house. It has to do with us inside it.

That voice you talk about, the voice inside my head, it won't stop hissing, "What is it? What is it? What is it?" But the stuff it comes up with isn't really answers.

For instance, you know how most people's parents seem to match up, almost like salt and pepper shakers? They've got the same color hair and eyes, or they lean toward each other when they sit together, or their speaking voices blend like notes in a song? Well, Mama and Daddy aren't one bit like that at all. Seeing them, you'd think they're married to entirely different people. If they were both parts of the same painting, a painting of a tree, for instance, he'd be the dark shadows at the roots and she'd be the leaves with sunlight shining on them. Except lately Mama shines too brightly, bright as fever eyes.

Here's what I mean. As long as I remember, she's bought books through the mail from some bookshop in New York. Good books, by writers you study in English class or read in magazines. She keeps them in a beautiful bookcase with glass doors, and when it gets full she carefully wraps the oldest ones in tissue paper and stores them in a cardboard box. She never gets rid of any of them. Every place we've lived we've had one closet crammed with Mama's books. This time when we moved to the house Daddy carted all her book boxes up to the attic. He's never been much of a reader, just his Bible and the newspaper. I don't think he's cracked one of Mama's books the whole time they've been married. Myself, I used to beg to read them, but she always said they were for grownups. Finally, I gave up asking.

I've come to think those books are Mama's food. She hungers for them like the singer in "Unchained Melody" hungers for his lover's touch—chewing her nails and watching for the mailman. When a book comes, she always acts so surprised and delighted you'd think it was a gift. She reads it slowly, savors it over several days, and tiny smiles twitch at the corners of her mouth. She sings when she does her housework and gets excited about things like buying all those bedspreads and curtains for the house. After a week or so, when she's finished the book, she gets quiet and pensive. After a while longer sometimes she gets a little sad. Then I guess she orders another one and starts waiting once again.

I asked her once, when a book hadn't come for a month or so, why she didn't just check them out of the library or buy them at a bookstore here in Atlanta. It's not like they're books nobody's heard of or anything. She gave a startled little laugh, as if it never crossed her mind I'd want to know, and said this New York place sold the best quality books at the best prices. I said they didn't look any different to me, and wasn't it the words that mattered anyway, and weren't the words always the same. She said sometimes the quality is in things you can't see. I guess sometimes that's true.

Anyway that's how things used to be. She'd read each book as soon as it got here, then put it in her bookcase and leave it there. But lately she pores over one until the next one comes, even if it takes weeks. Sometimes, too, she pulls other books out of her bookcase and leafs through them for hours at a time. She's not reading, really—just turning the pages, running her hands over the paper. Friday afternoon, when I got home from work, I found her sitting on the sofa surrounded by piles of books and an explosion of tissue paper. The attic stairs were still pulled down. She didn't even notice me until I spoke. Then she looked up, with some irritation, as though she didn't have the vaguest notion who I was—as though I had dragged her away from some whole other world.

It only lasted a split second, that look. Then she turned into my mother again, her voice ticking off the names of vegetables she planned to pick up from the market, even as she rewrapped books to go back in their boxes. Still, it scared me. I wanted to grab her by the shoulders and shout, "Stop it, stop it, stop it!" But what, exactly, do I want her to stop? Reading?

Sometimes my worries sound so silly, even to me. Still, that nervous, darting, hummingbird side of her grows stronger every day. She quit smoking after we left Mississippi, but she's started back. Not a lot, and only when Daddy's at work. But she's restless clear through, some part of her always moving just a little. Last Sunday at dinner, Daddy rambled on about the preacher's sermon, and Mama stared straight at him, nodding her head now and again, or smiling. But the whole time she kept rubbing her right index finger up and down the length of her butter knife, like a blind person trying to memorize her silver pattern. I sat there terrified Daddy would ask her what he'd said. I knew she wouldn't be able to tell him.

Tonight she pinned up the hem in a skirt she'd made me. I stood on a footstool and she sat on the floor with her shoes off and her legs folded. One foot twitched like a cat's tail. She was totally unaware of it.

This next part is another thing I've never told. Sometimes I daydream Mama is married to Robert Mitchum and that he is my father.

It's not like evening prayers, where I don't know why they're creepy. I know exactly why I picture Mama with Robert Mitchum. He's the only man I ever saw who, if he stood next to her, they would match up like they belonged together. They've both got the same identical heat inside them, like if you touch them you'll come away with blisters. I tried seeing her next to Gary Cooper, John Wayne, even William Holden, but they didn't work out at all. Only Robert Mitchum.

Anyway, I stood there while she measured my skirt hem with a yardstick and pinned it up with straight pins. She held the pins between her lips, their sharp points in her mouth. I don't know why they didn't prick her tongue. Each time her foot twitched, her nylons swished against each other, and for some reason I started thinking about her with Robert Mitchum, the two of them sitting on a picnic blanket in the woods, like in "River of No Return." He gazes at her a long time. Then he grabs her foot in both his hands, holds onto it like it's a nervous kitten that might get away—and I know he's going to keep on holding it and staring straight into her eyes until he makes that twitchy foot be still.

Suddenly, the room felt so hot I swayed on the stool. Mama asked, "What's wrong?" and I said I needed a drink of water. I climbed down, went in the kitchen and laid my forehead against the cool porcelain of the sink and stayed there a minute, gulping air.

All I could think was, what if I imagined her with Robert Mitchum because she was thinking something like that too? <u>What if everything I've been imagining is real?</u>

All I know is, Mama is here, same as always. But there is something haunting her, haunting our house, and I've got to find out what it is. I am afraid, to use your words, that it will bear on me.

This letter's gotten awfully long and strange. I hope it doesn't sound too creepy. I wish school would start. I wish Linda Sheffield were still here.

Here's the grammar. It's important. I should have put it first, I guess, instead of making you wade through all my problems. "Them" is a pronoun. You need to stop using it as an adjective. Say "We gave <u>those</u> books to <u>them</u>." Do <u>not</u> say, "You got them books yet?"

Also, remember about singular and plural verbs. Only say "was" when you're talking about just one person, place, or thing. When you're talking about more than one, always say "were." Except for one double negative and someplace you said "give" instead of "gave," those are the only mistakes I saw in your last letter. Your grammar's really getting much, much better.

Thanks for listening.
    Sincerely,
      Achsa

*   *   *

Atlanta, Sunday, July 24, 1955

Dearest E,

I wrote you a letter yesterday, and as soon as I dropped it in the mailbox at the end of our street I wished I hadn't told you all that stuff about Mama. I'm afraid you'll think she doesn't love me.

She does, I know she does. Even though I'm sure it isn't easy.

I used to think, how could someone so beautiful love a facial freak like me? Then one time she saved my life, and I decided she must love me after all. No matter what I looked like. And no matter what else she might ever do.

The first day of second grade, a girl sitting next to me threw up all over her desk. She must have had had a stomach virus, and I guess I caught it. For days I vomited up everything I ate. Regular as clockwork, after every meal. I've never since been able to eat spinach with chopped egg, or stewed tomatoes. I still remember how they came back up.

By the second week I was mostly bones. My eyes had sunk so far back in my head I looked blind. When I couldn't keep down even water, the doctor came to our apartment and left a bottle of pink medicine. I threw that up too. Something whimpered outside my bedroom door and I thought maybe he also left a puppy. Then I realized it was Mama.

The day was hot for September, but I wasn't sweating. All afternoon I lay in bed, watching a patch of sunlight on the wall turn from silver to gold to copper and then disappear. The house grew so quiet I felt sure Mama had gone away. I wanted water but I didn't want to vomit, so I just lay still.

I must have slept a little. Next thing I knew, the room was dark and Mama stood by my bed wearing a white apron and holding a blue and white dessert bowl. I thought I must be dreaming. She turned on the night light, sat down in my little desk chair, and placed the bowl on the nightstand by my water glass. It held a floating island custard, my favorite of all desserts. She dipped her index finger in the bowl, then laid it gently on my lips. The smallest bit of creamy sweetness slid off soft and cool into my mouth. Again, and then again, she touched the custard to my lips right where they met, big lip, little lip, all the time stroking my hair with her other hand. I swallowed. When I didn't vomit, she gave me water the same way, a drop from her finger. I took it, and she touched my lips with custard once again.

She fed me like that through the night. First the custard, then the water. From her finger, to my lips. And all the time with her other hand she stroked my hair. Finally, I must have dozed. I awoke at daybreak to find her sleeping in my tiny wooden chair, her head on my bed, one of her books in her lap—and the water glass and custard bowl both empty on the nightstand. The next day I was well.

She didn't have to do it, feed me like that the whole night. She could have let me die so easily.

I wanted you to know. I wanted you to know my mother loves me.

Sincerely,

Achsa

Chapter eleven

August 1–7, 1955

Tupelo, Monday, August 1, 1955

Dearest B,

Guess what!! Daddy and Satnin are meeting me in Little Rock day after tomorrow to sign the papers!!! I knew it yesterday. I waited till today to tell you so you could have a letter postmarked from where I was born.

I don't think bad about your mama. Sounds like she loves you very much. I'm sorry all that stuff is troubling you so. Maybe a doctor can give her some of ~~them~~ those new pills that keep you calm. I wish I knew what else to say.

Yours truly,
Elvis

*   *   *

Houston, Sunday, August 7, 1955

Dear Baby Girl,

Well, the meeting's come and gone. Colonel's never going to represent me. I'm never going to be a movie star, I'll never even have a real hit record.

95

Satnin wouldn't sign the papers. I'm mad at the whole ~~damn~~ world.

Reckon the world's mad at me, too. I hacked off some promoter when I only sang four songs in his stupid show. Now he's saying I told "off-color" jokes and "behaved in an unprofessional manner." Well, ~~shi~~ shoot fire and save matches. That's just tough. I don't want to do <u>nothing</u> no more, there's not no point to it. Except maybe slam my fist real hard into a wall.

We got to the signing and Daddy was all set for it. I thought Satnin was too. Then she started asking a whole bunch of dumb questions. Colonel and I both talked to her till we was blue in the face. The whole time she just stood there jawing, holding her pen right over the paper. It was all I could do not to grab that hand like you would an old person's and make it do the signing myself.

When she started going on about how was Colonel going to guarantee my safety, I knew it was all over. He still says she'll come around. Me, I don't know. Satnin just wants things back the way they was. Me driving a truck, coming home every night, going to school to be an electrician.

I saw Mr. Phillips later. That was really strange. He knew how bad I wanted Colonel to represent me. He knew me getting with Colonel would be good for him, too. Colonel could get him a good price if he was to sell my record contract. Anyway, I dreaded telling him what happened. I was sure he'd be real disappointed and sore, think it was my fault. But all he did was clap me on the shoulder and say, "I'm sorry, Elvis. I'm real sorry things didn't go the way you wanted."

Here's the strange part. I was looking right at him when he said it, and you know what? His face didn't look sorry at all. It looked like the face of a man that's just had a burden lifted off him.

There was one nice thing happened since I wrote you last. I'll close this letter with it so it won't just be me complaining the whole time. Friday night in Memphis I sang at the Country Music Jamboree my manager puts on every year. Last time, I hadn't ever sung on a big stage before. I got so scared. I started trembling all over, to where I almost couldn't hold the mike. To hide it I tried shaking just my legs, like Jake Hess with the Statesmen. Some girls started screaming, and I thought they ~~was~~ were making fun of me. They weren't. We'd only practiced two songs and we sang them both. They wanted us to sing some more, and we didn't have another one.

There's sure been lots of water under the bridge since then.

Still, I reckon it's not too late for me to wind up back home driving a truck.

Yours truly,
Elvis

* * *

Atlanta, late Sunday night, August 7, 1955

Dearest E,

I don't know why I'm even writing you this letter. It's just something really awful and embarrassing happened today, and it left me so ashamed and angry I can't keep it all inside.

If you're lucky, I will not have put this in the mail. If I did, you needn't read any further if you don't want to. I can't say I'd blame you. I'll even put the grammar up front so you won't have to look for it: Watch your adverbs. Say "I want it so <u>badly</u>," not "I want it so <u>bad</u>." Adverbs describe verbs and other adjectives ("<u>really</u> big show") and usually end in "-ly."

I <u>really</u> hope I don't mail this letter. Anyway, here goes.

I wrote you before about Betty Jean Puckett. She and I sit in the same Sunday school class once a week, but, as I think I've mentioned, we don't exactly run in the same circles. She mostly dates hoods and is generally thought of as really cool. We're pretty much the opposite of each other, if you want to know the truth. Which is why what she did this morning gave me such a shock.

We were both in the ladies restroom after Sunday school—she standing in front of the sink mirror brushing her wavy blonde hair over and over as though it wasn't already perfect, me trying to pin on this too-gimpy flowered hat Mama bought me to go with my white sundress and wishing I had hair one-tenth as nice as Betty Jean's—when without any warning she turned to me and said, "Hey, Achsa, want to go to Greene's and get a Coke?"

Just like that, like we were big buddies and hung out there all the time. She caught me so off guard I said OK. Which turned out to be a big mistake.

Greene's is where the popular kids hang out. It's a block from our church one way and a block from Dreamer Hills Baptist the other way. I pass by there every day on my way home from school, but I never go in except to buy something like Band-Aids or notebook paper I absolutely can't get any other place. They've got a jukebox but nowhere to dance, so the kids just sit or stand at the counter and sort of sway to the music. The going-steady couples hold hands in the booths and lean against each other with their eyes closed. Nobody ever speaks to me in there and I don't hang around.

Mr. Greene is a Jew, and Jewish people have their Sunday on Saturday, as you probably know. So his drugstore is the only one on our side of town that's open Sundays in case people need something in an emergency. It turned out Betty Jean wanted to go there so she could "accidentally" run into Carl Autry, who sometimes goes to the Baptist church. Carl is friends with Hank Lawson, the boy who said Penelope was Johnny Wooten's girlfriend. Carl took Betty Jean on a few dates—they even double-dated once with Hank—but he hasn't asked her out lately.

"I got to let him see I'm still alive," Betty Jean said. "I need him to start dating me again so we can be going steady by the time school starts." She made it sound like Rich's department store's after-Fourth of July bathing suit sale, where you've got to show up early to get a good one.

She snatched the hideous flowered hat from my hands and slammed it onto the mirror ledge. "Leave that ugly thing here," she said. That did it. I could have kissed her feet. Right then I'd have followed her anywhere.

I knew she only asked me so she wouldn't have to walk in by herself, but I didn't care. I thought maybe if people saw me drinking a Coke with Betty Jean Puckett they wouldn't think I was such a gimp after all. Church service started in half an hour, so we didn't have much time. We dashed out the door and down the street in our black patent heels and sticky-hot stockings. Our half-slip crinolines, stiff with starch, swayed our skirts like ringing bells. What pure joy, running fast as I could beside Betty Jean Puckett to Greene's drugstore on a sunny Sunday morning. Looking back, I can't believe I actually thought that.

When we got there, Betty Jean flung open the door and tossed her head, which got her bangs out of her eyes and at the same time let her take a quick look around. Carl was there all right, way in back at the newsstand, reading hot-rod magazines with Hank and a redheaded Baptist boy named Jimmy. Carl and Hank are only sort of hoods. Jimmy's a real hoodlum, and nowhere near as cool or smart as they are. Last year he got suspended three days for smoking in the boys' bathroom. Mama says Baptists keep you on their church rolls forever, no matter what, which probably explains why most of the hoods at Foster are Baptists.

Betty Jean pretended not to see Carl. She grabbed my arm, steered me to the soda fountain and ordered a small double-shot cherry Coke. I said "Me, too," even though I hate cherry. What I really wanted was a squirt of lime, but I didn't want to ask for it in case lime Cokes were a gimp drink or something.

The soda jerk, a pimply-faced boy who doesn't go to Foster and I think is Mr. Greene's son, handed us our Cokes in paper cups. We took them to the last booth, where anyone in the back who looked up from reading magazines couldn't miss us. Betty Jean started right in talking, staring straight at me and only now and then cutting her eyes around to where Carl was. "Sure wish Mr. Greene would let us play the jukebox on Sundays. It could use some hot new tunes, like the ones Avenue Al plays. I listen to Avenue Al every night before Penelope comes on. He's cool."

She was just talking so Carl would think she hadn't seen him—or maybe that she had and didn't care—and would come over to see what was what. In an effort to help her out, I asked why she thought WDDO never plays your records. She didn't know who you were, which really surprised me because she's so hip. When I told her, she sniffed and said, "Well, the reason they won't play any songs by this <u>hillbilly</u>, who is obviously <u>white</u>, is WDDO is a <u>colored</u> station and they only play songs by <u>colored</u> singers." She paused briefly, for effect. "Because if they didn't, all the colored people in Atlanta who want to hear 'Ain't that a Shame' would have to listen to <u>Pat Boone</u>."

Betty Jean made a "yuck" face, then grinned in triumph and started in singing the song herself, snapping her fingers and jerking her shoulders to the beat. I couldn't believe my eyes! Here came Carl Autry, sauntering right over and motioning Jimmy to come too. Betty Jean had made this impossible boy-thing happen easier than I could pass an English quiz.

Carl slid into the booth beside her. "Where you been, sweetheart?" he said, although it was really he who had been someplace else, according to Betty Jean. They started talking and giggling, all private and low, heads close together. I took a sip of my cherry Coke and thought how nice it would be, now that I'd served my purpose, if I could simply disappear.

Too late, the thought of heading back to church alone occurred to me. Jimmy, who until now had stood by, just staring at the floor, hands shoved deep in his pockets, plopped down on the other side of Carl, giving Carl an excuse to slide even closer to Betty Jean. Jimmy muttered something in Carl's ear, but Carl waved him away. Betty Jean took a last, gurgling draw on her cherry-Coke straw, peered in the bottom of her empty glass, then smiled up at Carl and fluttered her eyelashes. "I got the drugstore blues," she said. He thought that was so cute he put his arm around her and gave her a squeeze.

Things were starting to get awkward—shades of Ramey Lee and Nancy. I couldn't think of one solitary thing to say to Jimmy, and he certainly wasn't falling all over himself to speak to me. I didn't know where to look, either, since he was sitting right across from me, so I stared down at the table. Jimmy shifted in his seat, took a knife out of his pocket, flipped it open and started cleaning under his fingernails like I wasn't there. I almost suffocated from embarrassment. Maybe there was some rule of etiquette I didn't know about that said the girl had to speak first. All I could think to say was "How are you today, Jimmy?" which even to me sounded dumb beyond belief. I said it anyway.

Jimmy looked up, startled. Then he smiled a vicious red-wolf smile and said real loud in a put-on radio voice, "Hey! Nig—uh—Achsa! Read any good books lately?"

I can't believe I'm writing you about all this. Anyway, I wished with all my heart the floor would break open and swallow me. My face got hot and my mouth went so dry my tongue clicked sticking to the roof of it. My harelip scar throbbed tight and white, and I wanted more than anything to rub my thumb over it. What was I supposed to do? Say nothing? Or go ahead and give an answer, even though he was making fun of me?

Idiot that I am, I took a breath and spoke.

"Well, yes, as a matter of fact, now that you mention it, I have read a good book quite recently," I said, stalling desperately to come up with one that might remotely interest him. A single title came to mind. "The Iliad," I blurted. "I bet you'd really like it. It's full of battles and gore. We read some of it in Latin class and I read the rest on my own. Only in English."

My laugh sounded like a crazy person's. Still, I forged ahead. "It takes place in ancient Greece. It's even got a Penelope. She weaves all night. Or maybe that's The Odyssey. I read them both."

Jimmy stopped cleaning under his fingernails, clasped both hands around his knife, and stared at me like I was a large wad of Dubble Bubble he'd found stuck to his shoe. I looked down again, studied my hands in my lap. They were shaking. After what felt long enough for both of us to read the book in its original Greek and was probably about ten seconds, Jimmy grabbed Carl by the sleeve and just about dragged him out of the booth. "Come <u>on</u>, man, it's late, we got to go," he said.

Carl whispered, "See you later," to Betty Jean and hollered, "We're leaving, man," at Hank, who was still reading magazines in the back. Then Jimmy said something to Carl and they both ran toward the front of the store.

I reached for my double-shot cherry Coke and found nothing

in the cup but crushed ice. Something cold and wet was running off the table into my lap and dripping on my legs.

Betty Jean jumped up. "Oh, snot, Nig—Achsa! Jimmy slit your cup," she cried.

I looked at her in confusion.

"With his switchblade, dummy. Down near the bottom." She said it like it was all my fault, which I guess it was. For not knowing what to say to Jimmy. For being a gimp. For having a harelip. Please, God, don't let me mail this letter. But you know all that stuff already, anyway.

"Don't just sit there, we're late." Betty Jean said, yanking me out of the booth. "Oh, by the way," she added, "Carl's taking me to a movie Friday night."

When I stood up, the whole right side of my white dress was brownish pink and wet. I grabbed a handful of little paper napkins out of the dispenser on the table and tried to blot away the moisture, but they just turned to mush. Cherry Coke was dripping from my clothing all over Greene's black-and-white tile floor. It had soaked through my skirt and petticoats all the way to my skin. I looked up in time to see Hank following Carl and Jimmy out the door. He glanced at my dress and at the mess on the table and shook his head. "Oh, man," he said to Jimmy, "what'd you have to do that for?"

I stared straight ahead. If I didn't move, maybe none of it had really happened. Maybe I wouldn't have to walk back to church with wet brown stains all over the skirt of my white sundress.

"Come <u>on</u>." Betty Jean jerked my arm and pulled me toward the door.

The prelude had just ended when we slunk in. I scooted down a side aisle and slid in next to Daddy. He didn't notice anything, since the only place he ever looks is up at Mama in the choir loft. Mama didn't notice either, just stared down at her lap as usual so she wouldn't have to meet Daddy's worshipful gaze.

You have to stand up five times in our church service: once for the Doxology and the Apostles' Creed, once for the Lord's Prayer and the Gloria Patria, and three more times for hymns. Each time, I prayed to God to strike me dead so nobody would see my skirt.

When the service finally ended, I told Daddy I'd left my hat in the ladies room, then bolted down the back stairs, retrieved it and ran out to the car before anybody saw. When we got home, I pretended to search for my Bible in the back seat until both my parents had got safely indoors. Then I tiptoed in behind them and darted for the safety of my room, where I changed clothes and wadded up the horrid dress for the laundry hamper.

Crying was out of the question until after lunch, when I finally escaped to my backyard hideaway, but by then the tears had made such a hard little ball in my chest they would not come out. I had all afternoon to dread evening: Youth Fellowship, where Betty Jean and Hank would both know me for such a gimp that some stupid boy in Greene's drugstore would rather punch a hole in my cherry Coke cup with a switchblade than let people think he sat across from me because he wanted to. As it turned out, I need not have worried. When I got to Fellowship no one was there but Marlene Sprague. They'd all gone to the Baptist church for a revival.

That was my Sunday. Once I started writing, it just all came pouring out. I promise I'll write a more cheerful letter next time. Maybe about how great my life will be after I'm gone from here and living in New York.

Yours excruciatingly truly,
Achsa

P.S. Thank you for your concern about my mother, I appreciate it very much.

P.P.S. I'm very proud to have a letter postmarked from your home town.

Chapter twelve

August 12–26, 1955

Atlanta, Friday, August 12, 1955

Dearest E,

I'm so sorry about your contract. I don't blame you for being upset, although I'm sure your mother thought she was looking out for your best interests. You're a wonderful singer and you're going to be a fantastic actor. If this colonel thought so, surely someone else like him will think so, too.

This letter's awfully short and sort of wet. I'm writing it at work so I can drop it in a mailbox on my way home. I'll write more later and send a grammar lesson. Right now I mostly just wanted to tell you, don't lose heart.

Sincerely,

Achsa

P.S. I left several messages this week with some woman who answers the phone afternoons at WDDO saying to please ask Penelope to play one of your records. I haven't heard one yet, so last night I sneaked out in the hall after my parents went to sleep and called again. The

105

phone just rang and rang. Maybe Penelope doesn't answer when she's on the air.

*　　*　　*

Memphis, Friday, August 19

Dearest B,

She did it!! Satnin signed the papers!!!!! Daddy, too!

Didn't I tell you Colonel was smart? What he did, he got all these country stars to phone my folks and say what a great guy he is. When Hank Snow called, Satnin like to fainted. Sat right down on the floor and started fanning herself with her hand.

Now Colonel is officially representing me for three whole years. What that means is he's going to get me a contract with some big record company like RCA, and I can finally have a record that's a hit all over the country. After that, it's Hollywood!!

What it really means is, whatever happens from now on, we will never be poor again. Not me nor ~~none~~ any of my kin.

That's what I hadn't ever told you. Like you not telling me about your mouth. I feel some the same way about it, I guess. I spent my whole life trying to hide it. Sometimes we almost didn't have enough to eat. There was times we didn't have the rent money and had to move. One time the only place we could afford to live was in a colored neighborhood. I liked it there. Maybe that's how come I feel at home on Beale Street.

When we lived in Tupelo, most times I was the only boy at school in overalls. You learn to hang your head, stare at the ground and never look in people's eyes. That way you don't have to know who pities you, or who thinks you're not even worth the effort. You spend a lot of time at the movies, sitting in the dark where you don't have to see ~~nobody~~ anybody, and nobody can see you. That's how you get away from it for a little while.

From this day that's all behind me. I got no need to worry about ~~none~~ any of it ~~no~~ any more. Me and Scarlett O'Hara, we aren't ~~never~~ ever going hungry again. My heart's so light I might shoot right to the ceiling like a helium balloon. Stay up there all my life, my head knocking and my feet dangling down.

Still, it's a true saying, there is nothing in this world that ~~don't~~ doesn't cost something. My girlfriend and I broke up for good. She knew once I signed with Colonel there weren't any turning back. I'm not ever going to buy a furniture store. Or be a gospel singer. She gave me back my senior ring. It feels heavy as a lead pipe on my finger.

Your letter took my mind off my troubles some. Got me to thinking about <u>yours</u> awhile. Some folks is just mean and this Jimmy sounds like one of them. The way I see it, nothing that happened was your fault. You just got to learn to talk to boys is all. Boys are suckers for a compliment. You could of told that Jimmy how you really like red hair. Even if you don't. Leastways it would of put him off his guard and ~~give~~ gave got you the upper hand. As for that Betty Jean, I wouldn't want anybody for a friend that called me an ugly name.

I guess now I've set you straight I better go. I'm taking Satnin for a drive. Tonight's my last night home. Tomorrow night I got to be in Shreveport.

Yours very truly,
Elvis

P.S. I saved the best for last. Colonel's booking me into some towns I never been to. I'm pretty sure Atlanta's one of them. We'll finally get to meet each other. Bet I'll see a pretty girl.

* * *

Atlanta, Friday, August 26, 1955

Dearest E,

Congratulations on your contract!! Sounds like now you're really on your way to being a big star, like I always said.

I'm sorry things didn't work out with your girlfriend. I mean it, I truly am. I don't know what else to say.

If it's any consolation at all, you're coming along wonderfully well with your grammar. In your last letter you could have said, "It

would <u>have</u> put him off his guard and <u>given</u> you the upper hand."
But most importantly, you knew something was wrong with what
you wrote and you found a way to fix it. This next is more for writing
than speaking, because they both sound the same: Don't use "of" after
"could" or "would." It's "could <u>have</u> told," "would <u>have</u> put."

About your growing up poor, it's nothing to be ashamed of.
Thank you for telling me. I don't think any differently about you than
before. Neither should anybody else. If they do, they're not worth
knowing. That's <u>my</u> opinion, anyway.

When you come to Atlanta, you've got to promise me you
won't expect a pretty girl. I won't go backstage if you do. I mean it.
Mama made up my face tonight, made me as beautiful as she knew
how, as beautiful as I will ever be. Only I wasn't beautiful. I looked
grotesque.

Did you know that it's possible to go your whole life believ-
ing something without realizing it? I think that, all my life, some
part of me I didn't know about believed that Mama—so beautiful
herself—would one day make me pretty too. Or at least normal
looking, that would be enough. All the caterpillar has to do to be
a butterfly is wait. I waited without even knowing it. It's how I got
through every day.

Well, now the waiting's over.

This morning Mama stopped me as I headed out the door
for work and asked about the stains on my white sundress. They
hadn't come out in the wash. She pried it out of me about going
to Greene's and what had happened there. Then I asked her how to
talk to boys.

Something like panic crossed her face. "I never—we'll talk
about it later," she said and turned away.

This evening, after Daddy left for a deacons' meeting, she came
to me while I was drying dishes and handed me a book, <u>What Every
Young Girl Should Know</u>.

"I thought this would help you. With the boys," she said.

I barely looked at it. "I didn't want a book," I told her. "I wanted
you to tell me. I wanted <u>you</u> to tell me how to talk to boys."

She looked stricken. "I gave you the book because I don't know how to help you. Boys just always talked to me. I never had to learn." She said it like she was ashamed.

Poor Mama. You know how sometimes my mind's eye sees her with Robert Mitchum? Well, sometimes, in that same way, I see her with a different daughter. A girl my age, wearing a cashmere sweater set as fuzzy and pink as a bunny's ear. Her blonde hair falls naturally in a sleek pageboy, and she has a lovely, perfect mouth. When she goes on dates, Mama waits up for her. They stand talking in the kitchen with just the dim light on over the sink, while Mama fixes her a hot chocolate and melts a marshmallow on top. She tells my mother—her mother—about the movie she's just seen and where her boyfriend took her afterward to eat. Mama leans toward her, hanging on her every word like someone in love. Sometimes I think she wants me to be that girl so badly she forgets I'm not.

Mama stacked the glasses and dessert plates in the cabinet over the sink. Then she licked her thumb and smoothed my bangs down at the cowlick, like when I was a little girl. A light breeze played with the ruffles on the organdy curtains, the kind of breeze that tells you summer's going to end. Mama put her arm around my shoulders. "The senior girls wear makeup, don't they," she said.

I nodded.

"Come on," she said, gently turning me toward her bedroom. "I'll show you."

Fear and excitement ballooned inside me. In an hour I would know my future. I prayed, please, God, help me stand it without flinching. And without crying, especially without crying, whatever the results. Crying would break my mother's heart.

The warmth from her hand on my shoulder slowed everything to dream-time. She guided me to her dressing table, lightly pushed me down onto the round wooden stool that had outlived Great-aunt Achsa's old upright piano, cupped my face in both her hands and studied it soberly. Then she left the room and returned with a lyre-back chair from the dining room, positioned it opposite her dressing table and sat down.

The movement caused her hair to fall across one eye. She laughed, pushing it back, and in that moment I glimpsed the young, free, New York woman she must have been before my father came along. I willed all the clocks to stop so we might stay like that forever: her happy, and with her whole life ahead of her, me in the glow of her undivided attention, waiting to be made beautiful.

All my life, I had watched my mother at her dressing table perform unnecessary magic on her perfect face. Yet I myself had never once sat there. Even as a little girl I knew it was her throne—this small mahogany desk covered with a white cutwork scarf and topped with a piece of glass Daddy got cut to fit at a shop where they fix broken car windows. Everything on it sparkles and flings rainbow lights into the room: A pair of cut-glass lamps with white silk shades, a silver dresser set, a crystal tray, the graceful glass perfume bottles that line the wall beneath the large oval mirror edged with silver scrollwork that frames Mama's face like a cameo. Daddy bought her every bit of it, piece by piece, without her ever asking. I guess she wanted it.

This evening, on her crystal tray, she set out tubes and jars, pencils and brushes, lined them up like surgical implements. Seeing them like that—or maybe smelling all her perfumes at one time—numbed me, made me dizzy.

"I need you to face me," Mama said.

I spun woozily on the stool, turning my back to the mirror. Mama reached behind me to the crystal tray, opened a milk glass jar and smoothed cleansing cream on my face. Her fingertips massaged away the chill of it, and the sliminess. When she wiped it off, a corner of the Kleenex grazed my right eye.

She blotted away its watering. "A woman puts on her face every morning," she said. "It's something she gives to the world. And what the world expects from her."

"Why does the world expect that?" I asked.

"I don't know," she answered, creaming my face again. "Maybe the world thinks it's the best of what you are."

I frowned. She rubbed her thumb between my eyebrows until she rubbed the frown away. Her hands and voice smoothed away any further questions lurking in the still room.

Face makeup begins with creams: cleanser, moisturizer, foundation, highlighter, rouge. Every cream has a name. I had heard them all, all my life, but never said them. I tried to say them now, repeating each one as it touched my skin.

Eyes come next: the most painful part. Tweezers plucked eyebrow hairs growing in wrong places. A thumb gouged color onto my socket bones. Sharp pencils jabbed, an eyelash curler pinched. I winced, stifling an "ouch." All the while, Mama soothed me as one might a frightened child, describing every step in the same gentle singsong she had used long ago reciting Mother Goose rhymes. Finally, she opened a small, red case and spat delicately onto a tar-colored mascara cake, dug into it with a stiff little brush and swiped the brush along my lashes. Then she pouffed my face with peach-colored powder from a blue satin box.

Only my mouth remained. Which was everything, really. I could have begged her to stop right then, and she would have. But how would I have known my future? You would not have stopped her, would you? If you were me?

My calm left me. In spite of the cool evening, my skin prickled with sweat. The makeup on my face felt gunky. Mama smeared something from a white tube across my upper lip and powdered over it. She did not say what it was called. The tube said "CoverMark."

It was from Daddy I learned about my mouth. I was four, but I remember all of it. Until then, I thought people looked at me for the same reason they looked at Mama: because I was beautiful. The War had ended. Daddy had come home. We had moved into an apartment near a playground. One afternoon, while Mama was out shopping, he took me there. I'd never been to a playground. Mama always pushed me in my stroller, never stopping anywhere. Daddy and I walked. He held onto my hand and showed me tiny flowers growing in the grass and dirt around my feet. When we got there, he steered me to the sandbox and sat down on a bench nearby.

I was playing blissfully, digging holes and filling them up, when a bunch of kids charged over from the swings. They stopped at the edge of the sandbox, stared at me and giggled behind their hands.

"She looks like a nigger, don't she?" said a little boy in dirt-stained khaki short pants.

"She looks like a <u>rabbit</u>," a girl in a blue dress said.

"You're a rabbit," another boy chimed in.

I laughed with delight at this new game, raised my hands up to my head for floppy ears and began to hop around. The children laughed harder. And then came my father.

"Get on out of here. Leave her alone. Go on," he said, shooing them off like birds.

I stopped hopping, wondering why he had put an end to our game. Daddy squatted in the sand, reached over and took down my bunny-ear hands. Then he cupped my chin and rubbed his thumb lightly across my upper lip. "I'm afraid you'll never have an easy life," he said.

"Why, Daddy?" I asked.

He paused for what seemed an eternity to a four-year-old, then finally replied, "Because you don't look like your mother."

Something in the way he said it told me that no one, even mama, would ever love me, ever kiss my misshapen mouth. My father pulled me out of the sandbox and we walked home across the dirty grass. I sat down cross-legged on the living-room floor, and turned to face the wall.

My mother found me there when she came home an hour later. She stooped and gathered me into her arms. "You're my pretty girl," she said. Still, even that long ago, I dared not disillusion her, so I prayed she'd never know what I had learned that day. I also prayed that what she'd said was true. Even though she hadn't kissed me.

Mama pulled the cap off a deep, red lipstick from her crystal tray and swished the brush end of a slim gold wand across it.

"Make me beautiful" I pleaded, a prayer whispered so low she couldn't hear.

"Now we'll paint a lip line," she said, drawing with short strokes on my mouth as though it were a sketchpad. "Fire and Ice, that's a good shade for you, a nice dark red."

I could hear the crystal clock on her nightstand ticking way across the room, could hear a neighbor pushing a lawn mower one street over, hurrying to get his backyard cut before full dark. I could hear the sighing rush of red blood through my arteries.

Once, long ago, my mother touched her finger to the thin, white scar on my upper lip and said, "When God makes mistakes, He ought to rub them out." It's the closest she ever came to mentioning my mouth.

Now she rose, stepped back to survey my face, leaned down and smoothed my eyelids. Then she picked up the hand mirror from her dresser and held it out to me.

I gripped its icy handle, positioned it parallel to the floor and angled it up slowly. At first, it reflected only ceiling, then Mama where she stood behind me with expressionless blue eyes. I tilted it to reveal my face, one feature at a time. First the forehead. Then the Gypsy eyes I used to wear for trick or treat. Grown-up eyes now. Pretty. I smiled an unreflected smile. So far, so good. Next, sculpted cheekbones for a grownup face. And, oh, my bones were beautiful! The whole top half of my face was indisputably lovely. I held the mirror still until it trembled. More than anything I wanted to stop it there, drop it, smash it—keep the image of myself as Mama's pretty girl.

"Go on," my mother said. So I did what I had to. I tilted the mirror once again.

And there it was, my made-up mouth. A small, drawn-on, red, kewpie doll mouth, a cupid's bow. A death-mask mouth, bizarre and monstrous. My thick, lopsided upper lip, lightened and powdered the same shade as my face, crouched like a gargoyle above it. I smiled. My little red mouth smiled. I pouted. It pouted, too. I pursed my lips—a hideous kiss. A freak's kiss. Me.

"Thank you, Mama," I said. "It looks very nice." A disobedient tear crawled out the corner of my right eye. Blonde-pageboy, cashmere-sweater daughter hovered barely out of view.

That's when I recognized myself. I was Maizie, my first doll, my only doll with dull hair and brown eyes like mine. Maizie, whom I'd let fall into the space heater, the bottom third of her face melted, only her crimson, dead, cupid's bow intact. I hid her under my bed and never looked for her again. She still gives me bad dreams.

Mama put her hands on my shoulders and shook me ever so

slightly. She did not look twenty anymore. "Achsa, you will come into your own one day," she said. "I promise you. Beauty is not what it's cracked up to be. You will make up your face every morning and everything will be fine, believe me."

"No, it won't!" I screamed. Tears coursed down my cheeks, and I tasted the tinny strangeness of mascara. "You don't know me," I spat out between sobs. "I've got more in common with circus sideshow freaks than I ever will with you!"

"Achsa..." She reached out to draw me to her. I pushed her away, ran into my room and slammed the door.

I wish that once, just once, she would say out loud that I'm not like her, that I'm not pretty, that my mouth is deformed and ugly. Or that it even exists, that I exist the way I really am. Just once.

I cried so long I don't remember stopping. I only know I fell asleep and dreamed. I dreamed I was walking along a busy downtown street, wearing a mask of Mama's face. I was beautiful, yet nobody could see me. I shouted out to everyone I passed, yet nobody could hear. I grabbed hold of the mask with both hands and tried to pull it off. I ripped it, tore at it, and finally it came, taking the skin of my own face with it. At three in the morning I woke myself screaming. And then I wrote you this letter.

You said we could tell each other everything. Well, I did.
　　Sincerely,
　　Achsa

Chapter thirteen

September 7–
October 1, 1955

Somewhere in Missouri, Wednesday, September 7, 1955

Dearest B,

I want to thank you for writing me that letter, same as you thanked me for writing you about being poor. I wrote you stuff I never said, not even to Satnin. We got us something special, you and me. We truly do.

I'm glad your eyes turned out pretty. I like a girl with pretty eyes. I got to say I never paid much attention to girls bones. I'll take your word you got good ones. I thought some about your mouth. Maybe the only wrong your mama did was try and cover it up.

I got a story for you. I stammered ~~real bad~~ really badly when I was a kid. It pretty much went away when I got grown. Only, now and then I'd stammer some on purpose, just kidding around. One day I did it in a record session. Know what came out? "Oh, baby, baby, baby, b-b-b-b-b-b, baby, baby, baby, b-b-b-b-b-b," the start of "Baby, Let's Play House," and it sets all the girls to screaming. What

I'm saying is, maybe your lip is something, if you don't try and hide it, it can do you good later on. Like my stammer did for me.

As for your mama not talking about it, maybe in this one way she is like Satnin. Satnin thinks she wants to know every little thing happening to me, only she really ~~don't~~ doesn't. She doesn't want to know about girls tearing off my clothes, or me braining myself climbing onto a rickety stage in some cornfield ballpark, or how we ran into a car head-on last week driving to a show, which I had to tell her since it banged up the Fleetwood to the tune of $1,000. She ~~don't~~ doesn't want to know any of that stuff. Still it ~~don't~~ doesn't mean she doesn't love me. It means she loves me so much she can't bear thinking of me in any kind of danger.

Maybe your mama can't bear knowing how your lip makes you feel ugly and how kids call you Nig and Nigger Lip. Maybe those things give her too much pain, and that's why she won't talk about your mouth. Because she loves you too much. Just like Satnin loves me. So don't be too hard on her, that's my advice.

I'm glad to hear my grammar is improving, Teach. I owe it all to you. You be good going back to school, you hear? And don't you fall in love yet till I get there.

Yours truly,
Elvis

P.S. I bought me another car. A yellow '54 Eldorado convertible!! I'm a <u>really</u> cool cat now, driving everywhere with the top down. When I get to Atlanta I'll take you riding all over town.

* * *

Atlanta, Wednesday, September 14, 1955

Dearest E,

You're right, we <u>do</u> have something special. Or I do, anyway—a very wise friend.

I felt pretty low after I wrote you last. Each day piled onto the day before like one more gray wool blanket on a whole stack of them. I mostly just went to school and came home and curled up on my bed. Stared at the ceiling, never once looked in a mirror. I even made a "B" on a history quiz. Around Mama I tried hard to act my usual self—while "perky" does not exactly describe me, I have never been a moper. Still, even she sensed something was wrong. I said I'd come down with a cold.

Then on Saturday your letter came. I hid under the bedclothes and read it over and over the whole afternoon. That night and all day Saturday I listened to "Baby Let's Play House" again and again. By Sunday, when my parents left for church, I knew what I had to do.

I got out of bed, washed my face, combed my hair, and put on a pair of blue jeans and my favorite pink blouse. Then I went into my parents' room, where the morning sun spilled onto the floor, and sat at Mama's dressing table. A pretender to the throne, I didn't put quite all my weight on the stool as I picked through her top two drawers for all the makeup she used on my face. Then I went to work.

I'll tell you right off that in no way did I do an expert job. My eyes came out smeary and my cheekbones didn't look so well defined. But I could see improvement might be possible with practice. Eyes and cheekbones weren't the point, anyway. The point was my mouth.

I dipped a fingertip into Mama's small white jar of beige foundation cream and dabbed it on my upper lip, taming my nostril-to-lip scar into a little makeup-colored ridge just like Mama had done. Super! That left only Big Lip and Little Lip themselves. I wiped the makeup still left on my fingertip across them, banged them with a powder puff, uncapped the lipstick and rolled out its blood-red tower. Fast, that was the only way to do it. I knew I dared not stop.

I flicked a button on the gold wand that looked most like Mama's lip brush, and its bristles leaped out just like that Jimmy's switchblade. Appropriate. I slapped them back and forth across the lipstick till they'd worked up a thick, red lather, then I outlined my bottom lip and filled in color from the tube. More like "caked on," actually. Easy enough. I lathered up the lip brush once again.

And that was the end of me pretending nothing much was going on. My hand jiggled all over the place as I brought the brush toward my gargantuan upper lip. Then when I got there I couldn't touch it. No matter how hard I tried, I could force neither my hand nor my face to move that extra quarter-inch. I was paralyzed with fear.

Once in a great while, some phrase you hear every day suddenly means something. This one saved me living out my life stiff as a corpse in some stone-walled insane asylum, I am sure of it. "Paralyzed with fear," that's what I was. Furious something so dumb described me, I hurled the brush at Mama's mirror. It bounced off the silver frame, nicked the dressing table's glass top, and landed on the floor in a square of sun glare. Inside my head, what sounded like a horde of angry wasps had gone into a high-pitched whine. I snatched up the lipstick tube, stabbed it at my mouth, and ground its greasy redness everywhere inside my upper lip.

And there it was. Fire and Ice, blood and roses. My mouth. It was a hideous gash that I couldn't take my eyes off. I stared until it wavered mirage-like in my sight. Stared until—so huge, so stubbornly unshrinking—it turned beautiful. I looked away, looked back, and it was hideous again. I smiled. Several different ways. Most looked awful. One looked soft and lovely, but I could not remember afterwards how to make my mouth do that again. It is possible for one person to both cry and laugh out loud at the same time. Did you know that?

At quarter to noon I creamed my morning's work off my face and put away Mama's makeup. When they came in from church I said I felt much better. It had got boring lying around.

On Monday, when I went outside, everything looked bright and clean, even dark, dank, dingy Foster High. When I opened my locker, I nearly cried again, thinking how many times I'd dialed that combination through the years and how in a few short months I never would again. And I don't even like Foster all that much. Mostly, I like the first day, when they give out the books. I bring mine home, stack them on my bed, and page through each one to see what I'm going to learn. Then I just lie there, thrilled. I guess I really am the biggest gimp in all of Dreamer Hills.

I'm definitely going to college in New York, by the way. The counselor's office has a book that lists all the colleges and universities in the United States, and yesterday I copied down every one with a "New York, New York" address and wrote them for information. It should start coming any day. It's like I've always seen my future as a road stretched out in front of me, and now I'm finally walking on it.

Something else. I joined the Drama Club. They mainly just put on the senior play each spring, but this year around Thanksgiving they're doing another one. It's a comedy based on "Cinderella." My English teacher, Mrs. Rollins, is club sponsor. Anyway, when she stopped me after class today and asked if I'd join up and help her write it, my blood-and-roses mouth shocked me by saying, "That's just fine." Maybe it thinks it's a dramatic mouth and it <u>belongs</u> in a drama club.

Maybe my mouth is taking over my whole life. Ever since Sunday, almost every time I walk past a mirror or a window I cut my eyes to get a glimpse of my reflection. It's like I'm trying to catch myself unawares, to find out what I <u>really</u> look like, how other people see me. I stare at other people's faces, too, their mouths especially. Girls' faces, sometimes women's. White people, and Negroes too. Maybe I start out wanting to see how their mouths compare to mine, I don't know. From there I get all involved in trying to figure out who they are and what they're thinking.

Yesterday, this Negro girl who looked about my age got on the bus when I was going to the library. You couldn't help but notice her. She stood straight and tall and held her chin up like a princess. That long "Colored People Seat from Rear" seat in the back of the bus was empty. She sat down in the very middle of it and faced straight ahead with great composure. She looked so special it was all I could do not to crane my neck and stare. I wanted so very much to get up and sit by her and talk to her, find out everything I could about her, like with Mama that night in the car driving to Mississippi. That's what I mean. I didn't use to be like that until I painted my mouth.

Here's the grammar. It's correct to say "I don't," "You don't," "We don't," and "They don't." But it's "He <u>doesn't</u>" and "It <u>doesn't</u>."

Don't ever say "He don't," or "It don't." This is part of making sure your subjects and your verbs agree. And it's <u>important</u>!

    Sincerely,

      Achsa

P.S. I never knew singing was such a dangerous profession. Thank Heaven you're still alive!

P.P.S. Your new car sounds <u>super</u>!

P.P.P.S. Falling in love is very serious. You mustn't tease people about it.

*　*　*

Shreveport, Saturday, September 24, 1955

Dearest B,

    So you joined the drama club. Maybe one day we'll <u>both</u> be in the movies.

    Got by Memphis Friday and saw the Blackwoods at an all-night sing. After they ~~was~~ were done I went backstage to give my regards, and they got all upset I'd gone and bought a ticket. Said I should ~~of~~ have got in free. I'm not used to being treated different from other people. Them saying that made me feel strange, like I'd been let into some club I didn't know was there.

    I'm headlining the Hayride now. You know how you said you used to see your future like a road in front of you and now you're walking on it? Well, I reckon I'm running flat out on mine, everything's happening so fast.

    I like it how you looked at that colored girl and wished you could talk to her. There don't many white people really look at colored people, I don't think, else they'd never say all coloreds look alike.

    I stand by what I said earlier, by the way. I bet whoever looks at you they'll see a pretty girl. You're pretty <u>inside</u>, it can't help but show. And now you got this big dramatic mouth. Oh, excuse me,

120

ma'am. I forgot I'm not supposed to talk about you being pretty. Reckon it just slipped out.

I'm backstage at the Hayride and they're calling me. Time to go make a living. Catch you later.

Yours truly,
Elvis

*   *   *

Atlanta, Friday, September 30, 1955, 11:30 P.M.

Dearest Elvis,

The most terrible thing has happened. By the time you get this letter you will surely know.

About an hour ago I was listening to Daddy-O Radio. A record ended and Penelope didn't come back on. At first there was only silence. Then you could hear her talking, far away but getting closer. She was saying, "Something's gone wrong with our news machine. Can you hear it? 'Ding-ding-ding-ding.' It's driving me crazy. 'Ding-ding-ding-ding.' I got to put a stop to this." She put on Ray Charles' "I Got a Woman," and I went back to studying. A moment later the needle scraped across the record and the music stopped.

Penelope drew in a breath. "Oh, babies," she said softly, "somebody's died. That's what was happening with the teletype. It was letting me know someone important has just died."

You could hear paper rattling, then she began to read. It went pretty much like this: "'Noted Hollywood actor James Dean was killed at approximately 5 P.M., when the sports car he was driving collided head on with another vehicle outside Salinas, California. The 24-year-old Dean, who rocketed to stardom earlier this year as the tortured son in the movie <u>East of Eden</u>, had become a favorite of teenage fans. His second movie, <u>Rebel Without a Cause</u>, is scheduled for release in October, and he recently completed shooting on a third, <u>Giant</u>, starring Elizabeth Taylor. He was on his way to participate in an auto race when the accident occurred. Plans for a memorial service have not yet been announced.'

"I know who he is," Penelope said after a moment's silence. "Got that impish little grin on the covers of all those movie magazines. Looked like he'd be a real cut-up, he did." Her voice went soft and sad. "We got to play a record for him. Let's see, we got to find us a song to play for Mr. James Dean. The late Mr. James Dean, who passed away this evening in a tragic automobile accident. Here's one. I suppose it'll have to do."

She put on the Platters singing "Only You" and let it play through three times without stopping. I don't remember what she played after that. I was crying—crying because someone so young, with so much greatness in him, had to die, and because he won't be around to make any more movies for the rest of us to see. But most of all I was crying for you, because I know you will be sad.

Except in the most general sense of wanting to see you sing or to talk to you, I've never wished I was any place where you were. Not at any particular moment, I mean. But I do tonight. I wish I could be with you when you find out about James Dean, because I know how much he meant to you. I wish it with all my heart..

Sincerely,

Achsa

* * *

Gladewater, Texas, 4:30 A.M. Saturday, October 1, 1955

Dearest Baby Girl,

Something so bad is come to pass I can't hardly see through my tears to write of it. James Dean is gone. The Lord has called him home. I told people here to let me be alone. I'm grieving so bad I can't think of nothing else.

I can't believe he won't be with us anymore, Baby Girl. I depended on him. He was the one going to teach me acting for the movies.

I had it all planned out. I'd see every movie he would ever make. Again and again, like I did East of Eden. Keep going till I figured out exactly how he done it. How he could play-act some person on a movie screen and make that person seem so real just by being his own true self. I figured if I did that, went to school on him that way, then maybe one day I might be as good as he ~~is~~ was is.

Now that's not worth nothing. Cause he's gone.

You know, I used to lie awake nights thinking about him. Thinking how maybe someday him and me would star in a movie together. How I'd get to watch him on the movie set and see just how he ~~done~~ did it. Maybe I'd even get to be his friend. Carry him home to Memphis for a few days and we'd just hang out together. Take him to meet Mr. Phillips, take him down to Beale Street. Now that's not none of it ever going to happen, all what I thought about for so long.

I'm so sad right now I know why people say their hearts are breaking. My heart hurts like a pile of smashed glass in my chest. I'm glad I didn't find out tonight till I was done singing, else there's no way I could have got through it.

I wish you were here with me right now. We could lie down alongside each other, hold each other tight. Except for maybe Satnin, you're the one knows me best of all. It wouldn't bother me none for you to see me cry.

Sometimes when I think about you, it's like you're a warm, comfortable room all lit by candles. A room with a nice big bed that's got a thick, soft feather quilt on top. I wish I could be in that room right now, lying in that bed, your warmth wrapped all around me.

I don't mean nothing bad by that, I swear it. I don't really know <u>what</u> I mean exactly. Only, you give me comfort in my soul, dearest Baby Girl, and I love you. Promise you won't ever go away.

I think maybe I can get some sleep now. I hope you can too.

Yours always,

Elvis

Chapter fourteen

October 5–23, 1955

Dearest E,

Your dear letter lives in my nightstand drawer. I can't bear to hide it in the shoebox in the far back of my closet with the rest of them. It means so very much to me.

I've been thinking a lot about James Dean lately, about how his dying left a big, empty space. Somebody will come along and fill that space, sooner or later. I believe you are the logical one to do it. Nobody understands and appreciates him as deeply as you do. You're even the same age he was when he got his start.

There's this acting school in New York, the Actor's Studio. I read about it in a theatre magazine at the library. James Dean and Marlon Brando <u>both</u> studied there. And guess what? That place teaches exactly what you said—how to be a great actor just by acting like yourself. Anyway, I got to thinking maybe you should go there. Maybe it would be a little like having James Dean himself around to learn from.

As you can see, my mind is completely taken up with things

theatrical these days. I ended up writing so much of that Cinderella play that Mrs. Rollins wants me there every rehearsal in case anything needs changing. I wish you could see Betty Jean Puckett hamming it up as the fairy godmother. I dreamed up her character all by myself and wrote every one of her lines. She's like somebody's jolly old busybody aunt, who tries to do good and ends up tripping all over herself. Or at least all over her raggedy old ball gown.

Hank Lawson's girlfriend, a pale beauty who unfortunately can't act and won't take time to learn her lines, plays Cinderella. Prince Charming isn't any great shakes as an actor, either, but he <u>is</u> our quarterback. Mrs. Rollins told me she deliberately cast a cheerleader and a football player in the leads so lots of kids would come. So unfair!!! Yet I see her point. We're doing "Cinderella" to raise money for the senior play.

Well, that's the news. As for the grammar, it's getting harder and harder to find things to correct. In your letter before last you said, "I'm not used to being treated different from other people." You should have said "different<u>ly</u>," because it tells how you're treated. That makes it an adverb, and adverbs mostly end in "-ly." I think I wrote you about adverbs once before. Usually you do them OK.

Please think about what I said—about you going to the Actor's Studio and taking James Dean's place. I meant every word of it. I don't say stuff like that just to be nice.

> Quite sincerely,
> Achsa

*   *   *

El Dorado, Arkansas, Monday, October 17, 1955

Dearest B,

Congratulations on the play! That's really cool. If I ~~was~~ were came there to see it, I'd stand up and holler when you take your bow. They do let you take a bow for writing it, don't they?

I got some good news of my own. Colonel's hatched a plan to turn me into a big rock-and-roll star. Last night the boys and I did a show with <u>Bill Haley and the Comets</u> in Oklahoma City. Afterwards,

Mr. Haley came up to me and said I had "good natural rhythm." Imagine!! Mr. "Rock Around the Clock" himself!!!

Tomorrow we do a show in Cleveland with <u>Pat</u> <u>Boone</u>. Then we're off to St. Louis. Colonel's booking us into bigger and bigger cities. And here's the best part. Are you ready? One of them's Atlanta!! Colonel says we'll be there sometime in December. I'm going to get to see my sweet Baby Girl at last!!

By the way, what you said about me taking James Dean's place? That's the nicest thing anybody ever said about me being an actor, except maybe Satnin. James Dean's the greatest actor ever lived. There's not nobody can take his place, but maybe I can get to be some like him.

I want to thank you too for telling me about that Actors Studio. I have to say I don't think it's for me, though. A school like that, they teach everybody the same thing. James Dean and Marlon Brando, I expect they ~~done~~ did as good as they did in spite of it. Still, they might have ~~did~~ done even better if they hadn't gone.

I'm a different kind of singer. I'm going to be a different kind of actor, too. I'm not going to do ~~no~~ any singing in my movies ~~neither~~ either. I already told Colonel. I'm not going to be ~~no~~ any like Roy Rogers or Gene Autry. My inside voice is still telling me I'm meant to be a serious actor, and that's what I aim to do.

Yours truly,
Elvis

P.S. My folks moved last weekend. My new address is 1414 Getwell, Memphis, Tennessee.

* * *

Atlanta, Saturday, October 22, 1955

Dearest E,

Yippeeeee!!! You're coming to Atlanta!!!!!

I'll buy a front-row-center seat!!! And I <u>promise</u> I will come backstage. Not sure yet what I'll do about my parents. If I have to, I'll simply run away from home that day and face the consequences.

And you're going to be a rock-and-roll star!! Just like I wrote you eight whole months ago. No, I don't work for a radio station, but maybe a radio station ought to hire me, if for no other reason than because I am so modest (ha-ha, joke).

Now that you're hobnobbing with Pat Boone, I hope that doesn't mean you have to <u>sing</u> like him—find a song some Negro has already recorded and water it down for all the white people who only listen to white radio stations. If you're going to sing like Pat Boone you might as well just sing like Perry Como. Same thing. Actually, I bet you couldn't do that if you tried.

I'm <u>so</u> <u>glad</u> you told Colonel you won't sing in your movies. As for the acting, I hope you don't give up completely on the Actor's Studio. Lots of really famous <u>serious</u> actors and actresses who perform on the Broadway stage go there, and they all rave about it.

Speaking of serious acting (ha-ha), Cinderella rehearsals are really heating up—three afternoons a week. It knocks me out seeing <u>my</u> <u>very</u> <u>own</u> <u>words</u> turn into a play before my eyes. Cinderella says, "Forsooth, a fire burns for my prince within my very soul. He gives me fever," and I think, <u>I</u> <u>wrote</u> <u>that</u>!! And then a fire flames up inside me, too, only it burns for my words—the sound of them, and the marvel that people I've never even met will hear them.

The play's good for taking my mind off what's happening at home, but even then I can't ignore it. Mama's still acting very strange. Daddy, too. He makes her tell him every place she's going every time she leaves the house. And when she's home he never takes his eyes off her. Except when he's praying, which takes longer and longer these days. Last night he stayed down a whole hour.

Mama's gotten really jumpy, too, maybe from Daddy's eyes always boring into her. And she's busy every minute. Last week she went through all our closets, sewing on every loose button and stitching up every pulled seam on every piece of clothing we own. She's already finished making all my winter school clothes, and she's almost finished everything I need for spring. Last week she called me into the dining room, where she'd set up her sewing machine like the eye in a storm of pastel taffeta and satin that boiled over the backs of all the chairs and down onto the floor. "Pick a color for your senior prom dress," she said, smiling.

It shocked me speechless, since, one, I seriously doubt I'll be going to my prom, and, two, in the unlikely event I do go, I won't be needing a dress until next May. Finally, I found the words to ask her why she'd bought so many colors. She shrugged and said. "I wasn't sure what you'd like. Pick one. I've got dress patterns, too."

She looked so strange. Her eyes shimmered like tears were forming in them. I wanted to take her hand or something. But I didn't, because I was afraid I'd make her cry. Finally, I told her everything looked so lovely I couldn't choose and maybe she should. She chose blue.

Yesterday three books came, more than she ever got before. One was called The Rainbow, another was by a writer named Henry James, and the third was The Old Man and the Sea, by Ernest Hemingway. Today, I went to the library to find them, but they're all in the adult section, where I can't even set foot until I turn sixteen. Ugh! How much longer must I be treated like a child??!!

When I got home, Mama was sitting on the sofa, smiling gently. The Rainbow book lay open on her lap, and she was stroking its pages as if they were made of velvet. I threw my own books down on the table by the door so they made a big bang. I wanted to startle her, drag her back into our living room from wherever her thoughts had taken her.

Behind the glass doors of her bookcase all her other books lay jumbled, as if she'd got in a frenzy and pulled them all out like before. "Did you have a nice day, Mama?" I said.

She looked up. "Oh, yes," she answered dreamily, closing the book, running her hand one last time over the cover, and setting it carefully on the end table. "I guess I better go start dinner," she said. "Time slipped up on me."

Whatever's haunting her is like another person living in our house, a person slowly taking her away.

Sorry for running on about all this. It can't be pleasant reading. I wish I had a grandmother I could talk to, but they're dead. I don't have anyone but you. I wrote Linda Sheffield weeks ago and she never answered.

Yours truly,
Achsa

* * *

Atlanta, Saturday, October 22 again, almost October 23

Dearest E,

Why do I trust people? Why am I so naive?

I did something so stupid tonight I wish I ~~was~~ were <u>dead</u>. I mean it, I truly do.

None of it would have happened, except for this new girl in my history class, but that's no consolation.

You know how I said I was a gimp? Well, at Foster you're not just a gimp and that's that. It's more like there's this ladder, with each of us gimps sitting on a different rung, and you can rise or fall depending on what you do and who you're seen with, just like the cheerleaders and the majorettes on their ladder and the football players on theirs. Right now I'm finally pretty near the top of the gimp ladder, what with working on the play and all. But this new girl, Lucy, is fat, with greasy hair and pimples, and just smart enough to call attention to herself. In other words, she's way more of a gimp than I am, and she knows it.

I imagine that's at least part of why she asked me to go with her and her sister to the homecoming game. I was all set to say no, but she put her hand on my arm when she asked me, and I saw her ragged fingernails all bitten down to the quick and I started thinking about how just knowing you're a gimp can make you nervous all by itself, and how maybe it took real courage for her to ask me since she hardly knew me and maybe she was terrified I'd turn her down. Then I started feeling all clutched up inside from thinking she was probably feeling clutched up inside, too, and before I could stop myself I said, "Sure, I'll go."

I told Mama and, without me even asking, she loaned me her beautiful mother-of-pearl opera glasses she used to take to the theater in New York. Lucy's father drove us there but he didn't stay. When we got to the stadium, Foster's side was nearly full and we had to sit way up near the top—which I hated, since everyone can see who's climbing all those steps. The band had struck up "On, Wisconsin," and it was all I could do not to step—oh, so gimp-like—in time to the music. You can't imagine how relieved I was when we sat down in the middle of a clump of freshmen and I didn't see anyone I knew. Lucy's younger sister, a carbon copy of her, waved at a couple of the gimpiest ones and they waved back. The three of us took turns gazing through Mama's opera glasses at what was going on, even though not one of us understood a lick of it. I was feeling pretty safe, fairly sure not a soul I knew would ever see us way up there, when all of a sudden here came redheaded Jimmy, that awful boy who cut a hole in my Coke cup. He was running up the steps and staring straight at me.

I had a seat on the aisle. I figured he'd just go on past. But, of all the crazy things, he stopped right beside me, grinned and said, "Hey, Nig—Achsa, how you doing? Mind if I sit down?" like I was his long-lost buddy or something.

I'd give anything now if I had said something clever and insulting that would have made him melt into the crowd, something like, "You know, you owe me a cherry Coke, blockhead," or "Finished reading The Iliad yet, dummy?" Suffice it to say, I didn't. Any time anybody says or does anything that startles me, especially a boy, I freeze like a doe caught in headlights. Which is exactly what I did. I looked up at Jimmy with my eyes stretched so wide open they smarted and said, "Sure, go right ahead." He must have thought I was soft in the brain.

Anyway, he sat down and started watching the game and right away Lucy said she had to have a hot dog and did I want to come with her and her sister to the concession stand. I said, "No, thanks," figuring if I was going to get seen by everyone that would be the place, so they squeezed out past Jimmy's knees and headed down the aisle.

For my part, I figured this was as good a time as any to practice talking to boys, since I had absolutely no stake in the outcome.

It wasn't like Jimmy was anyone I had a crush on. Just the opposite. He squirmed a lot and his clothes stank of stale cigarette smoke and fried onions.

"Nice weather for a game, isn't it," I said without feeling too especially nervous or anything. It sounded like what somebody in my situation might say in a movie.

Jimmy snickered and said, "Yeah, sure."

I looked out of Mama's opera glasses.

After hardly any time at all, he said, "Hey, let me look through those things a second."

I said, "Sure," which is what anybody raised to be polite would say automatically. Soon as it came out of my mouth, I wished I could suck it right back in. Jimmy took Mama's opera glasses in his sticky hands, raised them to his eyes and peered through them a second. Then he jumped up, dashed down the aisle with them and disappeared, before I could so much as get my mouth open to ask where he was going.

I sat there dazed until Lucy and her sister got back with their hotdogs. Then we all sat there some more. We couldn't see much of the game without binoculars, and we really didn't have an awful lot to say to one another. After awhile it dawned on me maybe Jimmy wasn't coming back, and if I wanted Mama's opera glasses I had better go after him. I went running up and down the aisles, but mostly saw old football players who had graduated and gained weight and their dates or wives hidden behind huge gold chrysanthemum corsages. So I climbed back up to my seat. After the game ended, I made the two girls wait with me until practically everyone had gone, hoping Jimmy would show up. No luck. Finally, the girls' father came to take us home, so I had to leave.

I felt so bad about the opera glasses I wanted to throw up all the way back to our house. It didn't help that my window wouldn't roll down and their car smelled like maybe a week or so ago part of a greasy drive-in hamburger had got lodged under my seat. I made it, though.

Mama was in the dining room pinning a Simplicity pattern to the blue satin she'd picked out for my prom dress. When I told her what happened to her opera glasses, all she said was, "Don't worry, honey, it's all right."

I felt really fabulous for about half a minute, before I noticed she had their leather case out on the table waiting for them. Such a pretty case, all lined in blue velvet. Except for something white folded up in the bottom, it looked very empty. A tear hung in Mama's lower lashes, making me think about that girl in the leg brace at your gospel picnic. Mama's tear shimmered there forever, until it finally splashed onto the mahogany tabletop and I started crying, too. I told her I'd baby-sit or do anything to earn enough money to buy her another pair of opera glasses exactly like the ones Jimmy had stolen, but she said it didn't matter. She took the white thing out of the bottom of the case and used it to blot under her eyes. Then she gave it a startled glance and immediately stuffed it back where she found it. It looked like a man's handkerchief that had seen better days, all wrinkled and caked with dark brown mud.

"Is that Daddy's?" I asked her. "Don't you want to wash it?"

"No!" she said, like the very idea terrified her, and snapped the case shut. "Don't worry so about the glasses, Achsa," she added, a bit more calmly. "I've still got the case, so it doesn't matter."

But it does. It matters a great deal. I'll never forgive myself for letting that boy put his thieving hands on anything so precious to my mother. I didn't have a suspicious enough nature just three hours ago. But I do now, believe me.

Thanks for listening.
    Sincerely,
      Achsa

P.S. I forgot the grammar in my earlier letter. You caught every double negative but one, last time. Don't say "not nobody." Seems like they only get by you anymore when you get carried away about something. Except for that, it was a letter-perfect letter.

Chapter fifteen

October 28–November 15, 1955

Dearest E,

I saw <u>Rebel Without a Cause</u>!!

It was wonderful!! I've never seen anything like it! I cried so hard strangers turned around and stared. And the whole way through, I kept seeing you in James Dean's role and thinking, "That's the kind of movie Elvis will star in someday."

Speaking of acting, like it or not it looks like I'm about to get my big break. Betty Jean's flunking algebra and had to drop out of the play, so guess who's stepping in as fairy godmother? I'm not especially thrilled—as you can probably tell—at the thought of being stared at by an auditorium full of people, but Mrs. Rollins said it's too late for anyone else to learn the part. Except me, since I wrote it. Had my first rehearsal today and it's really not that awful.

That's it for now. I've got to run. Mama's driving me to Betty Jean's to pick up her costume. I promise I'll do grammar next time.

This was just a quick note to say I saw the movie. Hope you did too.

Sincerely,
Achsa

* * *

Shreveport, Saturday, November 5, 1955

Dearest B,

"You're tearing me apppaaaaaaaarrrrrrrrttttttt!!!!"

Rebel Without a Cause is the greatest movie ever made! And James Dean is the greatest actor ever was or will be!!

Did you really see me playing his role? That's so cool! If I can even just once play a part like that, I can meet my Maker knowing I ~~done~~ did the great thing I was meant to. Still, I wish he hadn't had to die.

Guess what? Looks like you and me are getting our big breaks at the same time. Colonel says RCA's about to buy my contract. He even put up $5,000 of his own money. That's so Mr. Phillips won't sell me off to someone else before it goes through. It touched my heart so much, Colonel believing in me like that. He is a truly great man. I only wish my Daddy was more that way.

I'm real sorry to hear your mama's still causing you worry. Can't you just come right out and ask her what's wrong? That's what I'd do if it was Satnin.

A couple boys from home rode down with me for the "Hayride," and I got to go keep them out of trouble. I'll let you know about RCA soon as I hear.

Yours truly,
Elvis

* * *

ATLANTA, FRIDAY, NOVEMBER 11, 1955, 9 P.M.

DEAR MR. PRESLEY,
I MUST INSIST YOU CEASE WRITING ME IMME-

DIATELY. AS A GOOD CHRISTIAN GIRL I FIND YOUR
LETTERS DISGUSTING AND OFFENSIVE. ANY CORRE-
SPONDENCE FROM YOU AFTER THE ABOVE DATE WILL
FORCE MY PARENTS TO TAKE LEGAL ACTION AGAINST
YOU FOR MAKING UNWANTED ADVANCES TO A GIRL
UNDER 18 YEARS OF AGE. FROM THIS DAY I REFUSE TO
COMMUNICATE WITH YOU FURTHER.
      YOURS VERY TRULY,
      ACHSA J. MCEACHERN

*   *   *

Atlanta, Friday, November 11, 1955, 11 P.M.

Dearest Elvis,
      Something terrible beyond believing has come to pass. And
it is every bit my fault.
      You are going to get a horrible letter written all in capital let-
ters and signed by me, if you have not already. Please believe I did
not mean a word of it!!!!!!
      My father made me write it, and you must do what it says, at
least for a little while. But please know I could never send you such
hideousness of my own free will. It would be impossible.
      What happened, Daddy found the letter you wrote me after
James Dean died. I so loved reading it, even just touching it, I had to
keep it near me. I did not realize what an incredibly stupid, careless
thing that was to do.
      Tonight, while I was drying the dinner dishes, Daddy went
looking for a pair of nail clippers. When he couldn't find them in
any of the usual places, he rummaged through my nightstand drawer.
And found your letter. For all he could tell from the envelope, it
came from "Evie," my "pen pal." He had no right to read it, but
that didn't matter.
      His voice, when he called me into my room, turned my blood
cold. I knew what had happened. He was standing in front of my bed.
Mama stood beside him, clasping your letter to her breast as though in
prayer. When I approached them, Daddy grabbed me by the shoulders

137

and shook me till my teeth rattled. We were a Three Stooges movie, him shaking me, Mama looking aghast, and me laughing in terror like a crazy person. Everything in the room bobbed up and down—the ruffled bed with my stuffed panda on it, the frilly window curtains Mama bought, my dresser mirror ringed with birthday and Easter corsages I've been taping up since I was ten.

Daddy kept on shaking me, screaming over and over, "Who is this man? Why is he writing you such filth?"

I tried to tell him it wasn't filth, but the words wouldn't come. He didn't want to listen anyway. He kept saying I'd lied about "Evie" so surely my lying had no end.

I started to cry, and he screamed the most shameful questions over and over into my ear: Why had I allowed you to pick me up, when did I sneak away to see you, where did we go, how many times had I gone to bed with you and, over and over, was I pregnant. When I didn't answer, he said you only wrote me so I would do nasty things with you, and I was just too dumb to know. That's when I threw up all over the floor.

Mama screamed and tore at Daddy's hands to get them off me. He shook me a while longer. Then he stopped.

My hands still held the blue checked dishtowel I'd brought from the kitchen. I wiped my face with it, blew my nose and told them, as calmly as I could, how I wrote you that first time after I heard your record and how you wrote back and asked me to correct your grammar. I said you are the closest, dearest friend I've ever had, even though I never met you face to face, not even when I saw you in Mississippi.

I told them all that—and it didn't make a bit of difference.

"We'll have no more of this," my father said. He snatched your letter out of Mama's hands and tore it into a million pieces. I let out a cry so loud and piercing it must have deafened God's ears up in Heaven.

Except He isn't there. Or anywhere. God's gone—if He was ever there in the first place.

They won't let me out of the house now, except for church and school. Daddy even tried to call Mrs. Rollins and get me out of the play, only Mama grabbed the phone. "You've done enough," she told him. Her eyes could have burned holes through glass.

He drew back a hand as if to hit her, then let it fall. "You're where she gets it from," he said.

That's when he made me write the letter. He told me every word to say and looked on to make sure I wrote exactly what he wanted. I printed, with all capital letters, because I could not form those hateful words in my own normal hand. And because I'm hoping against hope that when you get it and it looks so strange, even though I signed it you will know it didn't <u>really</u> come from <u>me</u>.

Daddy said I can't write you ever again, or he won't pay for me to go to college. Well, I don't care and I won't stop. I can get a scholarship. And he can go to <u>Hell</u>!!!

I mean it. He can go straight to Hades and burn there until all eternity. Mama, too. I'm writing you right now in their very house while they're both asleep, and they can't do one blessed thing to stop me. Monday after school I'll go to the post office and rent a mailbox, so you can write me back.

I'll let you know soon as I get my new "address." Meanwhile, whatever you do, please, <u>please</u> believe I never wrote that other letter—and that not a single word it says is real.

Very sincerely,
Achsa

P.S. Daddy flushed the pieces of your letter down the toilet, but they can never take it from me. I wrote out every word from memory.

* * *

Friday, November 11, late at night, on an airplane, somewhere in the sky between Nashville and Memphis

Dearest B,

Well, it's really happening!!! In just four days the RCA Victor record company is going to buy my contract. Mr. Phillips wants $35,000 and <u>Colonel</u> <u>says</u> <u>they're</u> <u>going</u> <u>to</u> <u>give</u> <u>it</u> <u>to</u> <u>him</u>!! Every nickel of it! That's more money than any record company in the world ever paid for a singer! They didn't pay that much for Frankie Laine, and he's <u>famous</u>. I ~~can't~~ can hardly believe it! And you want to know something else? It ~~scares the living sh~~ scares me half to death!

I mean, what if I let them down? What if I can't make them as much money as they think I can? Or even worse, what if they let <u>me</u> down? What if they can't record me good as Mr. Phillips and I really <u>do</u> turn out sounding like Perry Como?

I been two days in Nashville at the DJ convention and there wasn't ~~no~~ time to worry there. Now there's nothing going on but humming airplane motors and darkness and stars, and I'm making up for lost time. Reckon I ought to change the subject.

Here goes, and it's super news. I'm coming to Atlanta for sure!!

I even got the date. December 2. I'm doing a show at someplace called the Sports Arena, and I'm ~~asking~~ begging you to please, please, please, <u>please</u> be there. I really, really, <u>really</u> want to see you!!

I promise I won't spend ~~no~~ any time with anybody else, just you. I'll take you on that nice long drive I promised. We'll stop someplace and get a hamburger, sit around and talk all night. I want so much to see you it's all I can do to wait! I get so happy I could holler just thinking about it.

I got me a new song, too. It's about this hotel for folks with broken hearts. The minute I heard the demo, I said, "That's going to be my hit record for RCA." It will, too. Like you're always saying, "You heard it here first."

Right now I need to ask for a huge favor. I hope you don't mind. I wrote this telegram to send to Colonel after the contract signing. I've gone over it and over it till I got it how I want it. For my grammar lesson next time, I'd be really grateful if you'd take a look at it and fix anything I've said wrong. Here it is.

Dear Colonel,

Words can never tell you how my folks and I appreciate what you did for me. I've always known and now my folks are assured that you are the best, most wonderful person I could ever hope to work with. Believe me when I say I will stick with you through thick and thin and do everything I can to uphold your faith in me. Again, I say thanks and I love you like a father.

Elvis Presley.

I want to thank you so much, Baby Girl, for looking over this. It means a great deal to me. And for all the grammar lessons you already gave me I got to thank you too. If it wasn't for you I'd still be talking like a hillbilly, and probably not anybody would shell out $35,000 for me then.

Yours truly,
Elvis

*   *   *

Atlanta, Wednesday, November 15, 1955, 11:00 P.M.

Dear, dearest Elvis,

Ever since last Friday, I hoped against hope you had put one last letter in the mail and I could intercept it. When I rounded the corner onto Camptown Street today, the postman was three houses away. I caught up with him and stuffed your letter in my coat pocket before anybody saw. Knowing I had it there warmed me all afternoon.

And such a wonderful letter it is, filled with such great news! That's so terrific about RCA Victor, it takes my breath away!! I guess I really do know how to pick a hit, don't I. I picked you.

That's great about the song, too. But for me the very best news is, you're really coming to Atlanta!! Whatever happens, I will be there December second, no matter what! I'll ride the bus to town right after school and hide out in the movies until it's time to go to the Sports Arena for your show. I saved more money before they cut off my allowance than I'll need. Mama always says it's good to have a little something squirreled away, because you never know what might happen. She was certainly right on that one.

I'm so glad I got to see the lovely telegram you wrote. Your grammar is perfect all the way through. It reads like an A+ final exam; I didn't change a word. What you said should make Colonel very proud. I cried when I read it, because it came so straight from your heart.

You don't need me as your teacher anymore, you know. And that's fortunate, because I'm afraid I won't be able to do such a good job of it from now on. I went to the post office yesterday after school and tried to rent a mailbox, but it turns out if you're not eighteen your parents have to sign for it. I tried to bluff it out, told them I'd take the paper home and get it signed and bring it back, but they said my parents had to sign it there in front of them. Lots of luck. I tried to think of someplace else you could send your letters where I could pick them up, but there isn't any. Oh, how I wish Linda Sheffield were still here!!

So I guess your letter of November 11 is the last I will receive. I zipped them all inside my notebook Sunday night, then took them to school on Monday and hid them in my locker. Sometimes now all I want to do is curl up in a ball and sleep forever till I wake up dead. I don't want to study. I don't want to read. I barely want to listen to the radio.

I hate my father. I hate my mother. But most of all I hate my own <u>stupid</u>, <u>careless</u>, <u>unthinking self</u>!!!

I will still write to you, of course, but I won't put a return address on the envelopes, just my name. These past few days I've come to realize I can't <u>not</u> write to you. If I couldn't write you ever again—and if I weren't going to see you very, very soon—my life right now would be too sad to bear.

Sincerely,

Achsa

P.S. When you wish or wonder about something, the verb changes. Instead of saying "I wish he <u>was</u> here," say instead, "I wish he <u>were</u> here." I guess that's your last grammar lesson. I will miss your letters for as long as I live. I already miss them so.

Chapter sixteen

November 19–21, 1955

Atlanta, Saturday, November 19, 1955, very late at night

Dearest Elvis,

I miss you way too much to call you E. I want to write out your whole name.

Penelope's on the radio, playing sad songs. Or maybe to me all songs are sad now. I spent much of this evening twisting the dial, hoping desperately to pick up "The Louisiana Hayride" on some faraway station, but once again it was not to be.

It feels so strange writing you and you not able to write back—all dreamy and unreal, like writing in a diary. I used to imagine you backstage at some Legion Hut or high school auditorium, seated in an out-of-the-way corner on a rickety folding chair, using your knees as a writing desk. There'd be music, muffled by musty velvet stage curtains, and voices in the distance. But you'd shut out everything, fill your mind with the words you were writing to me. After a little while, someone would search you out and say, "Five minutes." You'd scrawl a quick last sentence and a "Catch you later," stuff the envelope in your jacket pocket, grab your guitar, and saunter out into that endless scream.

Now I don't know what to imagine. I don't even know if this letter will even get to you, or if you'll open it.

Did you know it's possible to go whole days without saying a single word to a living soul, even though you live in the same house with them? I do it all the time now. I can't bring myself to speak to either of my parents. Not one word. When they ask dumb questions like, "Did you have a nice day at school, Achsa?" I just shrug and turn away. A shrug can say a lot, I'm finding.

Mostly, I take to being cold-hearted, but now and then it really gets to me. The play was tonight. Daddy didn't come, of course, but Mama did. She took me early and I figured she'd turn around and go home. Then I saw her outside—a beautiful stranger shivering in a plain brown coat, waiting to buy a ticket. Pride that she was my mother and that she was staying borrowed my breath a moment. Then I regained control.

After curtain calls, she came backstage and hugged me. "The play was good. And you were good in it," she said. She sounded like she knew what she was talking about, not like somebody's mother. I wanted so much to ask her <u>how</u>. How was the play good? How was I good in it? Could I dare hope to be a playwright or an actress in New York? I wished more than anything I had found her stolen opera glasses, so she could watch me through them as she had watched the Broadway stars. But I just shrugged.

Mama's shoulders drooped. "I'll meet you at the car," she said and left.

The whole ride home, I had to fight really hard not to say something, for in spite of all my problems the play had turned out even better than I had hoped. Even making up my face wasn't too bad. I ended up looking OK.

The stage makes everything OK somehow. You want to hear something really nuts? I feel more comfortable on a stage than any-where else on earth. I'm not shy there, or frightened. Not even with all those people staring. When you're on a stage you never have to worry about what to say or what to do next, like I did that Sunday at the drugstore. It's all there in the script. Too bad real life's not like that.

Still, I have to say the best parts of tonight came when the actors said the lines I wrote and I heard the audience laugh, or gasp, or lean forward in their squeaky seats to see what happened next. The very first time a laugh came right where I intended, a thrill so intense shot through me that I thought, "This must be how God feels every moment," and I knew right then exactly what I am going to do with the whole rest of my life: everything that has anything at all to do with the stage.

I wish now more than ever you could write me back. I have so many, many questions. Do you love the stage the same way I do? Why do I feel so safe in the circle of the spotlight's beam? How do you take some other person's song and make it into a poem that's all your own? How does it feel to walk out toward an audience's single, perfect scream? Is it the same as walking toward their laughter? Or their leaning-forward-in-their-seats attention? I want to <u>know</u>. I want to know it all.

I miss you so much. I can hardly wait to see you and talk to you. Now that the play's over, that's all I live for.

Sincerely,

Achsa

P.S. I feel really odd writing so much about me and so little about you. Please don't think I'm like that, concerned only for myself. Here's some grammar, just in case you need it. Say "I'm going to <u>lie</u> down, and I'll <u>lay</u> the book on the table." Then, when you've done those things, say "I <u>lay</u> down this afternoon, and I <u>laid</u> my book on the table."

*　　*　　*

Atlanta, Monday, November 21, 1955

Dearest Elvis,

Ordinarily, I wouldn't bother you again so soon, but I have some news. Our evening paper runs a gossip column by this woman in New York, and guess what she wrote today? That RCA Victor paid "a record price of $35,000" for the recording contract of "an unknown hillbilly singer with the peculiar name of Elvis Presley." I guess you're <u>really</u> somebody now. I may get the swell head knowing you—especially since I had the scoop on that woman's "news" ages before she did.

Just seeing your name cheered me, which is something I could do with. It seems like ever since the play my time has all been taken up with worry. It rides on my shoulder day and night, a fat, black crow with its claws dug in.

Whatever's wrong with my parents, it's only getting worse. Daddy's grown so thin his ribs show through his undershirts. Every night he sits in his easy chair in the living room, immobile as a dead man behind his newspaper—except for his eyes, which dart toward Mama all the time. She's thinner, too. A translucent, blue-veined thin, as though she's got some bright, hot flame inside her burning everything away like candle wax. Every night, I hear them through the thin wall that separates our bedrooms. There's no talk, just bedsprings creaking. I'm not stupid; I know what they're doing. What I don't know is, if they love each other so much why do they both look so tormented? I thought when people loved each other life got easy.

I suppose I shouldn't write you things like that, but I don't care. They don't deserve any more privacy than they gave me.

This afternoon I walked home from school in a cold, gray rain. When I let myself in, the whole house was dark. At first I thought Mama must have gone to the grocery or something, but when I'd passed through the living room into the hallway, I looked toward their bedroom and saw her. She was sitting at her dressing table, just sitting there in a patch of rain-streaked window light—without a stitch of clothes on. Her skin glowed pale as marble in the gloom.

She hadn't heard me. I stopped out in the hallway, stood so still I almost didn't breathe. I didn't want to be there, and yet I couldn't leave or she would know I'd seen her.

Mama sat very straight, staring into the mirror, hands pressed against the sides of her face. As I watched, she moved them down along her throat and brought them together over her heart, fingertips touching. Then she pushed them apart and cupped a hand under each bosom. She stayed like that a moment, staring at her reflection. Half of me tried to squinch my eyes tight shut. The other half screamed that if I looked away I might not see the very thing I needed to see to help her. Then Mama moved her hands away, pressed them slowly down along her waist and hips, across the tops of her legs and out the insides of her thighs, until she sat holding her knees and rocking slowly. Only then did I realize she was crying—rocking herself in the dark and crying with her eyes wide open, so softly all the sound got lost inside the rain.

Blood pounded in my ears, and the skin on my face had gone dry and hot. Standing still was getting harder by the minute. A mean cramp coiled itself in the arch of my right foot. Very soon that—or something else—would force me to move and give myself away. Or Mama would look around and see me.

But instead something worse happened. Suddenly, she lunged across the dressing table, making my heart bang against my ribs. She snatched up one of her crystal scent bottles and hurled it against her mirror, shattering them both. Then she put her head down on the splintered glass, and sobbed.

I backed away through the living room toward the front door, opened it quietly, stepped outside and closed it behind me as softly as I could. Rain ran off the small roof of our stoop and flowed in muddy rivulets across the yard. A brown leaf washed past like a small rudderless boat and floated out of sight. Another followed. I stood shivering for what seemed like quite a long time. Then I flung open the front door so hard it banged against the wall.

Lights blazed in Mama's bedroom. She sat at her dressing table, wearing a housedress and mopping up spilled cologne and shards of glass. When I walked past she looked up and smiled brightly. A tiny, bloody cut marred her cheek. "The hook on the mirror gave way. It fell and broke, and smashed a bottle of my best cologne," she said.

I nodded and escaped into my room. I didn't close the door. I wanted her to come in and talk to me so I would know she was all right, but she didn't.

I wish so much you could write me back. What's happening

with my parents scares me. There's no one I can tell. I don't know where to turn for help except to you. And you are lost to me until you get to town.

Oh, hurry, please! That day can't come too soon.
Sincerely,
Achsa

Chapter seventeen

November 24–December 1, 1955

Dearest Elvis,

I hope you had a happy Thanksgiving. I didn't—but it was my own fault. I have no right to complain.

Mama keeps trying to win me back by being nice. This afternoon, she called me into the kitchen to witness some miracle way to clean silverware she read about in <u>Good Housekeeping</u>. You line your sink with that new aluminum foil and pile all your silver on top of it. Then you pour boiling water over it, sprinkle in some cream of tartar, whatever that is, and—voilà! (that's French for "ta-dah!")—it eats the guck right off.

Mama churned the water, pulled out a teaspoon shiny as new and said, "See? Magic."

It kind of was, but I just shrugged and headed toward the door. She grabbed my arm. "Achsa, there are a lot of things I should have taught you, and now there isn't time," she said. Her fingers hurt, and her voice sounded raspy and desperate.

I shrugged again, and right away I wished I hadn't. I wanted to say, "<u>Why</u> isn't there time? Is it because I'm going off to college? That's almost a whole year from now," but I kept still.

"Oh, go on. Just…just go on," Mama said, and turned away. I retreated to my room and didn't come out until it was time to eat.

It's got to the point I pretty much want to stop not speaking to her, only I never can find the right moment. I thought it might come during Thanksgiving dinner, but it didn't. Or maybe it did and I just didn't notice. Mama fixed all the foods I like, even sweet potatoes with marshmallows and mincemeat pie, which she usually saves for Christmas. And she and Daddy tried really hard to be cheerful, but that got me so sad all I wanted was to go back to my room and cry. I guess I should have broken down and made some conversation, but once I decide I'm going to do something, like never speaking to my parents again, I stick with it. Sometimes even way after I don't want to anymore. It's not necessarily something I'm proud of, I have to admit.

Right now it's ten at night. Penelope's just come on the radio. This very minute six days from now, you and I will be together. It's all I can think about.

Your show got advertised on <u>The Atlanta Constitution</u> movie page today, your name in big letters and a drawing of you playing the guitar. My heart did that jump-up thing like when I saw you in the gossip column. It wasn't a very big advertisement, but I'm glad Daddy never reads the movie page.

Sincerely,
Achsa

*   *   *

Atlanta, Tuesday, November 29, 1955, 9:30 P.M.

Dearest Elvis,

Well, it happened.

Mama knocked at my bedroom door this afternoon before Daddy got home. Three little taps, soft as if she had gloves on. "Achsa?" she said, "May I come in?"

I opened the door. She took a single step and stopped just inside it. She was clutching two manila envelopes. I knew immediately what they were. It was all I could do not to yank them out of her hands.

"May I sit for a minute?" she said.

I nodded.

She crossed the room and lowered herself gingerly onto the bed. I sat down beside her, but not close. She reached across the abyss and brushed my hair out of my eyes like always, which for some dumb reason made me want to cry.

"These came in the mail today," she said, placing the envelopes in my lap. One said Hunter College, the other said New York University.

"I wrote Barnard College, too," I said.

There it was. I had spoken to her. All this time I thought it had to be this big deal all carefully planned out, and now I'd gone and done it without thinking.

A smile spread slowly over her face. "I'm so happy," she said.

For one jubilant second I thought she meant happy because I was speaking to her again, then she got that faraway look. "New York is such a wonderful place to be young," she said. Her eyes were shining. "We can go to the theatre, all the museums. I'll show you everything."

"But you won't be there. You'll be here," I said.

An instant of confusion showed on her face. Then she said, "I'll come up and visit. That is, if you want me."

I smiled at her. "Of course I do," I said.

She put her hand over mine and we sat like that a moment. Then she said, "I'm sorry about your letter and that boy. For everything that happened."

I fought an urge to stiffen. "He's my friend, that's all," I told her.

"I thought so. He wrote you a lovely letter," she said.

My words tumbled over themselves then, like they had lost all patience waiting. "Why did you let Daddy do it? How could you let him tear up that letter? How could you let him make me write a letter full of lies?"

Mama took a long breath and thought a moment, then

answered slowly, "Your father tries to protect us both more than he should. I think it must be his way of loving."

I wondered if she believed that, wondered if it even might be true. I must have let out a pretty heavy sigh.

"I know," Mama said, as though I'd spoken actual words.

I smiled.

"I never spent as much time with you as I wanted," she said. "I'm sorry for that, too." She got up from my bed. "About the colleges, let me know if you need help choosing. If it were me, I'd pick Barnard."

I reached up and grabbed her wrist—and asked the question, like you told me.

"Mama," I said, "Something's been wrong between you and Daddy ever since before we moved into this house. What is it? Please tell me what's the matter." My head filled with a sound like the wind rushing past our car that night we drove to Mississippi.

She bent down, took my face in both her hands and looked into it sadly. "Oh, baby, nothing's wrong," she said. "It's just…I've had so much on my mind, so many things to think about, decisions." She paused, then went on, her voice brightening. "But I've thought everything out now. And believe me, it's going to be all right. Everything's going to be all right for all of us from now on."

I believe her. I believe whatever was wrong has been made right, or soon will be. My mother has never lied. When she walked out of the room, I swear I felt just like you did when Satnin signed your contract. So light I could float to the ceiling like a helium balloon.

Speaking of dizzying heights, I may have finally reached the top of the gimp ladder—or even vaulted off entirely. A cheerleader <u>and</u> a football player spoke to me yesterday in the halls at school. Kids I hardly know.

And in just 71 hours I'll be watching you sing once again, and then I'll go backstage and we will be together. I ask you, how much more blessed can any one girl be?

Most sincerely,
Achsa

* * *

152

Atlanta, Thursday, December 1, 1955, 11:30 P.M.

Dearest Elvis,

I feel really stupid writing you right now. I'll feel even stupider tomorrow, dropping this letter in the mailbox on my way to your show. I don't have anything really important to say, and for once I can tell you all of it in person.

But I want to write you. I don't want to stop. I want to write down every single one of my thoughts, describe every moment of this night-before-I-see-you. Then when this letter comes to you two or three days later, it will be like an historical document. "Absolutely, exactly everything Achsa McEachern thought the very night before her meeting with the great Elvis Presley, Number One Up-and-Coming Country Singer in the whole USA, whom she's been writing oh-so-very-long."

I'm way too excited to ever sleep. It feels like Christmas Eve. So quiet, the very air glowing like we've already got the electric window candles on. The clothes I'll wear tomorrow are hanging on the hook inside my closet door. I'll be the girl in yellow—a yellow lambswool sweater and the yellow pleated skirt Mama made to match it—sitting as close to front-row-center as I can get. I've put everything in my purse already: the money for the movies and the ticket and the taxis, the Sports Arena phone number so I can find out when the box office opens, a toothbrush and an almost-used-up tube of toothpaste because dinner's going to be a bunch of sticky movie candy.

Speaking of candy, I have a theory that you can tell a lot about people by the candy bars they choose. People who like Milky Ways tend to be cheerleaders and football players. People who like plain Hershey bars join the debate club or write for the school paper. There are others, too. I'm sort of a plain-Hershey person myself. What's your favorite candy bar? Don't let me forget to ask.

I ought to study. I've got a test tomorrow on the French Revolution, but right now I couldn't care less. Let 'em eat cake. Marat, Robespierre, King Louis, Marie Antoinette, the whole lot of them. Cake for all, I say! Devil's food cake!

This is turning into a really dumb letter. Feel free to stop reading it any time you want. It's just, I don't want to stop writing it. I want to keep on writing till I'm sitting in the Sports Arena and the lights go dim and everyone starts screaming and you run out on stage.

But if I weren't writing you, you know what I'd like most to do right now?

Sneak out in the hall and phone Daddy-O Radio and ask Penelope to play one of your records. Even with all the messages I left last summer, I don't think she ever did. Maybe I'll stop writing you and call her anyway. It won't take a minute.

Uh-oh. I just opened the door and Mama and Daddy are still awake. They're arguing, I can hear them. They're arguing about me.

Mama's telling Daddy I've been grounded long enough, that he had no right to read my letter in the first place. Daddy's saying she takes up for me because "birds of a feather flock together." His voice sounds really nasty.

I don't like this. Why, of all nights, does it have to happen now?

Daddy's saying I'm going to grow up just like Mama, he can tell. Well, I hope he's right. I hope I grow up <u>exactly</u> like her: beautiful, good, smart, with a boyfriend who buys me mother-of-pearl opera glasses and takes me to the theater.

But that's not what Daddy means. "Already she's a little whore," he's saying. Shouting, almost like he's forgotten I might wake up and hear. "A whore like you. How do I even know she's mine, Annette? You tell me. How do I know she's mine?"

Daddy sounds all high-pitched and crazy. It's scaring me.

Mama's crying, "Stop it, Warren. Stop it, stop it, stop it!"

Now there's no sound.

Don't let that mean he's hit her. Oh, please, God, if you're there, don't let that be what's happened. Don't let him hurt her, please! And please, please, <u>please</u> don't let her come in here and tell me, "Achsa, pack your things, we're leaving." Not tonight.

Mama's crying again, only softer.

Now there's quiet.

And now bedsprings creaking. Then it's done and there's quiet again.

And now sleep.

It's one in the morning. I just stuck my head out the door and heard my father's snores.

So I guess everything's OK. I guess I really will see you tomorrow. Yes, I <u>will</u>!

And by the time you get this letter it will all be over.

But I don't want to think about the being-over part. Not now. Right now I want to think about this one-and-only, standing-on-tiptoe moment when everything that's beautiful is yet to come.

Most sincerely,

Achsa

Chapter eighteen

December 3–8, 1955

Atlanta, Saturday, December 3, 1955

Dear Elvis,

Please forgive me for not coming. I wanted to so very much.

Yesterday, when the principal got me out of fifth period geometry, he said someone was waiting in his office. All I could think was, "It's Daddy. He knows. Somehow, though I never breathed it to a living soul, he's found out I've got money in my purse and what I plan to do with it and how I've spent the whole day counting every minute on the clocks in all my classes till I can get to you."

But it wasn't Daddy in the principal's office. It was Hank Lawson's mother, sitting on one of the folding chairs, twisting her brown leather driving gloves in her hands. She rose when she saw me and said, "Achsa, you must come with me."

The amount of kindness in her voice terrified me. I asked what was wrong.

"It's about your mother," she said, pulling at her gloves so hard the leather stretched like bubble gum. "You better get your coat."

The air outside was very cold. We were having one of those perfect, cloudless days with the sky as blue as it gets and the sun so bright it hurts your eyes even if you never look at it. Mrs. Lawson

drove rapidly and with great concentration. "I followed the commo-
tion and recognized your mother's car," she said, staring straight ahead
at the street. "It's the only black 1950 Chevrolet with whitewall tires
in all of Dreamer Hills. I called your father at the book bindery and
said I would bring you from school."

A faraway sound, like kittens mewling in a basket, turned
to sirens as she spoke. At the stop sign on the hill overlooking the
railroad crossing, I saw them. Fire trucks, police cars, ambulances,
poking like thorns out of a greasy black rose of smoke touched with
small licking flames. Half a block ahead of us, my father stood in
the middle of the street. "Excuse me," I said to Mrs. Lawson, and
jumped out of her car and ran to him.

He didn't see me. He was standing very straight, fists clenched
at his sides, staring at the wreck. He didn't move for what seemed
a very long time, didn't even blink. Then all at once he screamed, a
wild, suffering sound that will live in me forever. It's how I knew my
beautiful mother was dead.

My father started running, fast as he could, toward the smoke
and confusion. I tried to keep up, but tripped, fell, skinned my knee.
People with concerned faces bent over me, lifted me to my feet.

"It's my mother," I told them.

They all breathed in at once, like the audience at the Cinderella
play. Several moved to block my view, but not before I saw two firemen
grab my father to keep him from hurling himself onto the still-burning
car. "Annette, wait! Wait! Don't leave me here alone!" he cried.

Alone. My tongue rolled the bitter word around inside my
mouth. Without her, my father believed he had no one. I guessed
that made me alone too.

"I've got to go to him," I said. The caring people sadly shook
their heads and let me through.

As I made my way toward the wreck, its heat rolled into me.
By the time I reached my father, it had sucked the moisture from
my bones and stolen all my uncried tears. That same drive-in movie
calm as on the night Mama and I left for Mississippi seeped into me
again and the tragedy became made-up. Even I wasn't real.

I took my father's hand. It shook and his fingers were ice cold.

He looked down at me. "Achsa, we've got to help her. We've got to get her out," he said, as though she'd only pinned her foot beneath the brake pedal or jammed her door.

I glanced at the wreck. "She doesn't need us anymore," I said. Although it didn't cross my mind until much later, those were the first words I had spoken to him in three weeks. Still holding his hand, I felt his muscles tense, felt him gathering strength to break free of the one fireman who gripped his other arm. And then he crumpled; his hand went frail. He bent nearly double and started to sob.

I am ashamed of how I envied him. I longed only to keen for my beautiful mother who loved me and was dead, yet no tears came. The heat had turned them all to vapor and they'd slipped away.

Instead, my mind's eye showed me Mama at the moment of her death, her body lurching, her perfect features mashed against the car window by the train's grinding metal. I couldn't bear to look, willed my mind to turn away from it. That's when I saw her floating in the clear December sky, wearing her white summer nightgown, the one with all the tiny tucks, her face serene and smiling. I could tell she was dead by how the sky showed through the holes where her eyes had been—a sky their exact same shade of blue. And by how her billowing copper hair had turned to ropes of leaping flame that lifted her toward Heaven.

That's why I didn't come to see you.

Achsa

* * *

Atlanta, Thursday, December 8, 1955

Dear Elvis,

Mama is in the ground and our house is cold and empty.

At the funeral home, Daddy kept saying, "Achsa, what should we do?" until finally the man in charge spoke only to me. I chose a casket the color of Hershey bars, made from the same wood as her dressing table stool. And I asked the organist to play "Rock of Ages," Mama's favorite hymn.

We had the service Monday afternoon. Everyone from church was there. Aunt Jane, Uncle Henry and cousin Nancy drove from Mississippi, and Mama's oldest sister, Mavis, whom I had never met, flew down from New York. Seeing her was like seeing Mama if she'd turned out plain. Aunt Mavis has light brown hair, not blonde, and her eyes are gray, not blue. She's got Mama's nose, only fatter, and Mama's mouth, but thinner. Part of me, the part that can't believe what's happened, wanted more than anything to ask her what it's like to live in New York City, but I didn't. She left before anyone because she couldn't take but just that day off from her work and had a plane to catch. Before she climbed into the taxi, she gave me a hug and said, "You buck up now, you hear. For the living, life goes on." Then she was gone, before I'd lost the feel of her arms around me.

Later that day, we rode the train to Valdosta, on our way to Rachelville, which is where all Daddy's people are laid to rest. He and I sat with the other passengers. Mama rode in the baggage car. Before we boarded, Daddy asked me if I thought the engineer would let us stay with her. I said I didn't think so, and he patted my hand and climbed into the passenger car without mentioning it again. So many times since last Friday he has turned to me to ask what we should do about this or that. I always try to answer, but each time I get to feeling like I've somehow walked into the wrong house. It's a house that looks just like our house, with a man inside the exact image of Daddy, but it's the wrong house just the same.

A man from the funeral home picked us up at the Valdosta depot in a shiny black hearse and drove us the 30 miles to Rachelville. Aunt Dora came with him. I hadn't seen her since I was a little girl. She never did get married and now looks like a plump mourning dove with her gray hair and gray coat. Staying overnight in her house full of overstuffed chairs and crocheted doilies gave me comfort I did not expect. I guess because it's nothing like our home and so I didn't see my mother everywhere.

The next morning it was misting rain. Aunt Dora had a preacher at the cemetery, and a few people who knew Daddy when he was a boy. Daddy and I each dropped a handful of dirt in the grave hole onto Mama's coffin. After I let mine go, Aunt Dora held me fast and said, "Oh, child." But even then I could not cry. It's got to be the right time and the right place, I suppose. I've piled up so many tears that once I get started I may never stop.

Aunt Dora drove us back to Valdosta after the service. She said she'd try to come up at Christmas. It sounded like a word in a foreign language. How will we get through it without Mama?

At first Daddy wouldn't get on the train for home. I had to take him by the elbow like an old man. He kept saying over and over, "It's raining. Your mother will be cold." I sort of knew what he meant. It's hard to realize she's so far away, when our house, our clothes and even we ourselves still smell of her.

I better go cook dinner. It takes a long time because I've got so much to learn.

I'm sorry I missed seeing you, especially when I'd promised. It seems now like some other girl did all that planning and dreaming very long ago. I wonder if I'll ever be that girl again.

Sincerely,
Achsa

Chapter nineteen

December 11–21, 1955

Dear Elvis,

I think something bad is wrong with me. I can't stop thinking about Mama and the way she died. I think about it all day, then I lie awake nights and think about it some more. I flunked a pop quiz on Silas Marner Friday because I hadn't heard a word Mrs. Rollins said for days. My mind won't act right anymore. It just goes where it wants, and the only place it wants to go is to Mama in her car on that railroad track. But no matter how long and hard I think about it, I can't figure it out.

Mama was a careful driver. She always came to a full stop at stop signs and looked both ways at intersections, just like all the safety posters say. How could she not have heard the signal bells and seen a train bearing down on her? And if she saw it, why on earth didn't she get out of the way? You can drive across those railroad tracks quicker than a gnat can blink its eye. And why was she crossing the tracks there anyway? That road only goes to the highway. Nowhere else.

I've rolled all this around in my head for days, and there's only one way it makes sense. That's if it wasn't an accident. In other words, if Mama drove her car onto the railroad tracks and sat there waiting for a train to hit her.

And if that's what she did, I am the one who caused it. I killed my mother by not speaking to her for so long, by letting her believe I didn't love her. She allowed my father to deprive me of your letters, so I deprived her of my love—and it hurt her more than she could stand.

I did that. Stupid, careless, self-centered me.

I truly must be cold-hearted, as well. I still can't cry. Every time I think I'm going to, I just get sleepy. I don't mean tired or a little yawny. I mean sleepy, like I'm about to black out and fall into some horror-movie coma. Then at night, when I'm supposed to get sleepy, I'm wide awake and my mind's cranking out movies of Mama in the burning car.

The only good thing is, more than once I've listened to Penelope all the way to four A.M. when she goes off the air. After midnight she starts calling her listeners by their actual names and saying stuff like how she saw this one at Benton Brothers Barbecue drinking King Cotton wine with that one's wife. Sometimes that cat-purr voice of hers sounds like she's had a little King Cotton, too, but it's probably all play-acting.

You know what? I don't care if she's soused to the gills. I'm just glad she's there for me to listen to in the dark. Earlier tonight I sneaked out in the hall and called WDDO again to ask her to play one of your records, but no one answered. That's the fifth time I've done it since Mama died, and no one's ever answered. I keep thinking how maybe one night she'll pick up the phone and we'll start talking and I'll tell her about Mama and the way she died. Maybe she'll put on a record and just let it play over and over until I've finished telling her and she's through reassuring me it's not my fault, the way she played "Only You" the night James Dean was killed. She does that a lot late at night. I always imagine she's talking on the phone with someone that's not me, but she's probably only gone down the hall to the ladies room.

Daddy and I went to church ~~today~~ yesterday, and he made us sit way in the back instead of in our usual pew. He said sitting in a different place helped him remember not to look up in the choir for

Mama. He stared at the floor the whole time and twice broke down and sobbed. Everybody came up to us afterwards and said how sorry they were about Mama, even Hank and Betty Jean.

I hope you are getting along OK. I still think about you an awful lot. It's about the only thing that sometimes stops me thinking about Mama.

Sincerely,
Achsa

* * *

Atlanta, Monday, December 12, 1955, late at night

Dear Elvis,

I guess I shouldn't write again so soon, but something really spooky happened. A book came in the mail today for Mama, just like she was still alive. It's from that place in New York. I put it on the hall table like I used to, so I could stare at it and think how if she were here she'd run in the kitchen, grab a knife, cut the string, and unwrap the package. Then, cradling her new book against her chest, she'd dance into the living room, sit down on the sofa, open it slowly and say, "Oooohhh," excited as a birthday child.

After a couple hours I opened the package myself. I didn't want Daddy seeing it when he got home. It would only have upset him. It was a little book of stories written by a lady named Flannery O'Connor. I put it in Mama's bookcase with the rest. Soon as I can, I'm going to read every one of her books, even the ones up in the attic. Then I'll have lots of the same stuff in my head that she did. That way I can keep a part of her alive.

I know where ghosts come from, by the way. They come from us, when we can't believe somebody's gone. Part of you knows you're never going to see that person again, but the rest of you refuses to get used to it.

Last night for dinner I fixed Chef Boyardee spaghetti. Daddy only ate a couple bites before pushing away from the table and heading for the living room to sit in his easy chair and stare at the floor. After I washed up the dishes, I went in and turned on Ed Sullivan. I guess I hoped the jugglers and the trained animal acts would cheer him up some. Cheer us both up, actually. I sat down on my usual end of the sofa and watched a ventriloquist put doll wigs and lipstick on his hands and turn them into puppets. He was really sort of funny, and I liked it that all the puppets had lopsided mouths like me.

As I sat there, I got to feeling the exact same way I always ~~do~~ did when Daddy and Mama and I used to watch TV together—like nothing bad could happen, and even if I fell from some great height I'd land square in the middle of a fireman's net, bounce a couple times and that would be that. I had such a strong sense of the three of us I could have sworn Mama came in the room and sat on her end of the sofa the way she always ~~does~~ did after dinner. I caught a faint whiff of the rose sachet that clung to everything she pulled out of her lingerie drawer. I could even feel her body warmth and hear the rustle of her breathing. I was sure if I cut my eyes to the right without moving and startling her, I would see her. I did it, but of course she wasn't there.

Daddy felt her too, I know he did. He scowled and said, "Turn that thing off." Then he got up and stalked into ~~their~~ his bedroom and slammed the door. I stared at the blank TV screen, listened to the dry, hacking sound of him sobbing into his pillow, and envied him once more that he could cry.

Everything has grown so different in such a short time. Put one foot in front of the other and keep going, that's me now. It's as if, when Mama died, Daddy and I moved to some bleak desert country—just sand and rocks, never a tree or blade of grass or water anywhere. A mean sun burns and a hot wind blows all day, every night is bitter cold, and there's not one person in the whole empty place I can talk to. Even God is far away.

You, too. Are you out there? Do you still get my letters? Do you read them? Did you <u>ever</u> read them? Did you ever even <u>write</u> to me, and did I write you back? Or did I just imagine it? Have I always only written letters to myself?

Please, if you read this and you think about me as your friend, write to me once again. Daddy doesn't care about anything anymore, so I'm sure it will be OK. Please write me even just a note so I will know you're there. I feel very much alone.

    Sincerely,

      Achsa

* * *

Atlanta, Wednesday, December 14, 1955

Dear Elvis,

    Please, <u>please</u>, if you get this letter and if I mean anything to you at all, <u>WRITE ME</u>!!! Something bad is happening to Daddy. It scares me so much I can't keep it all inside.

    This afternoon when I was straightening up, I found a letter lying on Mama's dressing table. He'd pushed her comb and brush aside and written it, then left it right there without putting it in an envelope, as if he wanted me to find it. I didn't mean to read it when I picked it up, but the little bit I saw alarmed me. So now I guess I've done him just like he did me.

    It was a letter to God. I copied it out to show you, because you're the only person I know to turn to. I can't very well tell anyone who knows him. Here's what he wrote.

    Dear God:

      Forgive my presumption in writing, but I can no longer pray. Every time I try—as in every other waking moment and in all my dreams—I see only my wife, whom I shall never see again. I breathe her odors, taste her skin's salt. There is no worse pain.

      I loved her with all my being from the moment I first saw her. That she married me made my life holy. I worshipped her, and through her worshipped Thee.

      I am not an exceptional man. I have neither good looks nor great accomplishments. I never thought such bliss would come to me. I reveled in it.

      And then You took her just to show You could.

167

So now I damn You, God. I wish You dead, and all the universe as cold and empty as my days and nights without her. Cursed be Thee unto all Eternity. Amen.

Thy humble servant,
Warren McEachern

That's what my father wrote. I don't know what to do. Please help me.

Sincerely,
Achsa

* * *

Atlanta, Saturday, December 17, 1955

Dearest E,

I hope you get my letter postmarked December 14, and that you will answer it right away. Meanwhile, a true bright spot came into my life today. I heard from Linda Sheffield! I wrote her about Mama when we got home from the funeral, and at last she has written back!

It was an odd letter, very formal, like she didn't know quite what to say. She wrote that she is well and likes living in Jacksonville. She's seventeen now and her boyfriend wants to get engaged, but her parents won't hear of it. She said she was very sorry about Mama and that I must be very sad.

Here's the best part. She said that in summer maybe she can come see me, or I can go there. She wrote hardly a page, but it left me feeling like I had stumbled upon a cool spring and a shade tree in the middle of my desert.

I hope everything is going well for you. Every Monday afternoon I call Junior's and ask if you've made any more records, but they always tell me no. Every Saturday night I twist my radio dial for hours, hoping to tune in "The Louisiana Hayride," but I never can. At least once a week I screw up my courage and go in Greene's to check the magazines for articles about you, but the new ones haven't come in yet. I hope RCA and that Colonel are treating you right.

Please, <u>please</u> let me hear from you.
Sincerely,
Achsa

*   *   *

Atlanta, Tuesday, December 20, 1955

Dear Elvis,

Daddy drove me to church Sunday but he didn't go in. That's a first-ever. I guess he's given up on God the same as I have. Or maybe he's just given up on church. I went hoping for comfort, since everyone was so nice the time before. But now it's just like school—lots of people saying, "Hello, Achsa," in Sunday-go-to-meeting voices, doing their good deed for the day. Then their eyes slide sideways, and they look like they could take out running from the sheer terror I might tell them what it's like to have your mama die inside an ordinary day. The preacher's no different. He comes by the house and talks a blue streak, but Hell would have to turn into a frost-free Frigidaire for him to listen. Maybe Daddy knew something I didn't: that after that first Sunday they all hoped we'd disappear.

Maybe you're that way, too. Scared of me like they are, hoping I'll quit writing you and go away. Otherwise you would have written back by now. Well, too bad.

Daddy's not scared. He wrote God again. Left it lying out again, too. I copied down everything he said and put it back, same as before. I don't care if it is private. My own thoughts don't have room enough to sigh or turn over; there's no space left in me for other people's private things.

Here's what he said.

Dear God:

I have made of my wife a graven image, bowed down before her and worshipped.

169

We met on June 15, 1940, and from that moment I became her slave. I lived to lose myself inside her. And she let me, from that very night. Oh, yes, she let me, always. But when she closed her eyes, it never was from passion; it was to will herself into some other time and place.

Perhaps because of this withholding I became obsessed. Wanting her every moment of my waking hours and in all my dreams, I became a praying fool. 'Dear God, I have forsaken strong drink, all Godless thoughts, become a Deacon. Will you let her love me now?' But all You gave me was a child I never wanted. The first night my wife left our bed to quiet its crying, I prayed it would die. Thereafter, I withheld my love from it.

Annette was my soul, my only nourishment. The child took part of her away. I could not bear losing more. At night I began leaving my wife with tiny bruises in places others could not see—the aureole of her breast, the instep of her foot—marks that said she belonged not to herself but me. I did it so I would not die inside each time another man looked at her. But I died nonetheless, and so one day I struck her. She left me then. I brought her back from Mississippi, but I could not keep her, could not pull her from the secret place within herself.

This time, I prayed as constantly as monks pray. I had not lost my faith. Does that surprise You? I knew she would come back in time. I was sure of it. How could You take her from me after I had made my life a prayer?

But take her You did. So take me, too, Oh God. You owe me that. Strike me dead—<u>now</u>—so I can live with her throughout Eternity.

This is the last prayer You will get from me. And the sincerest.

Your humble servant,
Warren McEachern

That's it. I guess I shouldn't have read it. Parts of it I can't understand. Why did he bruise my mother, when he used to say it was up to him and me to protect her from all harm? And there's at least one part I wish I didn't know: that my own father prayed I would die. When he tried to hurl himself onto her burning car, he begged her not to leave him here on earth alone. I did not exist for him, as though his prayer had truly killed me.

I can't remember when I didn't know that a white-hot fire burned in Daddy's soul for Mama night and day. I always used to think that's what love was. Now I don't know anymore. I used to be so sure about so many things. Now I'm not sure of anything at all.

I wish I knew what to do. I wish I could cry.

I wish you would write me. I wish next Sunday weren't going to be Christmas.

Aunt Dora called long distance to say she couldn't come till after New Year's. She's the preacher's secretary at the First Presbyterian Church in Rachelville, and Christmas and New Year's are her busiest times. I said please, please come the very next day, then. She said she would try.

The postman brought another book for Mama. The Mayor of Casterbridge, by Thomas Hardy. I guess they didn't have it when she ordered it, so they sent it later. I left it on the hall table all day and pretended she'd gone to the store and would come home and find it any minute. I didn't put it in her bookcase until I heard Daddy coming up the walk.

I miss her so much. I miss you, too. And Linda Sheffield. I even sometimes miss Daddy how he used to be. Or how I thought he was anyway. Seems like everyone I care about, I miss.

Sincerely,

Achsa

* * *

Atlanta, Wednesday, December 21, 1955 [Written inside a Christmas card showing a shepherd looking down on the village of Bethlehem, above the words, "How silently, how silently the wondrous gift is given."]

Dear Elvis,

This afternoon I took your letters from my locker, locked

myself in a stall in the girls' restroom, and read them one last time so I could bear to leave them over the long holiday. In one you said God's plan is a mystery too big for any one person to understand. I'd like to believe that, but I'm not sure I can.

I hope you have a merry Christmas and a bright and happy New Year.

Most sincerely,
Achsa

Chapter twenty

December 24, 1955–
January 18, 1956

Dear Elvis,

Greetings on Christmas Eve. I hope you're home by now. What are you doing? Wrapping presents? Trimming a tree?

I've thought of you an awful lot lately. I sent you a Christmas card on Wednesday. Since then, I have written you 27 letters and torn each one of them up.

Last night my Sunday school class came caroling. They clustered together on our front walk in their wool mittens and mufflers. Their songs clouded the cold air. Last year I stood with them outside other people's houses, singing "Silent Night" and "Good King Wenceslas." It felt like a century ago.

Daddy wouldn't come out of his room, so I went alone to the door and spoke to them as if they were strangers: "Thank you very much for coming. My father thanks you, too. We wish you all a Merry Christmas," I told them, the same polite phrases the shut-ins said when I went caroling. All I really wanted was to scream, "Go away! We're not sick. We're not shut in. Leave us alone and go carol for

173

them." And yet, watching behind the frigid glass of our living room window as they shuffled away down the walk, I thought for the first time maybe Daddy and I were both those things.

So this afternoon I got out the electric candles, set them in the front windows and plugged them in. I couldn't stand a tree. I'd see Mama's face in every ornament. But I thought we needed something, and the candles make a pretty glow.

I wrapped the flannel bathrobe I bought for Daddy out of the grocery money and put it on the dining room table with the gifts Aunt Dora sent. There's also a package for me that came yesterday from Aunt Mavis, which was really a surprise since I never laid eyes on her before Mama's funeral and have never sent her even so much as a card. I hope Daddy comes out of his room tomorrow, so I won't have to open presents all alone. I wonder if he still prays I'll die. There's not much point, with Mama gone.

Before dark, I walked to the A&P and bought two turkey TV dinners for Christmas day. Hank Lawson was there bagging groceries, but I went through the other checkout line so he wouldn't see me and feel sorry for me. I hate having somebody I know feel sorry for me. It really gets me down.

~~I just read this letter, and I'm not going to mail it either. Although I don't think mailing it matters one way or the other. You never read my letters anyway. If you did, surely you'd write me. I bet you never think of me at all.~~

~~Very sincerely,~~

~~Achsa~~

December 25, 9:30 P.M.

Well, I guess there's no point in not sending what I wrote to you last night. Christmas Day is almost over now. If I had tunneled through it I'd be seeing light from the other side.

I'm feeling much better, thank you, although I can't say the day got off to the greatest start. I plugged in the window candles first thing, then I tried making all the breakfast smells I could—coffee brewing, bacon frying, bread toasting—but none of it got Daddy out of his room. I'd planned to heat the TV dinners for lunch, but he still hadn't come out, so I made myself a peanut butter sandwich and opened my gifts. Aunt Dora sent lots of underwear, but Aunt Mavis sent a beautiful red dress made of brushed cotton soft as swan's down. It fit perfectly. On the card she wrote, "Thought you might be needing a 'buck up dress' about now." I wrote her a thank you note and told her that someday I'm going to live in New York like her.

Daddy finally came out near twilight, and he seemed to like the bathrobe OK. Christmas dinner was no great shakes, but we could eat it. That's the good thing about TV dinners, they're dependable. I fixed ambrosia for dessert like Mama used to, but that turned out to be a mistake and just made Daddy sad. He ate one orange section, then got up and went back to his room. When he passed my chair, he said so softly I almost didn't hear, "You shouldn't have to look at me." It's the first time he's shown any sign he even thinks of me at all. It surprised me so much I stretched out my hand to touch him, but he'd already passed out of reach.

I cleared away the dishes and figured that was that, as far as Christmas was concerned, but then somebody knocked on the front door. When I opened it, there stood Hank Lawson holding Mama's opera glasses!

You can't imagine my joy at seeing them once more! God himself could not have come up with a better Christmas present!! Hank said he told Jimmy to give them back the night he took them, and he thought he had done it until he saw them in his room last week. Hank said Jimmy wasn't really a bad person, just sometimes mean and always careless. And that he hadn't done anything with the opera glasses, just stuck them on his dresser and forgot about them. Hank looked pretty sheepish about it all.

He also looked really cold, so I asked did he want to come in and have some hot coffee, and he did. He sat on the very edge of the sofa, like he might have to jump up any minute and light out for the Territory. When I brought the coffee, he hunched over it and held it with both hands. He's skinnier than I thought, so thin his Adam's apple shows. Turns out he did see me at the A&P on Christmas Eve. He's working there because his girlfriend's moving to Connecticut and he's got to get his car in shape to drive there pretty often. Right now it lacks a second gear. And a reverse gear.

I showed him Mama's books and told him he could borrow one if he wanted, since he'd returned her opera glasses and was probably pretty trustworthy. I figured Daddy didn't need to know. Hank smiled. He's got a nice smile. I think I told you once he looks a bit like you. He said that was really sweet of me and, yes, if I didn't mind, he did very much want to read The Old Man and the Sea by Ernest Hemingway and he'd bring it back next week. Then he drained his coffee cup and said he had to be going.

Afterwards, the clean laundry and shaving cream smells of him lingered, and the house felt larger because someone else had been here. I grabbed Mama's opera glasses off the hall table and held onto them so long the metal eyepieces got hot. I tried to pretend my hands were her hands and she was still alive, but I just got sleepy, like I do when I want to cry. So I put Mama's opera glasses away in their case, unplugged all the electric candles, put them back in their boxes in the utility closet and went to my room to finish writing you this letter left from yesterday.

I hope you had a good Christmas. And that you have a happy New Year, wherever you are.

Sincerely,

Achsa

*   *   *

Memphis, Monday, January 2, 1956

~~Dear~~ Dearest B, my dearest Baby Girl,

You been through so much it hurts my heart. I been trying to write you ever since you said it was OK. Only there wouldn't ~~no~~ any words come out, just tears.

I'd get to thinking about you with your Mama gone, and how if it was Satnin I'd be too sad to go on living. Riding that train of thought I'd get to crying, and I'd have to wad up the letter, toss it in the trash and go find me some people to be with quick, because I sure wasn't going to stay there alone. Even now I can't think too long about your mama being gone. My dearest hope is you will see it in your heart to forgive me. I meant to write you every day.

My only other excuse is I got some people traveling with me now, my cousin and this cat I went to high school with. Satnin likes it, ~~cause~~ because they keep the girls off me. Still, it ~~don't~~ doesn't give me much time alone.

Also, there's been a whole lot going on. Ever since I signed with RCA they've had me busy as a one-arm man hanging wallpaper. Reporters and photographers been coming out of the woodwork, and always there's some bash for me to meet some bigwig. If I was a drinking man, I could stay likkered up at them things till Gabriel blows his trumpet. Even if Gabriel's a jiving cat that doesn't blow till late.

We're recording "Heartbreak Hotel" tomorrow in Nashville, and come January 24 you can see my smiling face on your TV!!! Colonel's got me on The Tommy and Jimmy Dorsey Stage Show on CBS-TV in New York City <u>four</u> <u>whole</u> <u>times</u>!! He says there's more people will see me on ~~them~~ those shows than if I did the Hayride my whole life!

You can see I backslid some without your grammar lessons. I missed you every time I opened my mouth.

Still I got to say, that letter you sent telling me not to write you got to me real bad.

I reckon you don't know, but there's some people lately saying how I shake my legs is dirty and I ought to be locked up.

It's nothing dirty. You know that. It's just fun. I shake my legs and the girls scream. I laugh because they're screaming. They scream because I'm laughing. I leer at them a little and they scream some more. It's like we're all in on the joke. They know it's their job to scream, same as I know it's my job to shake my legs and give them a leer now and then.

Anyway, that one letter scared me so bad I just threw the rest on my dresser without even opening them. They got to be this big pile, and then Satnin saw them and said, "That Achsa person sure has wrote you a bunch of letters." Something in the way she said it, I opened them and read them every one.

The only thing, when you didn't show up in Atlanta I got mad and stuffed a few in my pocket without looking at them. I reckon I read about your mama a week or two after it happened. I started crying till I near couldn't stop. I remember it was right before a show. I went out and sang "I Got a Woman," fast as I could to get going. Still, I kept thinking about you and her, and nothing felt right.

My poor Baby Girl. I got to say, I really missed you. Please, please forgive me for not writing sooner. I will always write you from now on. I won't ever stop again.

Yours very truly,

Elvis

P.S. Your mama's death was by accident. Don't you go thinking any other thing. Remember that time you and her went to Mississippi, how at that diner her car door stuck and then the engine wouldn't crank? It stayed in my mind. I been in cars with stuck doors and balky engines, and I was all the time worrying I'd get trapped in them. That's what happened to your mama, you can count on it. Her car stalled on the railroad tracks and she couldn't get her door open to get out. It didn't have ~~nothing~~ anything to do with you! Not anything at all!

I should have told you that right off, only I didn't want to go crying again till I'd got done writing the rest of this letter.

P.P.S. There's something I been meaning to ask you ever since that first time you wrote me. In "Achsa J. McEachern" what does the "J" stand for?

* * *

Atlanta, Saturday, January 7, 1956

Dearest Elvis,

Your letter brought me a rising joy I have not known since Mama died. I treasure every word. Thank you especially for what you wrote about the car. It brought me some peace. I'd like to think you're right. Still, I wonder what she was doing on that railroad crossing in the first place. That road doesn't go anywhere but to the highway, so it's still a mystery.

I can't get over how much has happened to you since your letter of November 11! You truly have become a star! I feel shy writing you, embarrassed by how shamelessly and completely I unburdened myself these past two months. How desperate I must have sounded.

But that's over, it truly is. Aunt Dora has been with us since Tuesday, and already she's made changes in our household that have greatly improved my life. She's promised she'll stay until I graduate. She talks to Daddy like he's a little baby and fixes all his favorite foods. He's already coming out of his room some in the evenings. She tried to get him to take a few weeks off from work, but he says he likes it there. I look at his hands, at the scaly glue from the bindery peeling off them, and I picture him bent over the brittle, crumbly pages of some beloved family Bible, making them whole again. I can't see how this man could wish his baby dead. Let alone hit his wife, whom he ~~loved loves~~ loved with every fiber in his being.

I still miss Mama awfully. Remember what I said about ghosts? This morning I saw a glass on the drain board I didn't put there, and my heart got a split-second lift as if Mama had just walked out of the room and left it. But of course it was Aunt Dora. Sometimes at night I lie in bed thinking over all that's happened that day, and it's like I'm telling Mama and she's listening, only she's in the next room where I can't see her.

I guess I better close now. I don't want to write too much and make a pest of myself.

Sincerely,

Achsa

P.S. I hope you have a happy 21st birthday. It has slipped up on me, so I'm afraid I haven't sent a card.

P.P.S. The "J" stands for "Jessamine," as in Carolina Jessamine. It's a yellow flower. I was born with pale blonde hair.

* * *

Memphis, Friday, January 13, 1956 (very, very early)

Dearest B,

Well, I been legal since last Sunday. Free, white and twenty-one.

If some scrawny old black tomcat crosses your path today, you got to run find you a white one and pick him up real quick to change the luck. And don't go walking under ~~no~~ any ladders. A can of paint might fall and hit you in the head.

As for you writing me, you don't ever need to feel shy about it and you can write me however long a letter you want. There's so much changing in my life I got to keep some things the same. And sweet Baby Girl, I'd appreciate it if your letters can be one of them.

As for my letter here right now, you might just want to overlook it. There's no telling what I'm going to say. I just got in from Nashville cutting "Heartbreak Hotel," and I'm way too keyed up to sleep.

The RCA studio's got all kinds of professional stuff, and they do things real different from Sun. It takes a while getting used to. Sometimes it can get pretty tense. Like after we already did the song at least twenty times and the guys in the booth are saying, "This is it, we got it," and I got to tell them, "No, it's not right yet. We need to do it one more time."

I got to do a song the way I know is right. And I got to stay cool about it. Not just for myself, but for the boys backing me up and even for the city cats in the control room. Before I left Mr. Phillips, he told me RCA paid good money to get exactly what they got. He said I should keep on doing things exactly how I been, and he was right. They all look to me now. I can't let them down.

Anyway, the session's over and I'm bouncing off the walls. If we ~~was~~ were together talking, I'd be running off at the mouth.

It really got me about how your other name is Jessamine. Did you know, if people called you Jessamine instead of Achsa and you had a nickname, you'd be Jesse, same as my twin brother Jesse Garon? It's real strange you turning out to have his same name and us being so close. It's like you're him come back to keep me company.

Remember how I told you I used to sit by Jesse Garon's grave

180

and talk to him? Well, I'll tell you something else. When I was a little boy in Tupelo, lots of times on a warm night I'd go out in back of our house and ~~lay~~ lie down on the ground and stare up at the stars. Just lie there in a dead man's float, till I could feel my body lifting off the ground and rising up and up, drifting on air currents in the sky. Those warm currents turned me around real slow and stars would slide right past me. Every star was the soul of somebody who'd died. Most were souls of folks I didn't know. Only, sometimes one of them would be Jesse. He'd ease right up to me and say, "Hey there, Elvis Aron," and him and me would talk awhile. When we got done he'd drift away and hang out with the other souls up there. He was always my same age, except 30 minutes older. I reckon that's what made him wise. Or maybe it was being up there all the time with all ~~them~~ those other souls. I haven't talked to Jesse like that in a good long while. Lately I haven't had much chance to go up in the stars.

But you can. You can lie out in your backyard some summer night and get lifted up into the stars like me, and your Mama'll come talk to you. I know she will.

I'm starting to get sleepy. Reckon it's time to hit the hay.

     Yours truly,
     Elvis

*　*　*

Atlanta, Wednesday, January 18, 1956

Dearest E,

How you float among the stars and visit Jesse Garon is the most beautiful thing anybody ever told me. And you paid me the highest compliment anybody ever has when you said maybe I have his soul. I want to. I hope I do. I feel that close to you.

Our birthdays are just eight days apart, did you know that? I turned 15 on Monday. Aunt Dora baked a sheet cake and gave me a hair dryer from herself and a <u>Roget's Thesaurus</u> she said was from Daddy.

Last Sunday, at her suggestion, she, Daddy and I went to church. It was the first time Daddy and I had been since right after

181

Mama died. We sat in the back again and Daddy's body shook from silent tears through most of the service. One time he gave my hand a little pat and whispered, "I'm sorry," so low I almost didn't hear. I'm pretty sure he only meant sorry for crying, but I'd like to think he meant sorry he wished me dead. I just glanced at him and nodded. Sometimes you don't really want to know everything about something.

I would like to change the subject now. Actually, I've got a question. Since you appreciate my letters being something in your life that stays the same, does that mean I can still give you a grammar lesson now and then, even though you're about to be a big TV star?

I hope so, because in your last letter you said, "Him and me would talk awhile." You should have said, "He and I would talk awhile." "He and I" do things. "He and I went to the store." "Him and me" is what something gets done to, or for. "She went to the store to buy ice cream for him and me."

How's that for keeping everything the same?
Sincerely,
Achsa

Chapter twenty-one

January 26–
February 4, 1956

New York, Thursday, January 26, 1956
[postcard of Empire State Building]

Dearest B,

Thanks for letter and grammar. Through next week write me at Warwick Hotel, 52nd Street and 6th Avenue, New York, New York. This city is crazy. Rich people live on top of buildings and plant trees up there to get some shade.

I'm sending you the Empire State Building. Hope you like it. I stuck it in an envelope so no one would see. If I'd known you had a birthday, I'd have got you something <u>really</u> special.

Yours truly,
Elvis

* * *

Atlanta, Thursday, January 26, 1956

Dearest Elvis,

Something's happened. About Mama.

Hank Lawson stopped by Monday on his way to work to return <u>The Old Man and the Sea</u>. He said he really liked the book and I might, too. Then he showed me how it had weird little marks all the way through it. Some of the letters, c's, d's and such, were colored in. Others, like j's and t's, had dots under them.

"I wouldn't dream of marking up your mama's book," he said. "That's why I showed you, so you'd know I didn't do it."

I thanked him and slid the book in Mama's bookcase without thinking much about it. Then last night we had snow, and today all the schools are closed, so after Daddy left for work I took out <u>The Old Man and the Sea</u> and started reading. When I got to the pages with the marks, they really did jump out at me. It looked like toward the middle there was one on every page. When I finished the book this afternoon, I flipped back through and looked at all the marks again. I found where they started, about a third of the way in, and kept turning pages till I didn't see them anymore. Then I don't know why, but I went back and did it again. Only this time, as I turned the pages, I said each marked letter out loud.

About half way through, it happened. The letters spelled my name. A.C.H.S.A.

My mother had marked my name in a book in what looked like some sort of secret code. But why? Why did she do that? What else had she said about me? I grabbed a pencil and a sheet of notebook paper and wrote down all the marked letters in order. They made words, sentences. They read, "Yes. Come now. Bring Achsa. We will be a family." I read the words over and over. They told me nothing. Who was coming? Why were they bringing me? Where were they bringing me from? I stared at the letters until they shimmered and crawled across the page, stared so long my eyeballs dried and blinking hurt. Then in a flash I got it.

Mama didn't make those marks. Someone else did.

Inside my head everything got so quiet I heard the snowmelt

184

dripping off the eaves. Somebody I'd never heard of loved my mother. Loved her enough to go to a lot of trouble, possibly for a very long time, to communicate with her. Loved her enough to want not only her but me.

<u>Me</u>! The idea swelled my heart till my ribs ached holding it.

Who is he? <u>Where</u> is he? Did Mama love him before she met Daddy? Did she keep on loving him long after that? Did she love him until the day she died? I keep pressing my palms against my temples but it doesn't do any good. I can't stop my brain from shrieking, "I'm his daughter, I'm his daughter." What else can I be?

My earliest memories are of Mama when the books came, so happy she danced standing still. That's always when she loved me most. She even saved my life with the floating island custard on the day a book had come.

Do all Mama's books have notes in them? Daddy doesn't want me touching any of her things, not even her toothbrush, so I can't rummage through the taped up boxes in the attic. But I can look at the books down here in her bookcase. I will tonight, the minute Daddy and Aunt Dora go to sleep. Only one other time in my life—that school-day morning when I waited to see you, before they told me about Mama—have the minute hands on clocks crawled so slowly.

If my mother's soul burned night and day for a man who was not Daddy, it could explain a lot—even why she died headed for the highway out of town. But there are some things I still can't understand: If she loved this other man so much, how could she give him up and marry Daddy? If this other man loved her so much, how could he let her go?

And why didn't she bring me, like the message said? Why did I not die with her?

Sincerely,

Achsa

P.S. You were sweet to say that about my birthday. The Empire State Building made a lovely gift.

*   *   *

Atlanta, Friday, January 27, 6 A.M.

Dearest E,

Mama <u>was</u> running away! I'm sure of it! I checked her closet for the brown suitcase she took to Mississippi, and it was <u>gone</u>. It must have burned up in the car. I think she only didn't take me because she had to get away right then. Remember I wrote you I heard her and Daddy quarreling? Maybe he scared her so much she couldn't wait. Even for me.

I've been awake the whole night, paging through all forty-seven books in her bookcase. Only three had anything still written in them, the others were full of erasure crumbs. Inside a book I'd never heard of by Mark Twain I found "Please understand. It was the hardest thing I've ever done." In a book called <u>Sons and Lovers</u> was, "Do you need to ask? Each time I think of it part of me dies." The third, and saddest, message I found in her Bible. I almost didn't think to look there. She always kept its red ribbon bookmark at Psalm 100, because it came in the very middle. It fell open there when I picked it up, and in the column next to the 100th Psalm, in a Psalm with a verse that reads, "My heart is smitten, and withered like grass, so that I forget to eat my bread," he had spelled out with his markings, "Annette, you are my life."

This man has loved my mother longer than I've been alive. And she loved him in return. In one sense, he's been a member of our family from the start. Now he doesn't even know she's gone. And I don't know where he is to tell him.

I wish so badly I could cry. I squinch up my eyes, but nothing happens. Achsa McEachern has lost her tears and doesn't know where to find them. Do you think if I leave them alone they'll all come home? Did your mother ever say that to you, that rhyme about Little Bo Peep's lost sheep? Maybe if I find that man I'll find my tears.

I'm not making much sense, I'm afraid. I haven't been thinking too clearly these past few hours. There's school today. I better go get ready. As always, thanks for listening.

Achsa

* * *

Atlanta, Saturday, January 28, 1956, 10:30 P.M.

Dearest E,

You were <u>terrific</u> on Stage Show!! Now you <u>truly</u> have become a star!!

I was so afraid Daddy would do something to keep me from watching. But he shut himself up in his bedroom after dinner, and I just turned on the TV, natural as you please, and sat down. Aunt Dora sat down beside me with her knitting. When you came on, she took a look at you and said, "He's got a handsome face for such a greasy-looking boy." Then you shook your legs and the girls all screamed, and Aunt Dora said, "Oh, <u>my</u>."

I never saw your face up close before. You look exactly like the marble bust of Alexander the Great in my World History book. It's true. The resemblance is amazing!!

Watching you sing churned me up inside in those same odd ways as before. I sat with my arms crossed and clenched my fists inside my armpits where Aunt Dora couldn't see. When it was over I went to my room, shut the door, and just lay there in the dark.

Except for those few moments watching you, that poor man waiting every day for Mama is all I've thought about.

Sincerely,
Achsa

*   *   *

New York, Thursday, February 2, 1956

Dearest Baby Girl,

Your mama kept a powerful secret for a long, long time. If I ~~was~~ were you I'd try not to think too much about it. Still, I reckon that's hard to do.

Maybe you can do like me and get too busy to think. My life's like one great big giant all-night car sale nowadays. All bright lights and carnival rides. I never thought to pray for anything this big. I flat out could not imagine it! And Colonel's done it all.

I'm glad you liked the show. I must have done pretty good.

They want me two more times, six shows instead of four. You can write me at the Warwick till February 18. I'll be here every weekend.

I got to run. You take care now. And don't think too much about your mama and that man.

Yours very truly,
Elvis

*　　*　　*

Atlanta, Saturday, February 4, 1956

Dearest E,

A package came for Mama today. It was wrapped in brown paper and tied with white string, and it had a <u>return address</u> written on the front in blue ink: Jacobson's Books, 153 West 112th Street, New York, NY.

I ran with it to my room before anybody saw, copied the address on a strip of notebook paper and hid it in the picture section of my wallet. Then I undid the wrapping. Inside was a book of poems by William Carlos Williams called <u>Journey to Love</u>. Nearly every page had a marked letter. They read, "whereareyouwhereareyouwhereareyouwhereareyouwhereareyou," all the way from the start to the end of the book.

I bet anything that's his name. Mr. Jacobson. I bet he owns the book store. And I'm sure he hurts worse right now than even Daddy. Unlike Daddy, Mr. Jacobson still has hope. I can almost see him, waiting alone in the twilight by his shelves of books, after his store has closed for another day. Another day my mother didn't come to him. By now his hearing has grown keen as a wild animal's. With every footfall on the sidewalk, every car that passes in the street, his heart leaps and he thinks surely it's Mama. How on earth has he stood it for so many days?

I hid the book in my closet.

Sincerely,
Achsa

*　　*　　*

Atlanta, Saturday, February 4, 1956, 10:30 P.M.

Dearest E,

This afternoon I told Aunt Dora I had to go to the drugstore to get some notebook paper because I'd used all mine up during the snow. When I got there, I bought one package, which cost 30 cents, and gave Mr. Greene a dollar. He dropped two quarters and two dimes into my shaking hands, and I went over to the pay phone near the greeting cards, deposited one of my dimes, and told the operator I wanted to call Jacobson's Books, at 153 West 112th Street in New York City.

The time she took looking up the number seemed like half my life. I stared at the tiny holes in the worn black receiver and thought about what I was going to say when Mr. Jacobson came on the line and how I was going to say it and keep breathing. I forced myself to exhale very slowly and pictured my words getting sucked into the receiver holes, traveling through the stiff black cord into the phone box, and out along telephone lines strung between poles that marched from Greene's drugstore all the way to Manhattan Island.

Finally, the operator came back on the line. She said there wasn't any Jacobson's Books in all of New York City.

My heart dropped to the pit of my stomach. "There has to be," I told her. "I have a package from them."

She said, "Well, I don't have a listing for any store by that name."

I said, "But I have to find it. I've got to tell someone there my mother died." The words came very fast, without me thinking.

She didn't say anything for a long time. The connection was so clear I could hear her breathing. It sounded like Penelope's. Then at last the operator said, "I do show a Benjamin J. Jacobson at that address, but that telephone number is unlisted."

"What does that mean?" I said. All the sights and sounds of the drugstore had closed down to nothing but the mouthpiece of the telephone receiver and the operator's voice in my ear.

"It means I can't give it out," she answered.

"Oh." I said it very softly. I wasn't sure she heard.

She said, "Maybe you ought to write it to them in a letter."

"No, I don't think so," I said, "but thank you very much."

I replaced the receiver in its metal cradle very carefully, and a thought leaped into my head as clearly as if I'd read it on a billboard: I've got to go to New York, find Mr. Jacobson and tell him about Mama. It's what she would have wanted.

If you believe in ghosts, then maybe her ghost put that thought in my mind. New York's a long way off. I don't know how I'm going to get there. But I know that's what I've got to do.

Sincerely,

Achsa

P.S. In your last letter you said you must have "done pretty good" in your first Stage Show appearance. You should have said either "done pretty <u>well</u>" or "<u>been</u> pretty good." "Good" is an adjective, not an adverb.

P.P.S. You were even better tonight on TV than before! I hope next time you'll sing "Heartbreak Hotel." I can't wait to hear it.

Chapter twenty-two

February 11–March 2, 1956

Dearest B,

Satnin forwarded your letter. I'm telling you, forget about that Mr. Jacobson.

You don't know one ~~damn~~ thing about him, except here's a cat that can tell a lie just by writing his address. He doesn't own a bookstore. For all you know, he's a gangster hiding out under a phony name. Your mama probably had good reasons for not marrying him. And not taking you with her, too. If you ask me, you only want him for your father because you don't like the one you got. You better just leave him ~~the hell~~ alone.

I mean it, Baby Girl. There's bad people out there. You got to be on the lookout for them all the time.

The brass at RCA is finally letting me sing my song tonight. I'll think about you down there in Atlanta watching.

We been in North Carolina all this week. Some places we play, there's black people way up in the high seats. Every time I see them, I recall about you climbing to the colored balcony. You are a really nice girl. You know that?

You do like I said and take care. Nice girls need to be extra careful.

Yours truly,
Elvis

*   *   *

Atlanta, Saturday, February 11, 1956, 10:30 P.M.

Dearest E,

I <u>love</u> your <u>song</u>!! And you sang it with so much <u>feeling</u>!

What a haunting idea, a hotel where people go to die of broken hearts. The bus I take to the library goes past a place like that, a dingy old brick building on the south end of downtown, near the warehouses. Now every time I see it I'll think about your song. There's a potted palm in the lobby that's been dead for centuries, and next door is a really seedy bar where, one time while our bus was stopped, a man staggered out and threw up in the street.

Poor Mr. Jacobson could be that man, drinking to drown his sorrows. If I don't tell him about Mama, for the rest of his life he'll think she never loved him. And I cannot, <u>must not</u> let that happen. I've <u>got</u> to find a way to get to New York. That's all there is to it.

Sincerely,
Achsa

P.S. Every time I see you on TV you look more and more at home. Your first show was super, and you just keep getting better.

P.P.S. You said Mr. Jacobson was "a cat <u>that</u> can tell a lie just writing his address." You should have said, "a cat <u>who</u> can tell a lie...." Better yet, you should not have brought it up, since Mr. Jacobson is not that way at all.

P.P.P.S. Flash!!!!! I just heard "Heartbreak Hotel" on a <u>rock</u> <u>and</u> <u>roll</u> <u>radio</u> <u>show</u>!! You're not singing ~~hillbilly~~ country anymore!!!! You're singing rock and roll, just like I always said!

*   *   *

Atlanta, Sunday, February 12, 1956

Dearest E,

I did it! I did it! I did it! I got myself a ride to New York! Now I can find poor Mr. Jacobson!!!

Just a few minutes ago after church, Hank Lawson told me he finally got his car fixed and he's driving to Connecticut the first weekend in March. I sucked in my breath to get my courage up and, sounding cool as you please, asked him, "Can I hitch a ride with you as far as New York City?" It felt like hurling myself off a cliff into thin air.

Hank looked at me kind of funny, so I said Daddy wouldn't mind, that I had business there. I also told him I'd pay for all his gas and he could just let me out at Grand Central Station and I'd catch a bus back home. I said it all pretty fast. I picked Grand Central Station because that's where New Yorkers in books and magazines are always meeting, and I wanted to impress Hank that I knew my way around.

It must have worked—he said he guessed it was OK. I still don't know what I'm going to tell Daddy and Aunt Dora. Maybe that I got into a science fair up there or something.

I'm sure you are one hundred percent wrong about Mr. Jacobson being a gangster, by the way, and I will be proud to have him as my father. He loved my mother all these years and communicated with her the only way he could, and whatever reason they had for not being together, I'm sure it was a good reason. Maybe he fought in the war and got a wound like that man in The Sun Also Rises. You wouldn't understand and I'm not going to explain it. I read about it in a magazine.

The point is, Mr. Jacobson and my mother should have been together! They were supposed to be together! Because they couldn't, their souls burned for each other always, with a white-hot, never-ending pain too strong even for songs to tell. Mama's soul has been released. Now it is my Christian duty as their child to travel to New York and release poor Mr. Jacobson's.

Unless he's like Daddy. I don't think Daddy's soul will ever be released. Aunt Dora says if Mama were buried here instead of Rachelville, Daddy would just go lie down on her grave and die.

Last night he kept staring at me all through dinner like he'd just come to after getting hit on the head and didn't quite know who I was. This afternoon, when I had books and notes and cardboard spread all over the dining room table making posters for a history project, he came in, sat across from me and watched me very intently, moving nothing but his eyes. Just when I was starting to feel really weird from trying to act natural, out of the utter blue he asked, "What grade are you in?"

I said I was a senior.

"I thought you were fifteen," he said.

"I am," I told him. "I got skipped in grammar school, remember?"

He smiled a sad little smile and said, "I've always been proud of you."

I wish he'd told me earlier, like about 14 years ago. I wonder if it's even true. I'd say I hate him for not loving me, but when I think about it, all it makes me feel is sad.

It's late. I better get to bed. I still don't know if I believe in God, but you know something? I sort of do miss evening prayers—which, to be honest, is a real surprise. If it counts for praying when you don't kneel, I guess I pray some every night. And I always pray for you.

Sincerely,
        Achsa

*   *   *

Memphis, Sunday, February 19, 1956

Dearest B,

Looks like there's ~~not~~ no way you're going to cut out this ~~bullsh~~ nonsense about that gangster Jacobson. Here's $300 for a round-trip airplane ticket to New York and a hotel room when you get there and a good hot meal or two. I will not have you riding across state lines in a battered old jalopy with some boy who never once has asked you out and therefore doesn't give a rat's ~~ass~~ ~~butt~~ behind what happens to you. You won't look out for your own self, so somebody like me has got to do it. Call it a late birthday present if you want.

I am also putting in this envelope one ticket to my last appearance, March 24th, on "Tommy and Jimmy Dorsey's Stage Show" at CBS-TV. You say I'm getting better every time, and I thought you'd like to see me at my best. Anyway, the March 17th show is sold out. I also sent a backstage pass so you can meet me afterwards. That is, if you're not too chicken like in Mississippi.

My life is very busy now. I got no time to write a lot of letters jawing back and forth about this. If you can make up some excuse for your daddy so you can ride up to New York with that Hank hoodlum and stay the night Lord knows where, you can sure make up some excuse to fly up in a Super-Constellation airplane and spend the night at a decent hotel. May I suggest the Warwick. It is a very good one.

Yours truly,
Elvis

*   *   *

Atlanta, Sunday, February 26, 1956, 9 P.M.

Dear E,

I appreciate most deeply your concern for my safety, even though it did come with a certain amount of pique. I also thank you very much for the ticket. And the pass.

I assure you I will be at the CBS Studio at 8 P.M. March 24th. I also assure you I will come backstage after the show. At that time I will return your $300. It was sweet of you to send it, but as it turns out, I have a legitimate reason for going to New York, one for which both Daddy and Aunt Dora give their blessings and support.

Last Monday a letter came from Hunter College saying if I was still interested in applying and in the Beatrice Mason scholarship, I had better set up an interview with the Dean of Admissions. I immediately called long distance, thinking that's how such things got done, but was told I needed to present myself in person.

You would have been proud of me. Without skipping a beat I said, "Fine. I'll be there Saturday, March 24th." They said it had to be on a weekday, so I told them I'd come Friday, March 23. Next, I telephoned Barnard College and New York University to see if I needed to be interviewed by them, too, and I do. I go to Barnard Thursday morning, March 15, because the person I need to talk to leaves for a month in Paris that very afternoon. I get interviewed at New York University the following Tuesday.

The whole time I was on the phone, I thought about Mama coming into my room that time with the college catalogs. I miss her just as hard now as on the day she died. So why, why, <u>why</u> can't I grieve for her? I feel so full of tears that all I'd need to do is prick my finger and they'd come gushing out through even such a tiny hole. But I don't cry. Not ever. Not even in the bathtub. Or late at night when everyone's asleep. I'm like some kind of sideshow freak, "Human Teenage Girl without Tears."

The principal said he'd excuse me from school for my interviews if I kept up with my assignments. Then Aunt Dora said that, much as she hated leaving Daddy, she'd have to come along and chaperone me. I'd never get to Mr. Jacobson with her tagging along everywhere, and for a little while I really did lose heart. Finally, I remembered Aunt Mavis and suggested we see if she would take me in and be my chaperone, which she has graciously agreed to do. Aunt Mavis lives alone and works all day creating window displays at Macy's Department Store, so I'll have plenty of opportunity to locate Mr. Jacobson.

I wish I had time to read all the books he sent, but everything is moving too fast. I arrive in New York the evening of March 13. That's less than three weeks away. And in exactly one month minus one day and one hour from this very minute, you and I shall meet!

Thank you again. For everything. I can hardly wait to see you.
Sincerely,
Achsa

* * *

Pensacola, Florida, Sunday, February 26, 1956, 11 P.M.

Dearest B,
Hold everything!! We done got us a huge change of plans.

Colonel says I'm singing in <u>Atlanta</u> <u>March</u> 14th and 15th! So
here's what I got in mind. How would you like to see our last show
that Thursday and fly up to New York with me Friday? I'll get you
a room at the Warwick. I'll even get you in to see Stage Show. I'm
learning "sold out" doesn't always mean sold out if you got the right
friends, and seems I've got some lately.

You'll be there Friday, Saturday, even Sunday if you want.
That'll give you plenty of time to track down this Jacobson cat. I'll
even go with you and make sure you're safe. After all, he lied about
the bookstore. For all you know, he makes his living selling girls like
you into white slavery. I don't trust him worth a ~~damn~~ darn.

I'll tell folks you're my smart Atlanta cousin. You can give
me grammar lessons all you want. And please don't worry ~~none~~ any
about your mouth and how you look. Like I said time and again, it
~~don't~~ doesn't matter. Not at all.

Speaking of looks, I guess you saw on TV how my hair's some
different now. I dyed it black to show up in the lights. Thought I
better tell you so you'll know me. (Ha-ha. Joke.)

Write back first thing to say you got this letter. I can't wait to
see you in Atlanta and spend the weekend with you in New York.

Yours truly,
Elvis

P.S. I saved the bragging part for last. Guess what's <u>number</u> <u>one</u> on
<u>Billboard</u> magazine's country and western chart? Yours truly singing
"I Forgot to Remember to Forget." Since you won't listen to country
music on the radio, I guess I got to be the one to tell you that's a
pretty big deal.

* * *

Atlanta, Friday, March 2, 1956

Dearest E,

I suppose by now you have received my letter of February 26,
and will know I cannot possibly see you in Atlanta or fly with you
to New York.

Sometimes I think we are fated never to meet. It's way too late for me to even dream of unraveling all the careful planning for my college interviews. All I can do is hope and pray things work out for us the next Saturday, like we originally planned. I've still got my Stage Show ticket. And the pass.

I never thought being this close to having several of one's dreams come true would scare me, but it does. I wake up nights worried about everything. I've wanted to live in New York for so long. What if when I get there I don't like it? Or what if not even one of those colleges wants me? What if I don't find Mr. Jacobson? Or what if I do? I'm not pretty like Mama, what if he takes one look at me and turns and walks away? What if you walk away from me, too? I know you say my looks don't matter, but looks always matter. Why else would you have dyed your hair?

At least I think I'm going to like Aunt Mavis. I got a letter from her yesterday saying to bring warm clothes. She also said she's drawn me a diagram of the subway system so I can go places while she's at work. I took *that* as a real good sign!

The minute I get back to Atlanta, my whole life's going to change. Daddy wants to move to Rachelville as soon as I graduate, which is OK, I suppose, since I'll only be there for the summer. Aunt Dora will take her old job back at the Presbyterian church and I guess Daddy will get a job in a store or something. He's already started packing stuff. He says every day that he can't wait to go, so he can lie down on Mama's grave and keep her from the cold.

It's like he thinks she's under there alive. I worry Aunt Dora's right, that he'll just stretch out there and die. But I don't want to think about that now.

In twelve days you'll be here and I'll be gone. Isn't life strange? And then in 10 more days I'll be with you.

Sincerely,

Achsa

Chapter twenty-three

March 7–14, 1956

Memphis, Wednesday, March 7, 1956

Dearest B,

It's all my fault, things not working out for us in Atlanta. I got so much going on I didn't even know I was singing there till the day I wrote you. Anyway, you just come on to New York like you planned. I still can't wait to see you.

"Heartbreak Hotel" hit the Billboard charts last week. It's climbing like a rocket, and some big magazine wants to put my picture on the cover. Last weekend I bought my folks a house with a swimming pool! It's in the greenest, prettiest neighborhood you ever saw. And I'm getting the pink Cadillac fixed up so Satnin can learn to drive.

Seems like my every dream is coming true. I got money to give away, money to throw away, even money to burn. I'm not bragging, it's the gospel truth. If my life was a Bugs Bunny cartoon, I'd be buried up to my eyeballs in gold dollars till I flat couldn't move.

And I haven't even got to the best part. The best part is I'm going to <u>Hollywood</u> for a <u>SCREEN TEST</u>!!!!!!

Colonel made me promise not to tell, except for Satnin and Daddy. But I can tell you. It's with this really famous producer, Mr. Hal Wallis. He just got done making a movie called <u>The Rose Tattoo</u>, and folks still talk about a movie he made a long time ago called

<u>Casablanca</u>. It's exactly ~~them~~ those kinds of movies I want to act in. The Lord could not have picked a better man for me to meet. I guess He knows I'm not just doing it for me, that it's for James Dean, too. And most of all for Jesse Garon.

Sometimes late at night I get to wondering why the Lord has blessed me so. It's not like I'm a better person than everybody else, or anything. I reckon I'm not even good as most. Still, it just keeps coming and it ~~don't~~ doesn't ever stop. There's not a man alive that's <u>that</u> good.

It's crazy, but there's times I feel like maybe it's the Devil's work, and not the Lord's at all. Or maybe they're both in it together, and they're every minute testing me to see which way I'll jump.

You know something? I still think about how beautiful it felt singing all those gospel songs at that Fourth of July picnic. It seems like a whole lifetime ago, but it's really not even a year. There's times I wish I'd stayed with it and been a gospel singer from then on. That way I'd always know I was walking with the Lord, no matter what trials I faced.

A couple times I dreamed I'm done singing and I'm taking my bow. The fans are out there clapping and screaming and I'm thinking I'll give them one more song. Only, when I straighten up I'm not standing on a stage anymore. I'm on a narrow cliff. Nothing but sand and rock, like that place you went to when your Mama died. I look out to where the audience ought to be, and there's no lights, no spotlight, no people, nothing but darkness. It chills me through. Still, I start walking toward it, toward where the stage drops off, because I got no place else to go. That's when I wake up covered in cold fear and sweat.

But that's all just night stuff. There's not any of it real. What <u>is</u> real is I'm fixing to go to <u>Hollywood</u> and be in the <u>movies</u>! Just like my inside voice always promised.

Oh, Baby Girl, I can't wait to see you. I got so much I want to say. You hang onto that backstage pass, you hear? Don't you dare lose your nerve about using it, not for one little minute.

And don't you worry about anything, not anything at all. Things work out, they truly do. I am the living proof of it.

This is the best of times in all my life.
Yours always,
    Elvis

P.S. Uh, Teach, it's probably not my place to say anything, but in your letter of March 3 you wrote about your Aunt Mavis mapping out the subway system for you and how you took it as "a <u>real</u> good sign." If I am not mistaken, you should have said "a <u>really</u> good sign." Because good is an adjective. And because adverbs mostly end in "-ly." Gotcha! Ha-ha!

*   *   *

Atlanta, Wednesday, March 14, 1956, 2:30 P.M.

Dearest E,

Just a short note to say CONGRATULATIONS!!!

About the house. About "Heartbreak Hotel." And most of all about the <u>SCREEN</u> <u>TEST</u>!!! It's so exciting!! You really are going to be a <u>great</u> <u>actor</u>—for James Dean, Jesse Garon, and <u>all</u> <u>of</u> <u>us</u>.

Your plane is probably landing at the Atlanta Municipal Airport right this minute. In two hours my plane will take off. If I get up sufficient nerve, I will call you Saturday at the Warwick Hotel. I know they say a girl should never call a boy, no matter what. But when a girl and a boy who have written each other for as long as we have find themselves in the same city and he cannot call her because certain people might find out, I believe an exception might be made. Don't you?

I have just now packed a few last things, especially my radio, in the nifty blue suitcase Aunt Dora bought me. The next letter I write you will be postmarked New York City!!!

Sincerely,
    Achsa

P.S. Thanks for the grammar lesson. I deserved it. You have <u>truly</u> graduated now!

*   *   *

201

New York, Wednesday, March 14, 1956, 11:10 P.M.

Dearest E,

I'm <u>HERE</u>!!!!!!!! At last, at last, I am really and truly <u>here</u>!!

New York at night is as beautiful to me as the memory of Mama's face. Do you believe a person can be born in the wrong place? I do. I feel like I've been in exile for a lifetime and have only now at last found my way home.

Daddy and Aunt Dora put me on the plane in Atlanta. She waved the whole time, as it taxied toward the runway. Daddy mostly looked at the ground. After we took off I glimpsed them one last time, still standing on the tarmac and looking very small. The pilot told us the name of every city we flew over. By Philadelphia the sun had set to nothing but an orange streak on the horizon. After that, I didn't take my eyes off the view outside my window.

Before the pilot said a word I saw it, far off in the distance—a narrow oval, set inside a thin border of darkness and sparkling like a jewel-encrusted brooch. I knew instantly what it was. It tugged at me so hard my very heartstrings must have pulled the plane in for its landing.

Aunt Mavis met me at LaGuardia Airport, and we took a taxi to Manhattan. ("LaGuardia!" "Manhattan!") She lives in a teeny apartment with a living room, a bedroom, a guest room the size of a closet (which is where I am now and where her friend Nadine, an airline stewardess, sleeps when she's in town), and a kitchen no bigger than three orange crates behind a pair of folding doors. Considering she's got so little space, she's even nicer for letting me stay here than I realized.

And guess what? She lived in New York the same time Mama did. That really surprised me. I don't think they saw each other much. "We were sisters and we loved each other, but we led completely different lives," is what she said.

I asked her where Mama lived back then but she couldn't quite remember, only that it was somewhere uptown on the West Side. Then I asked her, as casually as I could, if she had ever met a friend of Mama's by the name of Mr. Jacobson. I'd never said his name out loud to anybody face to face, and my stomach gave an actual lurch at the sound of it.

Aunt Mavis thought a moment and then shook her head. "We didn't know any of the same people," she said. Disappointing, but not completely unexpected. What with her being the oldest and Mama the youngest, Mama and Aunt Mavis were pretty far apart in age.

Anyway, I've unpacked my suitcase, so I guess I'm settled in and I'm supposed to sleep now. That's a laugh. I can't stand to forfeit even one precious, waking minute. My mind feels quiet and excited all at once, if such a thing is possible. I may not close my eyes the whole time I'm here. Outside my window I see literally hundreds of other lighted windows, maybe even thousands. I hear taxis honking, a siren streaking by. And every one of them is saying, "Hello, Achsa! Welcome home!"

So good night from New York City, dearest E.

And good night dear, Beautiful City, good night.

    Love,

       Achsa

Chapter twenty-four

March 15–20, 1956

New York, Thursday, March 15, 11 P.M.

Dearest E,

Well, I had my first interview. At Barnard College.

It's uptown on the West Side, and I craned my neck at all the buildings, imagining Mama in every window—taking a big breath of New York air, setting a green plant on a ledge to catch the sun. I liked a boy once. He sat behind me in tenth grade history, and I stayed so nervous every day in class I dropped things and could barely write my name. That's how it felt being so close to where Mama lived such an important part of her life. I could tell by the street numbers that I was close to Mr. Jacobson, too.

My interview took place in a too-warm room with a hissing radiator and a ticking grandfather clock. Two women and a man asked me questions. They looked very elegant, like the New Yorkers one always sees in movies. When I said I wanted a career in the theatre and had already written at least half a play and acted in it, they leaned forward in their chairs. The admissions dean said I had good College Board scores. I hope that means they'll let me in.

I doubt I gave them any other reasons. Here I was, on trial

at the college I most want to go to, and all I could think about was poor Mr. Jacobson and how I was going to look for him the minute we were done.

He lives in a tall brick building on the corner of 112th Street and Riverside Drive, not at all the sort of place for a gangster. The lobby floor is brown marble and by the elevator there's a leather wing-back chair and a brass planter with a tall, green tree. Maybe Mama lived in that same building years ago and that's how they met. I checked the row of mailboxes near the door and found his: Benjamin J. Jacobson, apt. 913.

The elevator man was old and stooped and didn't say a word. The elevator was pretty old, too. I was its only passenger, and every jerky foot we rose I felt myself drawing closer to Mr. Jacobson. By the time I got off, my heart was pounding as though I had run up all nine flights of stairs in record time, which I probably could have done and got there faster.

Apartment 913 is at the end of a long hall. I pushed the buzzer several times, but no one answered. It was almost lunchtime, so I hung around outside his door awhile, in case he worked close by and came home to eat, but he didn't. I wanted to stay longer but feared the elevator man might set out looking for me. I'll come back again tomorrow. And Saturday, if I need to. Mr. Jacobson should certainly be home one of those days, I would think.

On my way to the subway, I stopped for lunch at a real New York delicatessen. I'd never heard of a single thing on the menu except eggs. The man sitting next to me at the counter ordered a hot pastrami sandwich, so I got one, too. It tasted surprisingly good, sort of like ham. Tonight Aunt Mavis treated me to dinner at a restaurant run by a family from India. Indian food must be an acquired taste.

I hope you are doing well, wherever you are. I will call you Saturday at the Warwick Hotel. By the time you read these words we may already have spoken to each other. I would like that very much.

Sincerely,
Achsa

* * *

New York, Saturday, March 17, 11:30 P.M.

Dearest E,

I went to Mr. Jacobson's yesterday and today, but no luck. I'm worried he may be out of town. Aunt Mavis says some people up north go south for the whole winter, though for the life of me I don't understand why.

I've got to see him now. By the time I come up here for college—if I even get to come—he could well have killed himself from sheer despair. I imagine he is already like one of the unfortunate guests at your Heartbreak Hotel, so lonely he could die. Macy's is closed tomorrow, of course, and Monday Aunt Mavis is off work, so I won't be going back till Tuesday. But I <u>will</u> go back. I <u>must</u> go back. And I shall <u>keep</u> <u>on</u> <u>going</u> <u>back</u> until I find him at home.

I phoned you before Aunt Mavis got back from work, but they said you hadn't checked in yet. Today has just been my day for missing folks, I guess.

This evening, Aunt Mavis had a friend to dinner, a bachelor named Tim who lives in the building. He's got wispy blond hair and crinkly eyes, and he's really, really nice. If he'd gone to Foster, he would have been called a sissy and a gimp. Here, he's a dancer. He knows almost everything about the New York stage. Tomorrow he and Aunt Mavis are treating me to my very first Broadway play!

Between dinner and dessert we watched "Stage Show." When you came out and started singing, Tim grinned at me and said, "Well, now we all know why we're tuned in to the Dorsey Brothers, don't we." I blushed, which I almost never do. He reached over, patted my hand and said, "My dear, allow me to commend you on your truly excellent taste." Aunt Mavis flashed him a look I'm pretty sure I wasn't supposed to see.

I guess it's safe to say Tim is not Aunt Mavis's boyfriend. In fact, I guess you'd have to call Aunt Mavis an old maid, since she's never married. It doesn't seem to bother her, though, which I find most encouraging.

They're still in the living room, or I'd try to call you again. They said they were going to finish off the wine. I feel quite roiled up inside just knowing that tonight you and I are in the very same city, and only a mile or two apart. Just think, in exactly one week minus three hours I shall be making my way backstage to be with you.

    Sincerely,

        Achsa

* * *

New York, Monday, March 19, 1956

Dearest E,

    Tim and Aunt Mavis let me pick the play we went to yesterday, and I chose <u>The Diary of Anne Frank</u>. It was wonderful! And guess what? The father of the girl playing Anne Frank founded the Actors' Studio, where I still hope you will go someday. Near the end, everyone pulled out their hankies. Except me, of course—although I was sobbing buckets in my heart. I brought Mama's opera glasses, and all during the play I wished more than anything she were with me. So many times I wanted to turn to her and say, "Mama, look." I still miss her so.

    Today Aunt Mavis took me to the top of the Empire State Building so I could "see all of New York at once." Now that I've been there, I will treasure the postcard you sent for my birthday even more. It was bitterly cold up there, but very clear—and you really could see everything. Staten Island, the Statue of Liberty, the Hudson and the East River, and Manhattan Island all the way up to the end. I got a lump in my throat thinking how this time next week I'd be gone, but <u>still</u> I could not cry.

    Tomorrow I go back to Mr. Jacobson's. Though I failed to mention him earlier in this letter, he is always on my mind.

    Sincerely,

        Achsa

* * *

New York, Tuesday, March 20, 1956 3:30 P.M.

Dearest E,

    I went to Mr. Jacobson's this morning, and once again he wasn't

208

there. I'm 99 and $^{44}/_{100}$ percent sure trying to see him on weekdays is useless, but I must take advantage of every chance I have, since my time is so short.

This afternoon I had my interview at New York University, and it went pretty well. Now I'm in the Sheridan Square subway station, waiting for the Seventh Avenue IRT. ("Greenwich Village," "Sheridan Square," "IRT,"—New York words melt sweet as baklava on my tongue.)

Being in the Village—that's what real New Yorkers call it—is like seeing the dream I've had for so long come to life. The narrow streets pull the buildings right up next to you, like friends. I've been walking all over, trying to pick which one I want to live in. It's all I can do not to stop everyone I pass and say, "Do you live here? What's it like? Before long you and I are going to be neighbors."

Everything moves faster in New York. It makes one's mind work harder, but I like that. Maybe I'll get through college faster here and live in Greenwich Village very soon.

While I was there, I went in a bookstore just like "Jacobson's Books" ought to have been. I bought a novel written by a French girl who's only 19. Its title means "good morning, heartache" in English, a sad and lovely phrase that made me think once more of Mr. Jacobson. I also bought that play about Anne Frank. I never knew you could buy plays in stores, never even imagined it. It's so exciting! Later, I stopped in at a pastry shop, which is where I had the baklava, the sweetest thing I've ever tasted, with a cup of jasmine tea with tiny flowers floating in it. A fat orange cat that seemed to have the run of the place curled up in my lap and went to sleep.

Aunt Dora called last night, and Daddy actually got on the phone and asked when I was coming home. I told him I'd be there Sunday, but I said goodbye and hung up before he could ask what time my plane gets in.

Friday is my last interview, the one at Hunter College. Right this minute there are just 77 hours until you and I meet face to face. An hour ago there were 78. If you don't get this letter before I see you, I can tell you in person everything it says. The last time I wrote those words, Mama was still alive. It seems long ago sometimes, and other times like yesterday.

Here comes the subway train. It's just a pinpoint of light deep in the tunnel, but the wind that always runs ahead of it is here. I love the subways, how it's warmer underground and how the rails sometimes sing for no reason. Knowing how to change between the IRT and the BMT makes me feel like a real New Yorker. Maybe by now I am!

Most sincerely,
Achsa

Chapter twenty-five

March 21–23, 1956

New York, Wednesday, March 21, 1956, 11 P.M.

Dearest E,

At long last I have met Mr. Jacobson.

It's true. I finally found him at home, and I told him about Mama, but it all turned out quite differently than I had hoped or imagined.

I went to his apartment early this afternoon and rang the doorbell, never thinking he'd be there. Then I heard footsteps. I thought for a moment I'd faint, only there wasn't time.

The door was opened by a quite distinguished-appearing gentleman, with deep-set eyes, thin lips, and what's called a Roman nose. His face did not look much like mine. Nor did his hair, which was dark and very curly and touched with gray. Also, he was tall. Still, I recognized him immediately as Mr. Jacobson. He matched up with Mama, just like Robert Mitchum. He had their same heat inside. It made you not want to stop looking at him.

"Mr. Jacobson?" I said. My harelip scar felt itchy and dry. I wanted more than anything to touch it.

The man nodded curtly.

"I am Achsa McEachern," I told him.

So great a joy leaped into his eyes I couldn't bear to look at it.

"Come in. Please. Please come in," he said. His voice rumbled deep and low, so different from Daddy's.

He threw open the door and I stepped into a beautiful living room with floor-to-ceiling bookshelves on two sides and a view of the Hudson River. I wanted to stand a moment and gaze at everything around me, but my poor, wretched message immediately came tumbling out.

"I have bad news about my mother," I told him. "She is dead."

The air rushed out of him as though he had been hit hard in the chest, and he turned his head away. In a faraway apartment on some other floor a phonograph played music that passed through the walls like heartbeats. When he turned back to me he was a different man, all welcome gone.

He nodded toward a pair of wing chairs separated by a leather-topped drum table and said, "Your mother was an old friend. I am so sorry to hear. How did it happen?"

I sat gingerly on the edge of the nearer chair. "It was an automobile accident," I told him. "It happened on December second. A train hit her car at a railroad crossing. The car exploded."

I hadn't meant to say that last part, except it came to me right then that Mama had died going to this man, and if he had married her she would still be alive. He had seated himself in the other wing chair and I watched his face, which looked like he was struggling with all his might to put a brake on some horrible set of gears that ground inside him. Or it might have been the way the snowy window glared behind him. Or even a shadow. Considering what passed later I can't really say.

A long moment went by before he spoke. "You must miss her terribly," he said then, perfectly composed. "It was good of you to let me know."

I nodded and stared down at my left hand clutching the green upholstered chair arm.

Mr. Jacobson jumped up. "Would you like something to drink?" he asked. "Milk? Tea?" He was already striding toward his kitchen.

"Tea would be nice," I said.

He stayed gone a long while and made very little sound. Maybe he just wanted to be by himself. I took the opportunity to look around the living room. <u>His</u> living room. Mr. Jacobson appeared to live alone. His furniture was the same rich, shiny wood as Mama's casket and smelled of lemon oil. A pair of gold-framed pictures on the wall near the door showed red-jacketed hunters riding past a castle. Beside the pictures hung a brass wall clock with a barometer. One of the bookshelves held a statue I took to be Don Quixote, a skinny man in knight's armor astride a skinny horse. Most of his books had to do with history. I had never heard of any of them. His head was filled with things I didn't know.

I stared shamelessly at everything. I figured I had a right to. If this man was my father, I had a right to know how it might have felt playing paper dolls on his Persian carpet, making forts out of his wing chairs, growing up in his apartment. Everything around me appeared very solid, which may be usual when people live so high above the ground. But I wasn't finding what I'd hoped for. Nothing connected Mr. Jacobson to me or said he was my father.

A tea kettle whistled, and eventually he reappeared, set a cup and saucer beside me on the table and returned to his chair. I thanked him, took a swallow. The tea burned going down.

Mr. Jacobson smiled at me, as though we were strangers on a bus. "You must tell me about yourself," he said. "How old are you? What grade are you in?" Polite questions anyone might ask.

"I turned fifteen in January. I'm a senior. I came here for my college interviews," I said.

He nodded. "You sound like a very smart girl," he said.

"Last summer I worked at a swimming pool," I told him. My mind's eye showed me the pool's concrete floor, where all those lost locker keys lay in the cold water, beneath the shadow of the diving board. If Mr. Jacobson and I were indeed strangers on a bus, we were coming to my stop. I sucked in a long breath and said, "I read your messages in the books. My mother was on her way to you when she died."

Mr. Jacobson's eyes went hard. His wall clock ticked. The distant music kept on beating in the walls.

"I want to know who you are and why you didn't marry her," I said.

He sat utterly still. So did I. After forever, he steepled his hands against the table top and said quietly, "You read my messages. And then you found me. You <u>are</u> a smart girl."

He sat so long studying his fingers I began to fear he might not speak again, that he would simply sit there until I got up and left.

At last he said, "My name is Benjamin Jacobson. I am a professor of history at Columbia University. I met your mother when we were teaching at the same West Side high school, before the Second World War."

Here it was, the beginning of what I had come for. "Was she beautiful?" I asked softly. Even I knew it for a strange question, but it was the one that came.

Mr. Jacobson considered it a moment. "Yes," he said, "I suppose so. All the men thought themselves in love with her, were struck dumb when she walked into a room, that sort of thing. I couldn't see it. I thought her far too pale." He shrugged a small apology. "But then I grew to know her."

"What was she like?" I said. The hole in me that all my life had gaped for Mama's answers opened wide.

He smiled slightly, whether at the impossibility of answering my question or at his memories, I couldn't tell. "She had set up a tutoring program for some of the slower students," he said, leaning forward as though drawing energy from simply speaking of her. "Nobody much would help her, since it meant staying late, but she wouldn't give it up. She was a stubborn and determined woman. When it became apparent she was going to do every bit of it herself, even if it meant working weeks upon weeks of eleven-hour days, I pitched in. She loved life, and learning, and approached herself and everybody else with a deep sense of respect."

"Why didn't you marry her?" I repeated, flattening out the words to have no tone.

He stared down at his hands a good while, then sighed and answered quietly, "I am a Jew. The war was coming. Nobody knew what would happen, even here. It was she who did not want to marry."

My surprise must have shown.

"I couldn't blame her," he added quickly. "Already there were rumors. It was no crime to be afraid."

So. My mother had brought about her own unhappiness, left him of her own free will. I let out a slow breath crowded with the hopes I had carried for so many weeks.

"And you are not my father," I said. It was not even a question anymore, it was an answer. It was why she didn't bring me. Because I wasn't his.

Now it was Mr. Jacobson's turn to look startled. "What? Of course not. Whatever gave you that idea?" he said.

I shrugged. I'm good at shrugging. "I don't know. Maybe that Mama got married two weeks after she and Daddy met," I told him.

He didn't look surprised, or hurt, or even angry. Maybe he already knew. Instead, something seemed to close off behind his eyes, as though a stage curtain had been lowered. He studied me, stared at me like that clerk in Junior's when I told him you were going to be a star—like I couldn't possibly know what I was saying. "Sometimes people fall in love that way," he said.

"I guess so," I answered. "Then why did you send her all those books?"

Mr. Jacobson shrugged. He was good at shrugging, too. "It was a way to keep in touch," he said, "a little harmless, nostalgic flirting, something grown-ups do."

Suddenly, I wanted more than anything to get out of there. I gulped the last swallow of my tea and rose to go.

"I just thought you ought to know about my mother," I said, pulling on my coat.

Mr. Jacobson looked relieved. "It was very thoughtful of you.

You'll have to come again sometime," he said politely at the door, the way people say something when they don't mean a word of it.

I nodded, started down the hall, and heard him close his door behind me.

So I guess that's that.

I got what I wanted. I found Mr. Jacobson, told him about Mama, and learned that he is not my father. I'm the same person I've always been. I don't know why I feel so sad.

I guess because he didn't love her more.

              Sincerely,
                Achsa

*   *   *

New York, Thursday, March 22, 1956, 5:30 A.M.

Dearest E,

I've lain awake all night thinking what a stupid, crazy, meddlesome person I am. How could I have confronted that man, Mr. Jacobson, like that?

I actually went to his apartment! Can you believe that? After I told him about Mama, I actually accused him of being my father!

I knew his address. Why didn't I just send a letter? I'm surprised he didn't call the police. He must have thought I was insane.

You too. You were right about me only thinking he was my father because I didn't like the one I've got. I really had no other reason. Just that one message about Mama bringing me, and that doesn't prove a thing. Maybe she was only planning to run away from home again. To someplace more exciting than Lydia, Mississippi. Maybe he'd offered to let her stay in his apartment, like I'm staying with Aunt Mavis, and she asked if she could bring me with her. She probably changed her mind because she knew she wasn't going to be gone long.

I ought to make a good living writing plays and stuff. I sure can imagine up a storm. Right now I just want to crawl way under Aunt Mavis's guest bed, curl up next to the wall and hide. Soon it'll

216

be light enough for me to look at my miserable self in a mirror and see what an embarrassingly stupid, melodramatic girl I am.

I am sorry for all my letters about Mr. Jacobson. They must have bored your socks off. I wish I'd listened to every word you said. Mr. Jacobson may not be a gangster, but he is not a very good man, in my opinion. My mother's very life turned on those books he sent, and all they were to him was "harmless flirting" and "a way to keep in touch." Mr. Jacobson was right, the way he looked at me—I really did know very little about him and Mama. Just enough to make me act like a prize fool.

> Yours truly,
> Achsa

*　　*　　*

New York, Thursday, March 22, 1956, 4:30 P.M.

Dearest E,

I just got back to Aunt Mavis's. I spent all day walking around in the Village, thinking it would cheer me up. It didn't do that worth a flip, but it did set me to thinking.

Maybe I really am the world's dumbest, most meddlesome, most melodramatic fool. But maybe I'm not, too. I sat for a long time in Washington Square Park and went over everything I know about Mama and Mr. Jacobson. A lot of it doesn't make a lick of sense.

For instance, everybody always knows where everybody else goes to church, so why didn't Mama know all along Mr. Jacobson was a Jew? Why would she pack up and leave all of a sudden like she'd just found out?

Why, if she didn't love him enough to marry him, did she always get that sad, faraway look whenever anybody even so much as said the word "New York"? Why did she only come alive when one of his books came in the mail?

Why, if he didn't love her all these years, did he send a coded message in a Bible telling her, "You are my life"? And why send it in a regular Bible, anyway, if he's a Jew?

Why, if there's not a Chinaman's chance I'm Mr. Jacobson's daughter, did Daddy say to Mama he didn't know if I was his? And why, if I wasn't Mr. Jacobson's and he and Mama didn't love each other anymore, had Mama packed her suitcase and headed for the highway on the day she died?

It has taken me awhile to come to this conclusion, but I am certain Mr. Jacobson told me lies. My mother loved him. All her life a hot fire burned for him inside her very soul. I felt it before I was even born. She would <u>never</u> have run out on him, not for any reason in this world.

I tried to call you at your hotel. Of course you aren't there yet, it's only Thursday. But I wanted so badly to talk to you I had to try. I always tell you everything. And I always listen to what you have to say. But I don't think anything you'd say this time will change my mind. I'm going back to Mr. Jacobson's. I'm going to tell him that I know he lied. Then I won't leave until he either proves me wrong or tells the truth.

Sincerely,
Achsa

*   *   *

New York, Friday, March 23, 1956, 10:30 P.M.

Dear Elvis,

Well, I went to Mr. Jacobson's, and of course he wasn't home. I sat on a bench outside his building and waited for him until I had to leave for Hunter College. I guess my interview went OK. I couldn't tell, my mind was elsewhere.

I've got my suitcase all packed and everything, and the minute Aunt Mavis leaves for work tomorrow I'm going back to Mr. Jacobson's apartment. I'll stay all day if I have to. Just sit by his door and wait until it's time to go see you. It's my only chance.

Tonight is my last complete night in New York. Maybe for forever, if I don't get in any of those colleges. It's cold outside, but I've opened my window a crack to let the traffic noise lull me to sleep. I wonder if I'll ever fall asleep back home without it.

In just twenty-one hours you and I shall meet.
Good night, my dearest friend, whom I will see so very soon.
Sincerely,
    Achsa

Chapter twenty-six

March 24, 1956

On the plane to Atlanta, Saturday, March 24, 1956, 11:15 P.M.

Dearest Elvis,

I am so sorry for my behavior I don't know what to say.

I am not a person who makes excuses for herself. I think people mostly are going to do what they are going to do, whether they can excuse it or not. However, given the way I acted and considering how long we have been writing, I believe you are owed an explanation. The only way I can give it is to write what happened. I have plenty of time to do that—this airplane doesn't get to Atlanta until after 2 A.M. And, as you wrote me one time from another airplane, there's nothing going on up here but darkness and stars.

This morning, when I said good-bye to Aunt Mavis as she left for work, and gave her the guest towels with the roses I embroidered as a thank you present, now seems like centuries ago. Big, wet snowflakes were already falling, turning the whole town quiet. I washed the breakfast dishes and put on the red dress she had sent me for Christmas. I spent almost an hour making up my eyes before dropping the makeup into my purse, along with my record of "That's All Right" I brought for you to sign. Then I put on my coat and scarf, picked up my blue suitcase, and walked out the door. It was almost eleven.

Snow was piling up by the time I got off the subway near Mr. Jacobson's building. The elevator man smiled at me this time. I'm sure by then he thought I lived there. I rang Mr. Jacobson's bell, but nobody answered, which I sort of expected. I stood there a few minutes, balancing on first one foot then the other. Then I upended my suitcase, sat down on it and leaned against the wall. I figured I'd wait there until six or seven if I had to.

Time passed, as they say. Lots of it. When I got tired of listening to the faint sounds of people living their lives behind walls not far from me, I ate two of the three Tootsie Rolls I'd brought and tried to recall the lyrics to all the songs I have ever known.

It was after 2 P.M., and sitting on one end of a not-very-large suitcase was starting to feel super uncomfortable, when the elevator door opened and Mr. Jacobson, wearing a plaid muffler and carrying a white bakery box by its string, rounded the corner at the opposite end of the hall.

Lucky for me he was watching his feet and didn't see me until he almost tripped over me. "Ah, Miss McEachern," he said then, smiling but not looking at all pleased. He eyed my suitcase. "Come to say good-bye on your way out of town?"

I nodded. "May I come in a minute?" I said.

"Of course," he replied, opening the door without much enthusiasm.

I went inside and took my former seat in the wing chair.

"Tea?" he offered, turning toward the kitchen.

"I'll take milk this time if you don't mind," I said, imagining it in a big glass and thinking he would have to be very rude to throw me out before I finished it, and that would buy me some time.

He disappeared into the kitchen, returned with the milk a moment later, placed it on the table and sat down stiffly in the other wing chair. "I was pleased to meet you the other day, but sorry it had to come from such sad circumstances. I hope your trip home is a pleasant one," he said.

It was drive-in movie time again. I watched myself take a swallow of milk and set the glass down carefully on the ceramic coaster Mr. Jacobson had put on the table. I watched Mr. Jacobson watching me and wishing I wasn't there. I leaned toward him, took a breath.

"I don't believe you," I blurted. "I don't for one minute believe my mother would not marry you. I saw her smooth her hands over every page inside every book you sent, for no other reason than that you had touched them. She would sit on our sofa, eyes shining like she had seen a vision. She loved you all her life. I've known it longer than always. I was born knowing."

Mr. Jacobson looked at me with fury. I gripped the chair arms to ward it off and closed my eyes against it. When I opened them, his face was contorted by another emotion entirely. He had jammed his thumb and forefinger in the corners of his eyes to hold back tears, but it was useless. With a gurgling cry, he brought his head down to his knees and began to weep.

"I am sorry," I said. It was true. My heart swelled with uncried tears for this lying man who was so angry and so sad, yet all I could do was sit dry-eyed and keep watch. Mr. Jacobson wept so hard and for so long I grew worried. I remembered how the firemen had to stop Daddy from hurling himself onto the burning automobile that was my mother's tomb.

Finally, I rose, stood behind Mr. Jacobson's chair and put a hand on his shoulder. "Can I bring you a glass of water?" I said. Such a pitiful offering.

He nodded, a small movement I almost didn't see. I went into the kitchen, filled a cut-crystal glass at the sink and brought it to him. He sat up and sipped from it and I went back to my chair. His tears were letting up.

"Forgive me," he said, gazing intently at his hands dangling limp between his knees and speaking so softly I had to strain to hear him. "I have lied to you when you deserved the truth. The truth is hard for me, but it is not yet impossible." His face clenched up again and he spoke haltingly between sobs. "I am not a Jew," he said, "I am a Negro. And I loved your mother with all my heart."

He looked me full in the face then. His eyes burned with pain. The rushing silence in the room made me think, absurdly, of

Mississippi, of riding in the car with Ramey Lee and Nancy with all the windows down. I opened my mouth to speak, because I could not stand such quiet.

"No," he said. "I want to tell you. I want you to know."

The snow fell soundlessly, as I listened to the saddest, loneliest story I have ever heard.

He was born Benjamin Jackson. His mother worked in the office of a white doctor in a Virginia city he did not name. He never knew his father. He was a smart child, with curly hair and olive skin. From the time he was ten, his mother sent him every summer to a camp for Jewish children in another state. On every application, she filled out their name as "Jacobson." When he turned thirteen, she enrolled him in a white private school in the northeast. At seventeen, he entered Harvard. That night, his mother boarded a train to California and never saw him again. Through the years, she occasionally wrote letters, pretending she was a maid keeping in touch with her former employer. The return address was always a post office box, a different one each time and in a different city. He always replied immediately, but nearly all his letters came back stamped "addressee unknown." The few that did not she never answered.

"So easy," he said, gazing toward the bookshelves as if they were a screen showing movies of his past. "Jackson, Jacobson. A little hiccup of the pen, and a black boy becomes a Jew, fulfills his mother's dream and loses her."

"Your mother's dream?" I said, my thumb tracing the scar on my upper lip.

"I didn't have much choice in the matter," he replied without bitterness. "I tell people my middle name is Jason, but it isn't. It's Jordan. From the moment my mother first laid eyes on me, she determined I would cross into the Promised Land, that I would grow up to be a white man in America."

"How could she have a dream that meant giving up her son?" I said. My eyes blurred with the false promise of tears.

"It was the truest mother's dream," he answered. "It was all for me."

I could not look into his face, see the pain of all he had lost. "She must be proud of you," I said.

He replied that she had died two years before. An attorney had sent a letter. It contained an opal ring that he remembered.

The wall clock chimed, in that muffled way even indoor things take on when it snows. "Do you ever want to…go back?" I asked.

"There's not a day goes by I don't think about it," he answered. "But I can't."

I looked at him without understanding.

"The others who pass, they always tell you, never get too close," he continued, speaking softly. "Don't read books by Negro authors, don't develop a fondness for jazz, don't become too good a dancer, don't buy the collards at the greengrocer's. Getting close only complicates matters. At worst you give yourself away. Well, I didn't listen—and I made a mistake."

"What kind of a mistake?" I said.

He reached a nervous hand to a leather box on the drum table, pulled out a Pall Mall and lit it with a matching table lighter. "A historian always has a specialty," he replied, picking a crumb of tobacco off his tongue the way I had seen Mama do. "An area of expertise where one writes and publishes, makes a name for oneself. I unwisely chose the slave trade in Colonial America, or perhaps it chose me. Every summer I travel to wherever I can spend my days studying ships' manifests, shipbuilders' drawings, lists of purchases, provisions. I want to know what was thought the minimum amount of food, water and floor space in the hold required to keep a human being of so many hands or stone alive during a middle passage of an anticipated duration. And what percentage of that did the trader, who was above all else a businessman, provide."

Those terrible gears I had earlier glimpsed in him ground again. He drew in on his cigarette to still them. "It's research with an importance far beyond me and my academic career. I dare not risk discrediting it. Were it to become known I had lied about something as basic as who I am, the question then would be, what else has he lied about?"

I nodded. I didn't understand completely, but I understood enough. We both sat quietly a moment. The light in the room was changing. It was well into afternoon.

"Did Mama know?" I said.

He nodded. "I prayed she would leave me when I told her, but she wouldn't. She stayed a long time after that."

He smiled sadly. "You asked the other day what she was like," he said, stubbing out his cigarette and going to the bookshelves across the room. He pulled down a black leather photograph album from the topmost shelf, brought it back and laid it on the table between us. "She was like this," he said.

He opened the album slowly, reverently, and ran his hands gently over its first page, the way Mama used to do with the books he sent. And there she was. My mother, in picture after picture she was unaware I would ever see. My mother on a Ferris wheel, licking an ice cream cone, hanging her stockings to dry over a shower rod, peering over piles of books spread on a table. My mother smiling, frowning, waving, laughing, running, sleeping. My mother with this man—dancing, walking, curled up on a sofa, at a sink peeling potatoes, crouched on a rose print linoleum floor, feeding a cat. The mother whose life I had divined and acted out with all my light-haired dolls.

I studied every photograph for a long time—not only Mama, but everything around her. Her dishes, her chairs, all the things she had looked at, touched, kept near. Mr. Jacobson did not rush me. When I came to the last photograph I looked up at him. "I want to cry," I said, "but I am not able."

He nodded, as though he understood.

On the next page, the last page of the album, wadded up and then pressed flat like a flower, was a woman's lace handkerchief. I touched it. It was held together by something dark and stiff.

"What is this?" I asked.

He stayed silent so long I feared he might not answer. "It was hers," he said finally. "We cut our wrists that last night we were together. Oh, not to die," he added quickly, seeing my alarm. "To commingle our blood."

My mind's eye showed me their two wrists bound together with a satin cord, blood running in a dark thread down each of their arms. "She kept your handkerchief," I told him, "with her opera glasses."

He pressed his lips together tight, fought once again for control. "It was her idea," he said finally. "She begged me, 'Please. Make me a Negro, so we can be together always. So nothing will stand in our way. The law says just one drop of blood. That's all it takes.'"

Tears welled in his eyes. "I told her it wouldn't change anything," he said, "but she refused to believe me. In the end I had to—had to—I had to send her away. I had to push her out into the hall and lock my door. Even then she would not go." His voice caught and he ground his teeth to steady it. "She screamed like someone dying...I hear her to this day."

Mr. Jacobson closed the photo album slowly, reluctantly, running his hands over the cover one last time. Then he returned it to the bookshelf and sat down. The room seemed smaller.

"Why did you do it? I don't understand," I said. "You <u>loved</u> her. She loved you. Why didn't you just marry her?"

He shook his head, a quick, nervous motion. "I couldn't risk involving her," he said. "People like me travel light—unless we cast our lot with someone like ourselves. I tried that early on. It didn't work. Only doubled the unease, the chance of discovery. Then later, there was the memory of your mother." He lit another cigarette and exhaled its smoke stream like a sigh.

"It was only the demands of circumstance, her circumstance, that finally changed me," he continued. "And it took a long, long time. She had planned to come at the end of your high school semester, and bring you with her. Then she got frightened and couldn't wait. We were going to send for you, when your school got out before Christmas." He choked on the words. "If only I had let her stay."

"She wrote me letters," he said, taking a slow breath. "All these years. I'd read each one and burn it. There seemed no other way."

I pictured Mama's words eaten by flames, turning to smoke and ashes.

"She loved you fiercely, much more than she dared show," he said then.

I nodded. For a long moment, neither of us spoke. Finally I said, "Am I your daughter?"

The question came to rest in that still room as gently as a snowflake on the window ledge. He paused, then answered softly, "Do you believe I would tell you if you were?"

I shook my head. He would not make me a Negro.

"I want to show you something," he said.

He rose and went to a coat closet, reached to the far back of its top shelf and brought down a large, gray metal strongbox, which he carried to the table. Then he took a ring of keys from his pocket, unlocked it with the smallest one, removed a photo album and set the empty strongbox on the floor. This album was smaller than the first. And older, its leather cover flaking like the Bibles Daddy mends. He placed it between us on the table and opened it tenderly. It smelled of must and age. The edges of its black pages had bleached to the color of dust.

"These are photographs of my mother, of her parents, and their parents, as far back as there were cameras," he said.

He named them all for me, told me their relationship to him, and their stories. I looked carefully at all their faces. They were strong and memorable, like the Negro faces you once wrote me about. I could not say if any one of them resembled me. Maybe they all did, a little. I looked at Benjamin Jacobson's long hands as he turned the brittle pages, at his slender, large-knuckled fingers so very like my own.

Snow was still falling hard and the sky had begun to darken by the time he closed the book. Beyond him, outside the window, my eyes fixed on a triangle of white drifting past the riverbank like a small, ghostly sail. "What is that?" I asked him.

He looked where I pointed and smiled slowly. "It's an ice floe," he answered. "Upstream, in the mountains, the river freezes over. Then the ice breaks and floats down. I like to think that's where spring starts. Up there in the cold, where you least expect it."

He rose. "Please let me buy you dinner," he said.

"I would like that very much," I replied.

Mr. Jacobson helped me on with my coat and gently wound

my wool scarf around my head and neck. I felt so cared for a lump rose in my throat. He gave the scarf one last tug, then lightly touched his middle finger to my scarred, misshapen upper lip.

"Was it difficult?" he asked, his face solemn. "To grow up with?"

I shrugged. Then I nodded.

"I thought so," he said.

For five blocks he carried my suitcase in the driving snow, the whole time firing questions at me about Mama. Did she still wear flowers in her hair? Had she quit biting her nails? When did she learn to drive a car? Did she still hate Henry James? What was her favorite thing to cook? Had I ever seen her run out in the rain and shake her fist at it and laugh? His questions were like his photographs, ordinary on the surface and yet filled with the most intimate love and longing. At some far away place inside the chambers of my heart, I sensed my tears gathering themselves together like storm clouds massing just below the horizon.

We turned in at a place called the West End Bar. It was crowded and warm, and smelled of spilled beer, wet wool and the hot food arrayed on a steam table near the door. He found a table in the back, motioned me to sit, then disappeared and shortly returned with two bowls of soup. "This is good to start dinner. It'll warm you up," he said, placing them on the table. The soup did look very good, thick with vegetables and large chunks of beef. And when I put my hands around my bowl, it warmed them.

He motioned a trio of young men he knew to join us. Students of his, they called him "Dr. Jacobson."

"I'd like you to meet the daughter of a dear friend," he told them. With a small spurt of pride, I realized he was showing me off.

I hardly ate even one spoonful of my delicious soup I was so excited. But I did not lack at all for nourishment. I have never heard such stimulating conversation as went on at our table that early evening. For the first time, I saw talk that was as much a sport as football, as entertaining as a movie. Ours ranged free of boundaries and touched on many more topics than I can even begin to remember.

I looked often at Dr. Jacobson's face in the dim light. So many varied feelings crossed it and with such intensity, like storms on the sun. Perhaps that's why he sought this public place, so it could hide them. In a few short days he had lost my mother and gained me. What did that mean to him? What did I mean to him?

When it became known I was from Atlanta, one of the students asked me how it felt to be a Southerner. I answered that I could not say, for I had never been anything else. Dr. Jacobson threw back his head and laughed uproariously. "I guess she told you, didn't she?" he said. He patted my hand and looked full into my face, and for the first time in my life I saw unqualified approval in someone's eyes. "She's going to Barnard next year," he said. "You boys better watch out."

I don't know how I let the time slip up on me. When I glanced at my watch and saw how late it was, I dashed to the door. Dr. Jacobson followed after me. Snow was falling fiercely. The few cars out in it crept along. "I have to find a taxi," I told him.

"All the planes are grounded," he answered. "Stay here, wait out the storm."

I must be honest. At that moment, I wanted nothing more than to do so, to stay wrapped in that bright, sparkling talk and Dr. Jacobson's approval all my days. I knew, too, that if I did so, I would never disappoint you, or disillusion you—I would always be your pretty girl. I turned, headed back toward our table, then I stopped.

I had made a promise. And I keep my word. "I am expected somewhere," I said. "Before the airport. I have to go."

Dr. Jacobson did not question me. He walked me to the door and flagged a taxi. "You will get into Barnard, you know," he told me as he handed me into it. I promised I would see him in the fall. "You make me proud," he said and shut the door.

We just flew over a cluster of lights the stewardess says is Charlotte. We'll get into Atlanta in an hour. I guess I better hurry up.

The taxi crawled through the blowing, piling snow. I reached in my purse and pulled out the eye makeup, but my hands shook so from the cold I couldn't put it on. I spat on the mascara cake, wet the brush, and swiped it across my eyelashes one, two, three times.

I groped for my tube of Fire and Ice, found it, and ground its color onto my mouth. That would have to do.

The taxi inched forward. At this rate I would never make it to the show on time. Four blocks from the CBS building I thrust some bills at the driver, threw open the door and ran through the snow-drifts as fast as I could, my suitcase banging against my shins. It was a long, slow journey, I wasn't used to snow. I fell once. Getting up took a long time, and time was precious.

I arrived at the TV studio panting and freezing cold, the last one let in before The Dorsey Brothers Stage Show started. My teeth chattered so violently I bit down on my gloved fingers so the noise would not disturb the people next to me. I sat through the parade of acts certain I would never again be warm. Finally you came out, bringing with you that same unbearably sweet pain I knew in Mississippi and turning all my cold insides to honey that had sat out in the sun.

And then the show was over. I clutched my pass in a daze and followed an usher's directions to the Green Room. You stood near the back surrounded by a group of girls. As I walked toward you I felt myself go shy. Suddenly aware of my wet coat, my blown hair, the inappropriateness of my poor blue suitcase, I stopped a few feet away.

From down inside me, far beyond the most distant view of my mind's eye, I felt something coming toward me like the wind rushing through the subway tunnel, felt it, as I stood there, just as surely as I had felt the cold inside my bones and then the honey's warmth. I stood watching you with your fans while that whatever thing drew nearer. How <u>good</u> you were with them, your arms and fingers touching them, on their hands, their shoulders. Three, four, five girls at one time, but you gave all your attention to each one as if she were the only one. And then you let them know so sweetly it was time for them to go.

When they had left, you turned to me. I said, "I am Achsa," so softly even I myself could hardly hear. You smiled and opened up your arms and I went into them, that strong, safe place. That's when my body shuddered, and what had been traveling toward me from so far away barreled into me.

It was my tears.

My tears had come home from wherever they'd been gone all those long months since Mama died. And there I stood, shuddering violently and sobbing into your jacket and your shirt, my spit-thickened Maybelline Velvet Black running all over them and my lipstick leaving streaks. I am so very sorry and ashamed.

I was only half aware of how you led me to a sofa, then sat down and held me like a sleeping child so I could feel the comfort of your heartbeat. You held onto me so tight I knew no wave that dared break over me would wash me loose. And so I cried.

I cried for Mama, because she went away before I knew her and her soft fingers won't ever smooth my hair again or hold a drop of custard to my lips. I cried for Daddy, because he loved her so long and hard he loved himself away and has no room for loving anybody else. I cried for Aunt Dora and Aunt Mavis, who were kind to me when they didn't have to be because they are my relatives. I cried for Dr. Jacobson, who knew my mother best and therefore loved her more than any one of us. I cried for him because he has no people he can claim, even in photographs, and because I know he is my father. I cried for you, because your arms were so strong where they held me and because I love you and you are on the brink of seeing all your dreams come true. And finally I cried for me. Because my life is sad and beautiful and it has only just begun.

And my tears were not yet finished with me.

I am surely not a child, and yet I didn't mind at all the way you shushed me, rocked me. Nor did I mind this once the way you called me Baby Girl, for right then I truly was.

I only vaguely heard the red-headed man coming to fetch you and how you said, "Not now." But when you waved him away, I felt the cold rush in where your arm's warmth had been. I burrowed closer and you stroked my hair. When he came back I heard more clearly, heard him say, "The reporter's here. What'll I say to him?" And you said, "Tell him I'm coming. He can wait." And still, my tears would not stop.

By the time the man with the paunch and the bald head came around, most all I had left in me was snuffling. I knew who he was, even before he said that about how "there's people have worked long and hard to bring this man here, son, so he can put you on the cover of his magazine. You got to talk to him right now."

I remember exactly what you told me then, and how my heart sank some but I was not surprised. You said, "I got to do it. Then I got to go get on the plane for Hollywood. That's what my life's like anymore. Like—this." You swept your hand in a wide arc that took in the Green Room, the reporter waiting somewhere in the building, the far off plane that would take you to your screen test.

I was almost all cried out by then, yet still I only faintly heard you ask someone to call the airports, check for flights to Atlanta. When he said I could make a delayed plane that was leaving from LaGuardia once they got the runway cleared, I even felt a bit relieved. In this day full of so many strange turns and surprises, my immediate future was now at least something I knew. When you blotted away my last tears with your handkerchief, I only for a moment feared they might return.

Your thoughtfulness, digging in your pockets and asking me did I have money, touched me deeply. I wish you had let me give you back your $300. I know you said I should buy myself something I really want, but I would only have to hide it. So I've decided I'll save it for something truly special—lessons at the Actors' Studio. Maybe I'll see you there.

This next is all a blur, someone saying they'd got a taxi and it couldn't be kept waiting, me saying "I'm sorry," you signing the record I had brought, us holding hands and running through the building and out past a clutch of fans still waiting in the snow. Then I was in the taxi and gone. And everything was quiet, even me.

After my tears, I felt washed clean through and through. My harelip scar tingled like when life and feeling flood back into cold hands held near a heater. Only then did I remember! I had reached up, taken your face between my hands, and kissed you full on the mouth, with my fat lip, harelip scar and all, the way any girl kisses a boy she loves. And you had kissed me back! The wonder of it filled my eyes with tears once more. But that wasn't weeping.

When I walked into the airport, its bright lights dazzled me and all its sounds came at me very sharp and clear. The plane to Atlanta wasn't boarding for another 30 minutes. I thought I better eat something, since I didn't guess they fed you on an airplane in the middle of the night.

The light wasn't quite so bright in the coffee shop, but there were mirrors everywhere, along the walls and on big, chunky posts. I went through a little cafeteria line and bought a cup of coffee and a slice of apple pie. The mirrors made it hard to figure out where I was going, so I sat down at the first table I saw. I wolfed down the pie. I had no idea I was so hungry. Then I took a couple swallows of my coffee and, for the first time since I'd sat down, looked up. Reflected in several of the mirrored columns was a seated woman in a brown coat, facing away from me. Her neck was long and slender, and her back curved at a graceful angle. Seen from behind, she appeared very sure of herself, like she knew exactly who she was and where she was going, and like she would get there. I thought that I would like to know her and wished I could see her face, for I imagined she was beautiful. I reached over to put down my coffee cup—and realized she was me.

My inside voice spoke to me then, clear as water. It told me I am a white girl and a Negro, a Presbyterian and a Jew, a Southerner and a New Yorker, with a deformed face that is beautiful, and I can become whatsoever thing I choose.

I did not know it until now, but I believe this is the last letter I will write you. I realized when you held me how easy it would be for me to have a fire in my soul for you and give my life to tending it, how easily I could become like Mama, Daddy, Dr. Jacobson. And, oh, I don't want to. I've got so many other things I want to do.

Your life's course is set now. You are going to become a big star and a great actor, like James Dean. You are a good man, a kind man. I have learned so very much from you, and I will love you past my dying day. I pray your every dream comes true.

This is hard for me. I want it to go quickly.
Love always and good-bye,
    Achsa

P.S. Please promise you will never forget to always remain on the lookout for double negatives. It is so very important.

Chapter twenty-seven

March 25–May 28, 1956

Atlanta, Sunday, March 25, 4:10 A.M., in a taxi going home

Dearest Elvis,

I cannot let you go without first telling you this.

By the time our plane landed it was nearly 3 A.M. I had meant to go straight home, but when I got in the taxi Penelope's velvet purr was coming from the radio, and I heard my inside voice say I had one thing left to do. I asked to be taken to radio station WDDO on Auburn Avenue.

The driver, who was probably just out of high school, gave me a look of pure disgust, popped a wheelie in the parking lot and didn't say a word. I guess he figured me for a Negro, but he took me where I asked to go. I'd hardly climbed out before he made a U-turn and sped away.

WDDO is on the first floor of an old stone office building with heavy glass doors that opened when I pushed them. I crossed the dark lobby and entered a dimly lit hallway from which came the muffled sound of someone's voice. Penelope's. At the far end stood a small, glassed-in room little bigger than a phone booth. Inside sat a woman who looked for all the world like the Chinese Buddhas on the handles of Aunt Mavis's silver coffee spoons, except she had dark skin. It was she who was speaking in Penelope's voice. Slowly, I walked to within five feet of the booth, then stopped. Penelope frowned, put on Little Richard singing "Long Tall Sally," and stepped outside. She had on a pink dress printed with large orange flowers and no belt. Her hair was pulled back in a tiny knot near the top of her head, and she smelled like gardenias, and faintly of fruit left to ferment where it had fallen.

She stood there, feet apart, arms crossed, and stared at me.

"What you want?" she asked sharply.

"I came to see you," I said.

"Well, here I am," she answered. "You surprised?"

"No," I told her, "not very much," which was true.

She laughed. "Well! You're smarter than most," she said. "College boys, fraternity boys, every weekend driving down from Athens, coming over from Georgia Tech. They take one look, their eyes bug out like flies' eyes."

She cackled—a sound nothing like her throaty radio laugh.

"They give some little wave," she said, "smile some sickly little smile, then high-tail it out the door and back to where they came from." She picked at the plum-colored polish on a long thumbnail.

"I'm sorry," I said somewhat uneasily.

She went on like she hadn't heard me. "People all the time think they know what they want. Most times when they get it they find out it isn't even real." Something in the way she spat the words out called to mind the straight pins Mama carried in her mouth to pin up skirt hems.

"But I don't care," she purred, Penelope once again. "I got me a good life. Yeah, it's real good."

I reached in my pocketbook and pulled out your record.

"What you got there?" she said.

I told her I had a record I wanted her to play.

"Humf. Daddy-O Radio doesn't play records by white boys like Pat Boone," she said.

"He's not like Pat Boone," I answered.

"Well, being as you're standing here at nearly four o'clock in the morning...." Penelope looked toward my suitcase. The Little

Richard record was nearing its end. "You just come in here and sit beside Penelope and we'll see." She entered the booth, settled herself in the announcer's swivel chair and motioned to a stool beside it. I wondered for a second if I was violating any Georgia Supreme Court laws by entering a radio control booth with a person of color, decided I probably was not and anyway it didn't matter, and sat down.

Penelope took a sip from a jelly glass on the console in front of her. Its amber liquid was what smelled like rotting fruit. "You got some place to go to?" she asked.

I nodded.

"This hour, that's a good thing," she said. "What did you say your name was?"

"Achsa," I told her, "Achsa McEachern." She didn't laugh at it.

"Well, right now, Achsa," Penelope said, "you're going on the air."

She flipped a lever on the control board and put her mouth up right next to the microphone, like I always imagined she did.

"Guess what, babies," she said. "We got us a surprise visitor this morning. We got young Achsa McEachern, right here with us in the studio. You want to tell us where you go to school, Achsa McEachern?"

She tapped the microphone soundlessly with a plum fingernail, and I spoke into it, so scared I wasn't sure my voice would come. "I go to Foster," I said softly.

"You hear that, babies? Miss McEachern goes to Stephen Foster High School," Penelope crooned. "All the way out there in Dreamer Hills."

She paused, letting the knowledge I was white sink in. Then she went on. "I look up just a minute ago, she's standing here with her little blue suitcase. Looked like she was moving in. Says she's on her way home from the airport, and just <u>had</u> to stop. Because she's got this record, and nothing will do but she wants <u>your</u> Penelope to play it."

Penelope took a long breath then exhaled as she spoke. "And you know what, babies? I am going to. Just this once. I'm going to play this record Miss Achsa McEachern of Stephen Foster High

School has brought. You speak right here into the microphone, tell us the name of the record. Just go right ahead."

I did. I said, "It's called 'That's All Right, Mama,' and it's sung by Elvis Presley." My voice was calm and clear, but my hands were trembling.

"Elvis Presley?" A giggle erupted through her nose. "Elvis Presley? That's the funniest name I ever heard. I don't think I'll forget a name like that any time soon."

I handed her the record. She turned it over, looked at both sides.

"Well, I'll be. This song's been written by Mr. Arthur Crudup," she said with admiration. "He's all right. We'll just put it on the turntable here right now, and we'll all listen to what this Mr. Elvis Presley's got."

I watched as she placed the needle on the record and spun it once around, her hands so sure of every movement. I heard your opening "Weeeellllllll," then she flipped a switch and I couldn't hear you anymore.

"See?" she said. "I'm good as my word."

"What happened to the music," I asked. "Is it going out over the radio?"

She tapped a fingernail against a dial where a black needle bounced from side to side.

"You see this needle move? That's what tells how loud it is. Mr. Presley, he's singing plenty loud," she said. "Now I'm going to flip this switch so we can hear it in here. But when I do you got to be real still. Every sound you make will go out on the air."

I nodded. Penelope flipped a silver lever and the little room filled up with your song. "Ah, da-da dee-dee-dee-dee, I need your lovin', that's all right. That's all right now, Mama, any way you do." She listened a moment, then smiled and put her thumb and forefinger together in an "OK" sign.

I sat there beside her, so close our upper arms sometimes touched as we watched your record spin around on the turntable. The little room smelled of her perfume, and of cigarettes and hair oil, dust, face powder and whiskey. I looked through the glass, and my

mind's eye saw your music moving through the studio like mist, past
the hallway and the darkened lobby and out into the cold night air. I
watched it spread throughout the city, all the way to Dreamer Hills
and beyond, drifting down into the windows of the sleeping houses.
The dark ones, and the ones that keep a light on in the night.
  Love always,
    Achsa

*   *   *

Memphis, Monday, May 28, 1956 [never mailed]

Dearest Achsa, dearest B,
  I miss you, Baby Girl.

Notes and Acknowledgments

For a long time I wanted to see how close I could fit fiction up against reality without distorting what was real. Peter Guralnick's superlative two-volume biography of Elvis Presley, *Last Train to Memphis* and *Careless Love*, and his collaboration with Ernst Jorgensen, *Elvis: Day by Day*, gave me the consummate tools. Although young Achsa McEachern, her world and the story she tells are pure fiction, the twenty-year-old Elvis Presley she uses as a sounding board is as real as I could make him. His fictional letters reflect his true itinerary and the public events (concerts, business meetings, etc.) that occurred during those pivotal months of his career. In addition, Guralnick's biography and Elaine Dundy's *Elvis and Gladys* provided me with valuable insights in creating the "private Elvis" he reveals to Achsa in his letters. Other helpful books I consulted for the novel include Pete Daniel's *Lost Revolutions: The South in the 1950s*, David Halberstam's *The Fifties*, Dave Marsh's *Elvis* and Bobbie Ann Mason's *Elvis Presley*.

Thanks go to Terry Kay for his interest in the early manuscript and his friendship through the years; to Harvey Klinger for his work on behalf of the book; and to publisher Matthew Miller, editor

Deborah Meghnagi and all the folks at *The* Toby Press. The care and affection they've shown the book is every writer's dream.

Thanks also to Larry Webster for information on commercial aviation flight times and scheduling in the mid-1950s; to John William Neuberger for sharing his encyclopedic knowledge of 1950s automobile engines and what might cause them to malfunction in specific ways; to manuscript readers Jean Bogas, Sandy Carlson, Nancy Davis, Joyce Dixon, Verna Jones, Jo Thurman and Pat Williams; and to the Elvis fans with whom I communicated on the Internet, who, without exception, graciously went out of their way to track down information I sought.

Finally, I am grateful for an opportunity to recognize my teachers—David Bottoms, Pam Durban, Carol Lee Lorenzo and Tom McHaney—and to thank the many fine writers with whom I have worked on this book in reciprocal critique settings: Christena Bledsoe and Donna Warner, friends through most of my adult life, for the loving attention they lavished on my first draft; in Florida, group leader Dawn Radford, Nora Collins, Anne Cowles, and Beth White; in the mountains, Al and Mary Ann Clayton and Gene Wright; in Atlanta, the members of the Midtown Writers' Group, who nurtured me for numerous years with their unsparing evaluations on this and other projects: founder Linda Clopton, Eric Allstrom, Skipp Connett, Thomas Cook, Nora Harlow, Jim Harmon, Carla Jennings, Dee Kite, Anne Lovett, Frank McGuire, Jill Patrick, Charles Ross, Marilyn Staats, Jim Taylor, Anne Webster, Fred Willard and Gene Wright; and, in each of the above settings, my husband, Bill Osher, who had faith in my ability as a fiction writer long before I believed in it myself, who inspired me with his own disciplined writing habits, and who saw me through with his unflagging support.

I owe much to you all.

About the Author

Diane Thomas

Born in California and raised in Atlanta, Diane Thomas graduated from Georgia State University and earned an MFA from Columbia University. She reviewed films and plays as entertainment editor of *The Atlanta Constitution* and wrote features as an editorial associate at *Atlanta* magazine before becoming a freelance writer/ editor. She and her husband divide their time between the Georgia mountains and an island off the Florida panhandle. *The Year the Music Changed: The Letters of Achsa McEachern-Isaacs and Elvis Presley* is her first novel.

The fonts used in this book are from the Garamond family

The Toby Press publishes fine writing,
available at leading bookstores everywhere. For more
information, please visit www.tobypress.com